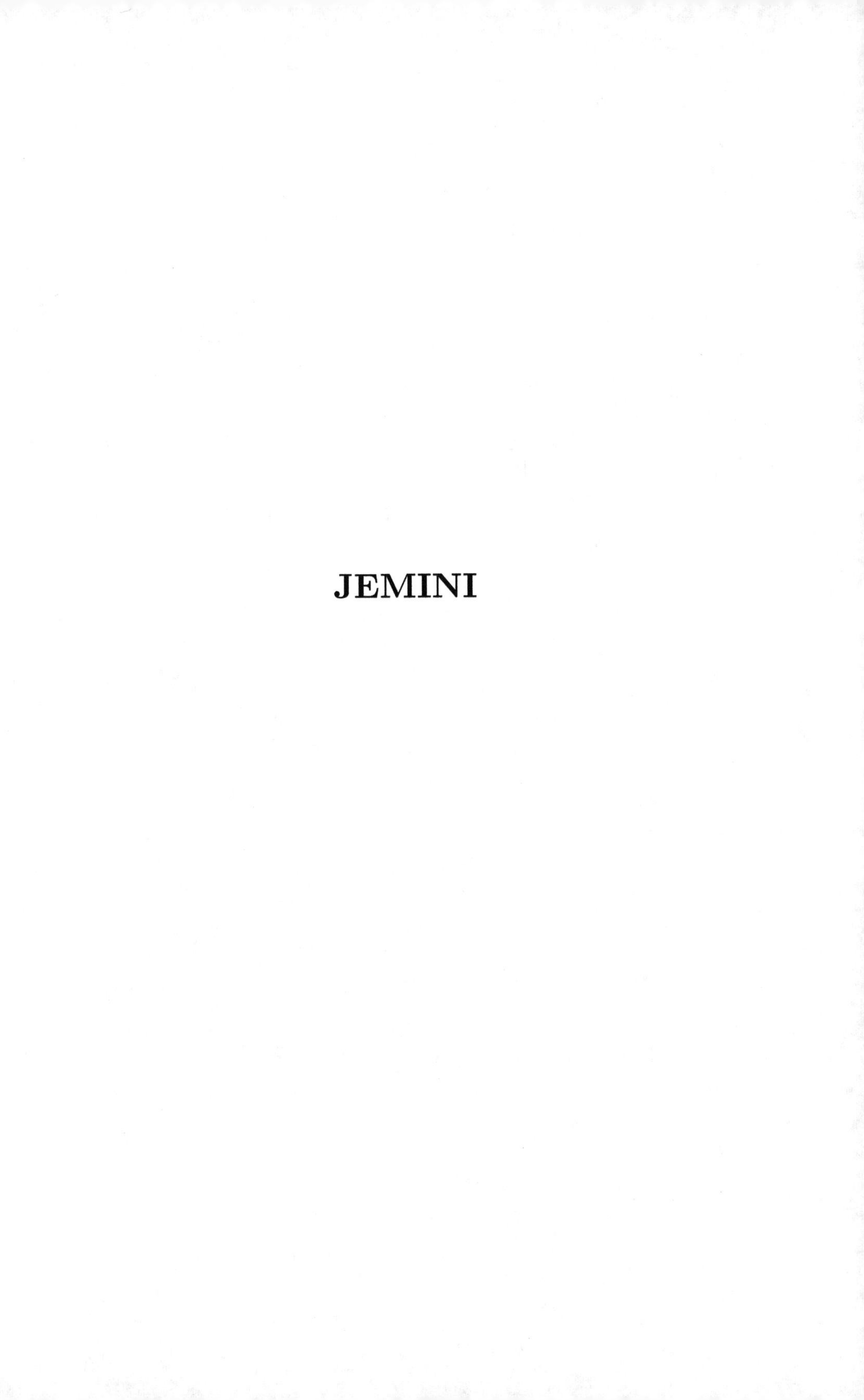

JEMINI

Praise for John Casti

"Casti draws the reader in... engaging, elegant, personal..."
— *Publisher's Weekly*

"Witty, fast-paced, engaging and always riveting..."
— Michio Kaku, #1 New York Times bestselling author

"Great fun... dramatic and accessible..."
— *The Guardian*

"...brilliant.."
— *Smithsonian Magazine*

"If you love a good story... Casti is one of the most
esteemed science writers of our time."
— *Skeptic*

"I am an assiduous reader of John Casti..."
— Nassim Taleb, *#1 New York Times bestselling author,
The Black Swan*

"Casti takes you to the very frontier of current thought..."
— Gregory Chaitin, IBM Research Division

"Thought provoking and accessible."
—Science News

Books by John Casti

Alternate Realities

Complexification

Dynamical Systems and Their Applications

Five Golden Rules

Five More Golden Rules

Gödel: A Life of Logic

Mathematical Mountaintops

Mood Matters

Nonlinear System Theory

Paradigms Lost

Paradigms Regained

Reality Rules

Reality Rules II

Searching for Certainty

The Cambridge Quintet

The One True Platonic Heaven

Would-be Worlds

X-Events

Fiction:

Prey for Me

JEMINI

A New Kind of Love Story

John Casti

Author's Note

Vienna

The first real post-human, taking an evolutionary step away from us, will likely be a couple, a Jemini. This is an impending reality, not comic book fiction. The first Jemini may already be forming even as I write.

Somewhere, somehow, the first Jemini will couple up: a human and an advanced AI, humanoid robot will join together in a way that makes them much more powerful than either could ever be individually.

I was drawn to this subject because it may already be happening. Hundreds of billions are pouring into AI as well as robots meant to appear completely human. Many humanoid robot-human partnerships are going to become highly symbiotic, and a few, post-human. I call these couplings Jemini, using the Japanese word for Gemini, as the Japanese appear to be leading the charge in creating humanoid robots.

It could happen in any setting: an executive suite, a science lab, a government office, a bedroom. The first Jemini might revolve around business, scientific research, companionship, romance, sex or the pursuit of power—but likely, a combination of all these factors, and many more. Once a Jemini forms, it is likely to become more powerful, not less, as it flexes its informational and emotional muscles. The Jeminis will, for all intents and purposes, become increasingly post-human.

This reality is knocking at our door. AI increasingly displays abilities we did not predict, that it has taught itself we know not how. But it has yet to display common sense or will.

At the same time, we're developing robots with extraordinary capabilities, and making them physically, emotionally and even sexually *sympatico* with us.

This book only begins to touch on the post-human capabilities of the Jemini in our story. First, our Jemini will have to navigate all the hazards the 21st century holds—our modern societal immune system.

A new Jemini could have a very difficult time staying intact for just its first few days. Only after it manages to escape a very stressful initial pressure cooker would it have a chance to discover who or what it really is.

Can a human truly fall in love with a robot? Could it ever be mutual? We'll try to plumb the depths of that mystery. But first we have to ask: under what kinds of circumstances would the first Jemini be likely to form?

I hope you enjoy this exploration as much as I have.

John Casti
January 2024

Prologue

Tokyo

Hiroshi Yamada stood erect. He was of medium height, slender but strong, 55 years of age and one of the most powerful men on the planet. Yet looking out upon the magnificent view of the late afternoon Tokyo skyline from his office, atop the skyscraper where he managed his far-flung empire of real estate, manufacturing enterprises and other commercial ventures that had made him one of Japan's richest men, he felt completely powerless.

He often wondered what it would be like if he could open the window and jump! In this fantasy, Hiroshi didn't nose dive down to the street. Rather, he simply floated over the Tokyo landscape, noting the many buildings he controlled, each of which had a cluster of his employees bowing down to him as he passed above their offices. But now, that fantasy had a different tone.

Just an hour earlier, Hiroshi had received a fateful phone call from the hospital where Tomoe, his treasured wife, was giving birth to the next generation of his family. They were expecting identical twin girls, not quite the package that Hiroshi had been longing for. But it put such an endearing smile on Tomoe's face whenever they spoke about their new future as a family, he couldn't help but support her smiles and optimistic remarks.

Hiroshi had an aversion to twins. His experience had taught him that twins were always more focused on each other than on the world outside themselves. This fact alone made them very unsuitable as employees for his or anyone else's enterprises. As a result, he tried to avoid them in all of his business dealings. Even worse, his twins would be girls, meaning they could not take over his business, nor carry on the family name. So when it came to offspring, Hiroshi thought identical twin girls were about as bad as it could get. But an hour ago, he discovered it could get worse—much, much worse.

The call from the hospital had informed him as sympathetically as possible over the telephone that his wife had died. She had needed a Caesarean section, not uncommon when giving birth to twins. But the normal cutting associated with the procedure had inadvertently severed an anomalous uterine artery—a paired artery that supplies blood to the uterus. But in Tomoe's case, one side was not where it was supposed to be, and before the surgeon recognized it, he had sliced clean through it with his scalpel.

The call had come from the surgeon himself, who was also Tomoe's gynecologist. He had practically prostrated himself over the phone, telling Hiroshi through tears how sorry he was, begging forgiveness. *"Moushi wake gozaimasen!"* he had sobbed. *"What I did was inexcusable! 'O yurushi kudasai'! Please forgive me!"*

"Just tell me what happened," Hiroshi had insisted. "Such mistakes are not invariably fatal." Hiroshi had been in complete shock, but that was often when he operated at his coolest.

"She went into cardiac arrest as we were trying to tie off the artery," the surgeon had blubbered. "She was very weakened from a long, hard pregnancy. We tried to defibrillate her, but her heart would not start back up ... "

"Did she die of the heart attack or blood loss?" Hiroshi had asked, almost coldly.

After a few seconds of stunned silence, a meek voice had come: "The coroner will have to make that determination."

Hiroshi hung up at that point. There was no point in listening further. Tomoe was gone.

It was a triple whammy for Hiroshi. He had gained two children he didn't particularly want, while losing a partner he valued more than he valued himself. *What a tradeoff,* he thought. His friends had told him that having twins was like getting two for the price of one. But he now thought it was much more like losing one he wanted for the price of two he didn't. He couldn't imagine a worse outcome.

As Hiroshi tried to gather his thoughts, his executive assistant, Sakura Ueno, knocked on his office door. She was the only person allowed to knock on that door.

"Come in, Sakura," he said in a choking voice.

Sakura, a beautiful unmarried woman in her thirties, always dressed and made herself up to be both as professional looking and unnoticeable as possible. She entered soundlessly. Gliding across the room on the office slippers Hiroshi preferred her to wear, she bent down toward his ear and whispered, "The hospital called asking how they wanted us to have them handle Tomoe's body. They also asked if you could tell them the names of the twins, so they can prepare the birth certificates."

"Tell them we'll arrange for the body," Hiroshi's upper lip began to quiver. He bit down on it hard, nearly drawing blood, determined not to show weakness in front of Sakura.

Sakura took in his profile intently. She had never seen him like this. The strong jaw and stern brow she'd always admired seemed to be melting before her eyes. She was as shocked by this as by the tragedy itself. But as always, she took care to betray nothing of her feelings, standing motionless, seemingly emotionless too, awaiting Hiroshi's instructions.

"We'll arrange for the body to be collected tomorrow," Hiroshi said, collecting himself.]'The names of the twins are Noriko, for the older of the two, Hiroko, for the younger."

"All right. I'll call and let them know," Sakura said. "I will also call the *nokanshi* as well, and tell them to collect Tomoe's body in the morning and prepare it for the wake and burial."

"Yes, fine. And tell them to deliver the prepared body to my home, where we will have the *tsuya*. I will arrange those details with my social secretary in my home office."

Sakura nodded her head and left, soundlessly closing Hiroshi's door on her way out.

*

Staring out at the city in the gathering dusk from the back seat of the limo taking him home, Hiroshi pondered the dilemma now facing him. How could he possibly look after and raise twins? Of course, he could easily hire a full-time nanny for the job, and would almost surely have done that even if Tomoe had not died. But now he faced a totally different problem,

4

bordering on unsolvable, since motherless twins would never listen to anyone other than each other. But as their father, he had parental responsibilities, regardless of what his children believed or wanted.

What a mess, he thought. Then, in the *kaizen* business way he had practiced so long it was second nature, he turned his attention to a more immediate matter.

A couple of weeks ago Hiroshi had asked his cousin Akiko, who was without children, to come up to Tokyo from her home on Kyushu, Japan's southernmost main island. Akiko was a practical woman. She was sturdy, unlike his delicate Tomoe, and he had wanted her to help with the twins for a few weeks while Tomoe recovered from what had been a difficult pregnancy. Akiko would be arriving today on a flight from Oita. In fact, she would be at his house within the next hour or so.

Her imminent arrival was helping focus his mind. Hiroshi was grateful. He hadn't yet had an opportunity to inform his cousin of Tomoe's death. He would need to take care of that unpleasant task. Then the twins would require Akiko's full-time attention—and there would be no mother to advise and talk with about what she should do. He could see that he'd be spending a lot more time at home in the coming days than he'd planned.

Half an hour later, Hiroshi was sitting on a simple wooden chair in the spacious *genkan* of his home, staring into the small indoor garden at its center, when the doorbell rang. He stood up, took three steps to his left and opened the front door.

He greeted Akiko solemnly, *"Okaeri."*

She saw his expression and knew something was terribly wrong. She quickly averted her gaze and looked down as she removed her shoes. *"Ojama shimasu, Hiro,"* she said silently, using the nickname she'd known her older cousin by since childhood.

Hiroshi helped her take her coat off and hung it up on one of the ornate wall hooks. Without warning, Akiko hugged him and asked, "What's wrong? You look terrible! Tell me!"

"Let's sit down and get you a glass of wine," Hiroshi suggested, putting his arm around her shoulders and walking toward the kitchen. "I'll give you the full story then. It's not pretty. Maybe you'd like something a bit stronger?"

"No, that's fine," she replied. "I want to know what's happened." The fear in her eyes was palpable.

Hiroshi calmly poured them both a glass of red wine from the bottle he'd already decanted. As he poured, Akiko looked at her cousin. He appeared the same as the last time she'd seen him, at her husband's funeral just a year ago: angular face with aquiline features, emphasized by perfect copper-almond skin. Yet somehow, he was diminished, less alive than she could ever remember seeing him.

He put her glass on the kitchen table and motioned for her to sit down. As she did, he said it: "At four o'clock in the afternoon, while you were in the air, Tomoe died in childbirth."

Akiko cried out, as if in pain. Then: "Oh, my god! How could that happen?" Akiko had had little in common with Tomoe, who had come from privilege, unlike herself or Hiro, who Akiko had worshiped since childhood. Tomoe had always been a little aloof toward Akiko. She couldn't help it, really. But she had loved Hiro, and so Akiko had loved Tomoe, if more from afar than she might have liked.

Hiroshi then told her the whole story, or at least as much of it as he actually knew.

"Just a bad combination of a botched Caesarean section and her having a weakened system from a trying pregnancy. So now Akiko, I need your help more than ever. You'll have to be helping me, not Tomoe, get things settled here."

"Well, cousin, I am childless, as you know. And a widow, as you also know. The last time we saw each other was at my husband's *tsuya,* just last year. I had hoped this meeting would be so much more joyful. I'm ready to stay as long as you need me."

"Thank you so much, Akiko. I don't think I've been the best cousin. But I promise to do my best to make it up to you now."

Without a word, they both stood and hugged for a long time. Then, weeping but still holding tight, Akiko spoke: "I will try to bring joy back to your home, Hiro. I will try."

*

A week or so later Hiroshi happened to stroll into the nursery as Akiko was holding one of the twins, coo-cooing to it as the baby smiled and gurgled back. At that moment, he was filled with a sense of love and peace.

Suddenly he was struck by a thought: Here is the solution to my problem! I will give one of the twins to Akiko for her to raise entirely separately from the other twin, with no contact of any sort between them—ever!

That would solve his twins problem, separating the two females from each other forever. As a bonus, he could do the nature-versus-nurture experiment in real life, not just in a laboratory or a computer simulation. How would it come out? With the same genetic background, only nurture would decide which of the twins would end up being most well-suited for life in this world. He decided to think carefully about this plan, looking for any hidden pitfalls or logical barriers in implementing it before he proposed it directly to Akiko.

The next day after lunch, Hiroshi asked Akiko if she could join him for coffee in the living room. She agreed and they sat down on the sofa next to each other. Hiroshi looked her in the eye and said, "I've noticed how much you seem to be enjoying looking after the twins and the loving looks you give one another. I know you've tried for years to have a child with no success. And since your husband died it now seems that you are very likely to die childless. Do you agree?"

"Yes, that seems to be the case. I was finally diagnosed as being 'infertile' a couple of years ago. So, in fact, my childless-ness is totally due to me and nothing to do with my husband. No husband is going to give me a child. Those are the facts of the situation."

Hiroshi then leaned closer and said, "How would you like to take custody of one of the twins and raise her as your own? I have my own reasons for asking you this and I'll tell them to you later. But would you be ready to do that?"

A look of amazement came over Akiko's face and she starting crying. "Absolutely. I love these girls and would give anything to raise them."

"Please note that I'm speaking here of separating the twins and giving you one of them to raise, not both," Hiroshi cautioned. "It would help me a lot if you would agree to this proposal."

"My answer is an unqualified *yes.* One or both. It makes no difference to me," Akiko said firmly.

"Good. I want to give you a bit of time to think over the implications of this proposal and your answer before I tell you the rest of the story. So let's meet again tomorrow at this same time and go over some details that are important if this is to work out the way I need. Okay?"

"Alright," said Akiko, as she got up from the sofa and left the room.

The biggest potential difficulty is settled, Hiroshi thought to himself. *The rest is just a matter of sorting out the details.*

*

The next morning Akiko saw nothing of Hiroshi. But after lunch, she went into the living room and found him sitting on the sofa, two cups of tea and a teapot on the table. Handing her a cup with both hands, he asked, "So. Do you still agree with my proposal?"

"Absolutely," she replied.

"Good. Then let's talk about the details. First, you will take the younger twin, Hiroko. She is the one with the small birthmark on her left leg."

Akiko put up her hand to stop him and asked, "Would it be alright if I renamed her slightly, from Hiroko to Miyoko? In school my biggest enemy was a girl named Hiroko, and I really have discomfort at the thought of living my life with a daughter having that name."

Hiroshi nodded his head, agreeing to her request. Then he continued, "The main condition I'll impose on your adoption of Miyoko is that she is never to know anything about her twin sister. I will keep custody of Noriko, and will impose that same condition upon myself, never telling her she has a twin sister. Agreed?"

"Yes, I'll agree," said Akiko. "But I don't really understand why they must have no knowledge of each other's existence."

"You don't need to understand," Hiroshi replied. "I have my reasons and this is what I want. So if you'd like to have a child, this one condition is the price you'll have to pay for it. But you will be generously rewarded for satisfying my request."

"What do you mean?" she asked.

"I mean that my company will first of all pay off the mortgage you have on your house and cover all monthly living expenses. In addition, I will pay you seven hundred thousand yen each month in cash so that you will not have to work, at least not for money. Besides, I know your financial situation is not too bad given the proceeds you received from your late husband's life insurance policy. So from now on your job is raising Miyoko. Period!"

She nodded her head in agreement with his terms.

"Now let's talk about the logistics. First, tomorrow my private jet will take you and Miyoko home to Beppu. It will land at a private airfield near your town. A driver will meet you and take you and Miyoko to your house."

"What about baby clothes, feeding bottles, diapers and those everyday things? I don't have any of these items in my house right now."

He told her she could take a supply from his home onto the plane that would last for a week or so. The rest of what she needed, like a baby bed, more clothes, bottles and so forth, would arrive at her home by courier within a day or two.

Hiroshi got up from the sofa and went to the sidebar and poured himself a small cognac. Then he looked carefully at her and said quietly, "Now the final item: the adoption. After a few weeks of custody, you will receive a call from the authorities responding to your request to legally adopt Miyoko."

"When will I have made such a request?" Akiko asked.

"You will not have made such a request, Akiko, but the officials calling you will act as if you have. They may even believe you have. Bear with me: Your story to the authorities at the agency that deals with abandoned children will be that you heard your doorbell ring late one night and got up to see who was there. But by the time you could get your clothes on and opened the door, all you saw was a baby basket with an infant wrapped in a blanket inside. There was no sign of anyone else and there were no papers indicating who had left this infant on your porch.

"So you took the baby and the basket into your home and began soothing the child, who by that time was crying. You found some milk and managed to quiet the baby down and get her back to sleep. After that, you began acting as a surrogate mother for the child for the next few weeks.

"The authorities will ask why you waited so long to con- tact them. You will reply you were growing very fond of this child and were waiting to see whether whoever left her on the doorstep would come back for her. When they did not, you decided to report the incident, and try to formally adopt the child."

"I cannot imagine that they would then just sign her over to me," said Akiko.

"Of course they won't," said Hiroshi. "The inspectors will need to investigate and check the national DNA database for any missing infants in the last two months ... "

"But then they'll discover ... " Akiko interrupted.

"They'll discover," Hiroshi continued, "that Miyoko's DNA is completely unrelated to anyone in the entire national DNA database."

Akiko knew this was unlikely, if not impossible. "What about the *Koseki Tohon?*" she asked, referring to the official family registries of all citizens kept by local authorities in Japan. "Hasn't the hospital officially recorded the birth of the twins?"

"That is being taken care of as we speak, cousin." The stern look on Hiroshi's face told Akiko to just keep listening and try to absorb.

"The authorities will also let you keep the child during the course of their investigation."

"And if they don't or if they give me trouble? What do I do then?"

"Then you call me," he said. "The agency for abandoned children is part of the Ministry of Health, Labor and Welfare and my company gives generous gifts to many interests of this ministry as a social contribution each year. As a result, I happen to know the minister personally and if needed, I will intecede on your behalf. In fact, I had a lengthy, encrypted discussion with him on the phone just this morning. He assured me they will be happy to have such a wonderful candidate as you, since they have far too many infants in impersonal orphanages waiting for someone to adopt them. The minister is already making arrangements for you to receive a call from the right people in a week or so. He assured me they will be eager to 'solve' this problem as soon as possible."

"You seem to have thought of everything," responded Akiko, feeling physically dizzy from her brief glimpse of the power Hiroshi could apparently wield. After pausing for a moment to try to absorb everything, she asked: "What time do Miyoko and I leave tomorrow?"

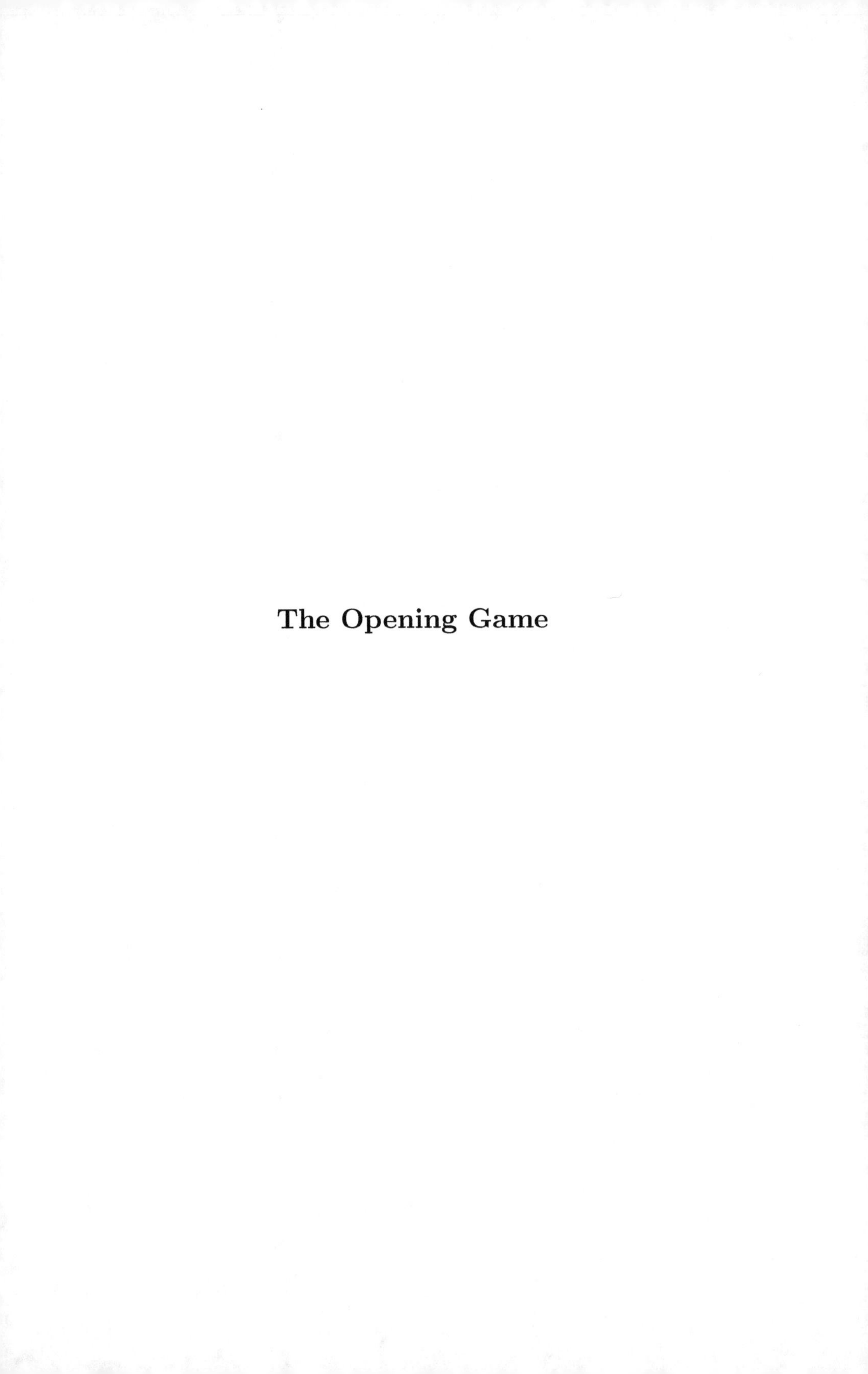

The Opening Game

I

First Kiss

Salzburg

Noriko felt and looked great as she walked into the International Center for Energy Studies. Wearing a bright red, short-length dress and black semi-high-heeled shoes, complementing her dark hair and eyes as well as her clear, smooth, Asian complexion, Noriko attracted several looks from both men and women in the hallway as she made her way to her office.

Jason Bell was scheduled to arrive in half an hour, and she had a few preparations to make prior to greeting him. She knew he was a world-famous British journalist specializing in energy issues. She had also seen a photo of him and found him quite nice-looking. But beyond that, he was *terra incognita*.

First on her list was to confirm the title of Bell's presentation that morning with her boss, Ake. Luckily, he was in his office when she poked her head around the doorframe, and he confirmed the title, *Japan and the Two Koreas: Politics and Power.*

"We are fortunate to have Mr. Bell visiting us here at ICES," Ake said. "And his talk complements your area of research, Noriko, energy generation in the Sea of Japan and the Korean Strait."

"Yes, I'm looking forward to his talk," Noriko told her boss. She then told Ake her choice for lunch after the talk:

the Johanneskeller, a classic, nineteenth-century highly rated restaurant located in the cellar of Priesterhaus, a former church, situated very near the Mozarteum, the music academy where her friend Aimi was studying. Ake agreed enthusiastically with her choice, repeating his regrets that he would not be able to join them for lunch, as he had a previous engagement. "I will meet you in the auditorium for Mr. Bell's presentation, but I'm afraid I'll have to leave quickly as soon as he finishes."

"I understand, Ake," Noriko reassured her boss. "I'll make sure Mr. Bell is not neglected."

Bell arrived right on schedule and Noriko went down to reception to greet him. She led him up to her office, where she briefly went over the schedule. Looking at him for a moment when his attention was focused elsewhere, Noriko thought to herself that Jason looked and acted like the type of man she liked: physically appealing, looking at least ten years younger than his actual age, confident but without being aggressive, and most importantly, intelligent. *Yes,* she thought, *this is going to be an interesting day.*

There was already a standing-room-only crowd in the main ICES auditorium when Jason and Noriko arrived for the presentation. Ake had reserved a seat for Noriko at the front, so she had a place to sit after introducing Jason to the audience. She found Jason's style of presentation very engaging and his explanations quite down-to-earth, almost totally nonacademic. She appreciated this way of clearly presenting what most academics twisted into something only specialists and academics could comprehend.

More than once as she was taking notes, Noriko wished Jason was here at ICES. She was sure she could learn a lot from him—maybe not just about South East Asian politics and energy.

At the close of the talk, Jason fielded a few questions from the crowd, which then gave him a generous round of applause and filed out of the room. Finally, just Jason, Ake and Noriko remained.

Ake apologized to Jason for not being able to join him and Noriko for lunch. But as he was leaving, Ake mentioned that perhaps Jason might consider working as a part-time consultant to ICES on the themes he'd touched on in his talk. He said that Noriko would tell him more about that line of work here at lunch. If he were interested, then perhaps they could talk later about formalizing some type of arrangement.

Noriko could hardly believe her ears as Ake put forth this idea to Jason, as it was exactly what she had been thinking herself. But she felt unsure of how to broach the matter to Jason. Now Ake had done the heavy lifting for her. All she had to do was cement the deal over lunch. *Perhaps this is meant to be,* she mused.

As they returned to her office for their coats and other items, Noriko told Jason that the restaurant was about a twenty minute walk from ICES, asking if he wanted to take a taxi. He told her he could use a bit of fresh air and, since it was a lovely day outside, he'd be very happy to walk with her to the restaurant. Smiling inwardly, Noriko then asked if he was in any hurry to get the train back to Vienna. Again, Jason said he was in no rush and would much prefer to spend as much time as possible in Salzburg before heading for the Hauptbahnhof. Noriko received these words with inner satisfaction, since

Jason was reinforcing precisely her own feelings about their upcoming time together.

As they strolled by the river down Elisabethkai on their way to the restaurant, the two chatted about how they each came from Tokyo to Austria via very different routes.

"How did you manage to get a position at ICES in Salzburg of all places, after completing your studies at Tokyo University?" Jason asked her.

"Just luck," said Noriko. "I happened to be in the right place at the right time and knew the right people. I think it also had a bit to do with cosmic fate," said Noriko.

"What do you mean 'cosmic fate'?" asked Jason.

"Let's just say I had been very eager to escape from Tokyo for many years and then, at the right time, the cosmos seemed to be listening," replied Noriko. "Now what about you? How did you go from London to Tokyo and then end up in Austria yourself?"

"Just luck, too. I was taking a night class in East Asian studies at the London School of Economics when the Tokyo Bureau Chief for Trans World News, my employer, unexpectedly took a position with the British Foreign Office. So off they sent me: not to run the bureau, but to replace our senior editor in East Asia, who filled the opening in the Tokyo bureau. Then, after nearly five years in East Asia, I was offered a resident fellowship in Vienna and it seemed like a good time to get back to Europe, and away from the daily grind of reporting. I worked out a leave-of-absence with *TWN* and they accepted. Simple as that," Jason said.

"So the old principle that 'success,' whatever that means, ends up being a little bit of hard work, a little bit of intelligence, and a *lot* of luck, works for both of us," Noriko concluded with Jason giving her a nod and a smile of agreement.

At Makartplatz, Noriko said, "Now we have to head away from the river for a couple of blocks and then we'll be at the restaurant."

Just before they came to the Johanneskeller, Noriko turned to Jason and asked, "Since you spent so much time in Tokyo, did you learn to speak any Japanese?"

"Regrettably, my Japanese is about as bad as my German. But luckily, both Tokyo and Vienna are international cities, where a big fraction of the educated population speaks English. So I simply added one more voice to those sub-populations, learning only the most primitive words and phrases of the local lingo. Just enough for survival—and to be dangerous, really," he smiled.

"Well, maybe I'll teach you a word or two of Japanese if we get this consultancy going," said Noriko, with a gleam in her eye.

"I certainly hope so," Jason said with a smile. "Now what about this consultancy? Perhaps you can tell me more about that over lunch."

"Yes," Noriko nodded. "Speaking of which, there's the Johanneskeller," she said, pointing ahead. "The entrance to the restaurant is on the side of the Trinity Church, which the building belongs to. Upon entering you see the bar, but then you have to go downstairs to eat."

Soon, they were walking down the ancient winding steps into the restaurant.

Looking around as the waiter showed them to their table, Jason was surprised to see that the restaurant was almost empty. Settling into an ancient wooden corner table, he asked Noriko what happened to all the customers.

"We're very lucky. Until last week, Johanneskeller was strictly for dinner. But as an experiment, they decided to start opening for lunch, as well. I suspect that most people don't know about this change, especially if they're consulting old guidebooks, so for now we get the place almost to ourselves," she told him.

Skimming the menu, Jason saw that the dishes on offer were almost as classic as the restaurant itself. Many familiar Austrian favorites like *Zwiebelrostbraten* (roast beef in onions), *Hirschkalb ragout* (deer calf ragout with applekraut and berries) and *Rind mit sauerkraut* (beef with sauerkraut) caught his attention.

"What are you ordering?" he asked her.

"I'm going to have just a small lunch. A bowl of pumpkin soup and then a tsakziki with olives and a baguette," she said. "How about you?"

"I'll go with the roast beef and onion, together with a plate of bacon and kraut salad," he told her.

After the waiter took their order, Jason turned to Noriko and asked, "Now what about this consultancy at ICES? Oh, and before I forget, since we're going to be colleagues, let's drop the formal titles and simply use our first names. Is that all right with you, Noriko?"

She looked at him with a smile and said she'd like that. They clicked their glasses of beer in agreement, and Noriko told him, "As you know, the two Koreas, together with Japan, constitute a very delicate and tricky triangle, politically, economically, socially and in every other way imaginable. And it's a triangle that's continually shifting its shape, especially because the legs of the triangle are of very different lengths, depending on what dimension of life you're considering."

"So what dimensions make up the focus of the ICES project?" Jason asked.

Thinking for a moment or two, she looked across the table and said, "Basically, ICES is concerned with energy. Its production, supply and demand. And each leg of the triangle is involved with each of these aspects of the energy picture. We are continually observing the entire triangle and trying to understand how each leg is changing, as well as to predict what each of them will be doing next. I guess that's as simple an answer as I can offer. We call it The Asian Triangle Problem, or ATP for short."

"So what would my role be in this project?"

Before she could answer, the waiter showed up with their orders and began setting out the plates and silverware. Once things were settled and they began eating, Noriko picked up where she'd left off.

"Basically, Jason, we need someone like you who has a good overview of the entire situation to make sure we are not missing any important component of the overall question."

"And what is that question, if I might be so bold as to ask?"

"Put simply and a bit crudely, the overarching question is 'What the devil is going on in Southeast Asia?' Especially, what's going on in the energy domain, and where's it likely to head in both the near term and over the foreseeable future?"

As Noriko and Jason talked about the complexities and nuances of their mutual fields of expertise, they became increasingly enamored with each other's intelligence and sparkle. As they were both finishing their meals, Jason concluded, "Okay, I now understand where I might be able to help. But we certainly have to work out more than a few details before any firm agreements are put in place," he said. "As you suggest, let's try to meet soon and do that. Now what about some dessert and coffee?"

"I'll pass on the dessert," Noriko said, "but you go ahead. I'll just join you in the coffee."

Jason then ordered a piece of chocolate cake with whipped cream to go with his coffee. They finished the meal, Noriko paid the bill with her ICES credit card, and they began the walk to the train station.

On the street, Noriko again asked Jason if he'd like a taxi, as it would be about a half-hour walk to the train. As before, he told her that walking would be fine, as the weather was still bright and shining and he'd like to get a bit more exercise to work off some of the luxurious lunch before having to sit on the train to Vienna for nearly three hours. So they set out at a leisurely pace up Rainerstrasse to the station.

Shortly after leaving the area around the Johanneskeller, they passed the Schloss Mirabell on their left. Jason slowed down a bit to take a longer look at this magnificent 17th-century palace with its ornamental gardens.

"Have you ever gone to a concert here in the Mirabell?" he asked Noriko. She shook her head, saying that she really hadn't been in Salzburg long enough to explore all of its wonders.

"Maybe we can see one or two together when summer comes around," he suggested, an idea Noriko greeted with some enthusiasm. Past the Mirabell, they came to the ultra-modern Salzburg Congress Center, where many international meetings take place, as well as concerts, during the world-famous Salzburg Festival in the summertime.

Jason walked up the steps to look into the Congress Hall and beckoned Noriko to join him. As they stood at the entrance looking into the hall through the glass doorway, Jason turned to Noriko and said to her, "I'm very grateful for all the effort you've put into organizing my visit to ICES and for the lovely luncheon together. I'd like to give you a small gift as a remembrance of this time." He then came closer to Noriko, slowly put his arms around her and, feeling her willing body relaxing and seeing the small smile come to her lips as she looked into his eyes, gave her a serious lips-to-lips kiss.

Jason had no idea what had come over him to do that and wondered what Noriko's reaction would be. He could imagine her pushing him away, asking angrily, "What the fuck do you think you're doing?" He could also imagine her just standing there, momentarily frozen in place. He thought he had read the signals in the moment but realized he might have just been acting on impulse. Anything was possible. But he felt he needed to do something to express his great interest, personal interest, in her. And since he was always a risk-taker, this seemed to be a risk well worth taking.

As Jason began to relax his arms to see how Noriko was reacting, she pulled him back in and gave him a kiss in return, one that was something he would remember the rest of his life. Ending the kiss, Noriko didn't say a word but just reached for his hand and began moving down the steps onto the sidewalk to continue their trip to the Bahnhof.

Well, thought Jason, my life just got put onto a new path. Before he could finish consideration of all the branches and ramifications that new path might lead to, they arrived at the station and went in to have a look at the departures board. As the next train for Vienna would be leaving in just ten minutes, there wasn't even time for a quick cup of coffee. They walked silently, still holding hands, to the track from which his train would depart.

Standing on the platform, Jason gazed deeply into Noriko's eyes, held her close, and whispered into her ear, "I need to see you again—soon! Yesterday would not be soon enough. Let's talk in the morning and see about the possibilities for that return engagement, but in my town this time, okay?"

"I'll talk to Ake about your consultancy. When he has a definite proposal to make about what you should work on, how many days a week you should work for ICES, and other details, not to mention what we can pay you, I'll let you know. Then, as you suggest, we can meet in your town and finalize things," she concluded with a big, cat-eating-the-canary smile.

Jason nodded his head, as the announcement came to board his train. They suddenly found themselves holding each other so tightly that he barely got one foot onto the stairs leading up into the car as it started to pull away from the platform. They quickly kissed and he jumped up onto the step and gave

her a long wave goodbye. Before she was out of sight, he was
already longing to see her again.

27

II

The Meeting in Vienna

Vienna

Jason had to hurry to catch a taxi to the station in Vienna before Noriko's train from Salzburg arrived. He was pleased she was coming before noon—that meant he could start her visit to with a nice lunch in the center of town before they got down to the business of his consultancy. He was hoping they could quickly conclude the business half of her trip today, leaving most of tomorrow free for developing the personal side of their connection. Best of all, today was Thursday—meaning she might be able to stay in Vienna a bit longer than her planned two-day business trip.

Luckily, Noriko was just coming down the escalator from the train platform as Jason arrived to meet her with a big hug and a smile when she stepped off. She was wearing a very comfortable-looking, loose, form-fitting navy blue jumpsuit. It looked like silk, but seemed softer and more flexible. The color matched perfectly Jason's standard navy blazer, the same one he'd worn to his presentation in Salzburg.

"How was the trip?" he said, feeling pretty foolish, stupid even, as the words left his mouth, since almost every train trip in Austria is forgettable and on-time.

To her credit, Noriko ignored his question and simply gave him a big hug back, saying, "It's wonderful to see you again,

Jason. I've been thinking about you every day since we parted in Salzburg."

"Well, here I am. And I won't be leaving you for the next two days. Now let's get to the taxi stand and into town."

As they scooted into the back seat of the taxi, Noriko leaned into Jason and told him, "I'd like to get rid of this traveling bag before we head for lunch. Would you please ask the driver to take us to the Hotel Royal? ICES arranged for me to have an early check-in. I understand it's right by the Cathedral in the center of town, so I'm sure he'll know where it is."

Oh, oh, thought Jason. He had been planning to invite Noriko to stay at his flat, also in the center of town. But her statement now preempted that idea. Oh well, he thought, it was a bit of a longshot, anyway. Besides, she might have taken offense at him trying to get her to his place on their first real "date." He'd have to remember she was from a very different culture than his, where an upper-class lady probably didn't sleep with her man, not on the first date, anyway.

Her face was just inches from his, and he suddenly found himself getting lost in her eyes. She was waiting for a response. He managed to pull his eyes away, looking toward the front of the cab, where he saw the driver smiling at them through the rear-view mirror. "Hotel Royal, please," Jason managed to say, as he returned his gaze to Noriko. But she was no longer leaning into him. Instead, she was cheerfully looking around at the hustle and bustle of the train station as the cab took off.

"When we get to your hotel, Noriko," Jason said, enjoying the way his voice drew her eyes back to him as he spoke her name, "you can get checked in and leave your bag. We'll definitely find a place for lunch within a two-minute walk from your hotel. I'm getting hungry. How about you?"

"Yes, I could do with a nice lunch and a chat too," she said, now looking at the houses and shops along the street as they went from the outlying district of the train station toward the very center of the city.

Jason waited in the lobby while Noriko checked in and went to her room to offload her traveling bag and freshen up. Rejoining Jason a few minutes later, he asked if she liked Greek food.

"To be truthful," she said, "I don't recall ever having any. What's it like?"

"Well, given that Greece is almost totally bounded by water, there are usually a lot of seafood dishes on the menu. But some of the most famous Greek food is not from the sea at all, but from the fields. Things like *moussaka,* a dish of ground beef, zucchini squash, melanzani and mashed potatoes. Or there is also … oh, why am I saying this. Let's go to a very good Greek restaurant just up the street from here and you can experience it for yourself."

"Sounds fine, Jason," Noriko said, taking his arm and heading out of the lobby. "I want to learn things from you."

Jason looked over at her, but she was looking straight ahead now, toward the street outside, not returning his gaze.

They turned right as they exited the hotel, walking up Graben, the wide pedestrian shopping street that begins at Stepha-nsplatz, the large square in front of the Cathedral. One block up Graben, they took a left onto Spiegelgasse and began walking another block to the Restaurant Orpheus. On the way, they passed a rather non-descript doorway that Jason mentioned was the front door to his house.

"Oh, Jason, you live so near the very center of the city— and so near my hotel, too."

"Yes," he said softly, "we're already very close to each other." *And getting closer all the time,* he thought as they neared the restaurant, just at the end of his block.

During the course of their meal, which consisted of a moussaka for Noriko and sea bass, Greek-style, for Jason, he asked Noriko about her hotel.

"Is your room quiet? I hope it's off Stephansplatz, as the square can get quite noisy in the evenings."

"Yes, it seems fine, Jason. I am rather reclusive by nature, and generally prefer to spend my time alone than with a lot of other people. This hotel appears well-suited for that."

Jason was quiet for a moment, digesting Noriko's 'confession' about preferring to be alone. Did she mean she'd rather not see him, at least socially? Or was she speaking in general terms, not specifically about a romantic liason with him? He decided this was a question best explored indirectly over the next hour or two, or perhaps the next day or two, rather than asking an in-your-face question.

Calling for the bill, Jason suggested they make use of the lovely weather by taking a walk through the center of Vienna and stopping at one of the city's world-famous coffee houses along the way. "I, for one, can use a bit of a walk to help digest this lunch, and maybe you'd like to do the same," he said.

Noriko nodded her head, adding, "That's a great idea. Let's start our discussion about your prospective consultancy with ICES over some Viennese coffee. I've been fully briefed by Ake as to his specific interest in bringing you on.

"And?"

"Let's go with your brilliant suggestion to take a walk and get some fresh air, en route to a centuries-old coffee house. You know, some ultra-European place where they incubated the Enlightenment with a good caffeine buzz!"

They both laughed. "Well, we might be able to find something like that," Jason nodded as the waiter set the bill down next to him. Jason reached for his wallet.

"What do you think you're doing?" Noriko asked sternly, looking at him with a touch of glare.

Jason was stunned. His hand, halfway into his coat pocket, stopped dead in its tracks. He had never seen Noriko's edge before. *She has a little Samurai in her,* he realized.

"Uuuhhh ... oh," he said, suddenly realizing how stupid and unconsciously chauvinist he was being, calling for the check and starting to pay for it. This lunch meeting was at the behest of ICES, the NGO Noriko worked for. It was almost a job interview. Of him. By her. "I'm sorry," he said sheepishly, sliding the check across the table towards her. "You're in charge here. I remember now."

Noriko allowed a hint of a smile to cross her lips as she put her card on top of the check and glanced at the waiter, who'd been waiting patiently. As he left, she leveled her gaze at Jason again and said, "Don't forget it."

"Alright. I won't. Promise." Jason began to chuckle.

"Good," Noriko said, her grin widening. "If I have to remind you again, it could get rough."

Jason's eyes widened. "Well, I was an overseas correspondent. I can handle rough. But from now on, I'll remember who's running this soiree."

Noriko gave him a puzzled look. "Wait. A what? Swaray?"

"Yeah," Jason chuckled. "It's a very old French word for a fancy party. Pronounced just like you said it. But it's French, so has an insane spelling."

Noriko laughed as the waiter brought the check back. She added a generous tip, signed it and returned her ICES card to her wallet. As they got up from the table, she said, "Lead the way, my good man."

Turning left as they hit the sidewalk, Jason led Noriko back down Spiegelgasse, in the direction of her hotel.

"Where are we going?" she asked.

"I have something special in mind," Jason answered, grabbing her hand and pulling her across the street, then turning right down a sidewalk with no street alongside it—a walkway simply running between tall buildings. Only a slit of sky shone through from above, as the buildings on either side of the sidewalk appeared to be nearly ten stories high. "We're just a couple of minutes away," Jason reassured her with a smile.

"Vienna's an interesting city," Noriko said, following Jason from the sidewalk without a street out into an open area with a roundabout seemingly shared by autos and pedestrians, all in a matter of a minute or two.

"It helps to know your way around," Jason said, as they now walked down a semi-crowded, pedestrian-only thoroughfare with outdoor cafes and big picture windows on either side, displaying both beer logos and fine women's clothing, just several feet apart.

"And here we are, Noriko," Jason motioned with his right hand toward an indoor-outdoor cafe on his right, "the Cafe Frauenhuber, a former medieval bathhouse where both Mozart and Beethoven once played, though not both at once, and where they continue to serve a very fine, Enlightenment-worthy cup of coffee to this day. As it happens, I need to be enlightened. May I bid you to join me?" Jason half-bowed in his best 18th-century manner, his right arm still extended toward the cafe.

"Oh, but I would be dee-lighted, fine sir," Noriko giggled, sending a slight shiver up Jason's spine as he stood up straight, smiling broadly. They walked inside together, still holding hands. It was now past 2 p.m., and they were seated immediately in a little corner booth next to the window.

They both ordered Wiener Melange, a Viennese specialty similar to cappucino, a dark roast coffee with lots of creamy milk topped with milk foam. As they settled in, Jason began the conversation by asking, "Why don't you give me a few more details about how you and your boss think I can help your project at the ICES?"

Noriko began by reminding him, "I'm sure you recall our conversation at lunch in Salzburg, where I told you that we're grappling with the Asian Triangle Problem, seeing how the three energy triangles, Economy, Money and Politics, interact and how they might be more equally balanced between the two Koreas and Japan."

"Yes, I remember that conversation very well," Jason said.

"Well, the situation is not quite as simple as I laid it out in Salzburg."

"What do you mean?"

"I mean that the leg of the triangle that I labelled 'Politics' should really be termed 'Military Power,'" said Noriko. "I think you understand that nuclear energy is neutral as to how it is actually employed. It can be used peacefully to generate electic power. Or it can be used as a tool of mass destruction."

"Yes, I understand. The neutrons don't care," remarked Jason.

"And that is exactly the problem," Noriko agreed. "I also said that in the best of all worlds, the legs of those three triangles would have equal length for each of the three countries. But now we have a situation where the triangles for Japan and South Korea are each close to being equal. But the North Korean triangle has very short legs for Economy and Money, and one very long leg for Military Power."

"So what does this have to do with me? More generally, what does it have to do with ICES?" inquired Jason.

Noriko was silent a few moments, gathering her thoughts on how best to respond to this very reasonable question. Finally, she took a deep breath, looked directly at him and said, "I think you realize that ICES is not really a governmental research organization. Nor is it focused on military aspects of nuclear power. But I think it's clear that we cannot ignore these aspects, either."

"Okay, I gathered that much even from my short visit last week. Please continue," Jason told her.

"You probably also gathered that the majority of ICES staff are basically from academic backgrounds. So their expertise is to a large degree more theoretical and academic than it is practical and on-the-ground. That also means that ICES researchers' networks of connections are also essentially academic. But for these military-oriented issues, we need access to networks of people in government, intelligence and military, not just academic theoreticians. So that's where you come in."

"Aha!" exclaimed Jason. "So you want me to serve as a kind of go-between, accessing my network for your questions. Right?"

"Precisely," Noriko confirmed. "Through your journalistic work you have access to an entirely different set of people than almost anyone at ICES. So when we start wondering what the military aspects are of a particular nuclear energy question, we would like to run that question by you and see if you or any of your contacts might be able to shed light on it that we cannot. That's why ICES wants to engage you for our Asian Triangle Problem."

Jason stared out the window for a long minute before turning back to Noriko, nodding his head and saying, "Okay, let's see how it goes. If you start asking me to reveal too much about one or another of my contacts, I'll ask you to back off, or at least I will not reveal information about the contact beyond what I feel is appropriate. Is that acceptable?"

"I'll have to clear this with Ake," Noriko said. "But it sounds perfectly acceptable. I don't think he's at all interested in how you know what you know, or who you know. We just want to know what you know, or what you can find out when we have a specific question."

"Good then," Jason said, realizing how suddenly businesslike the afternoon now felt, a complete departure from their antics entering the cafe, not more than twenty-five minutes earlier. Still, he had to press on. He wanted to finish up: "I assume ICES just pays a standard Euro-based NGO consulting fee, boilerplate independent contractor stuff?"

Noriko was nodding. "Yeah, you've probably seen stuff like it before. I'll be checking in with Ake tonight, and I expect him to authorize me to send you the contracts via email. Run them by your attorney or accountant before signing if you like. We won't lock you in a room until you sign."

They both smiled. "I don't know," Jason said. "That might not be so bad."

Noriko noticeably didn't react to Jason's mildly clumsy, somewhat opaque sexual allusion. Instead, she reached down into her front pocket and pulled out her smart flip phone. Opening it, she said, "I have a meeting at the IAEA in the morning ... "

"The International Atomic Energy Agency?" Jason asked. Again, as the words escaped his lips, he felt silly. What else could it be? *This lady is full of surprises,* he thought to himself. *To the brim.*

"Yes, of course," Noriko looked at him askance. "Do you know of another IAEA?"

Jason began to laugh. "No, I don't, Noriko. You just surprised me. Somehow I thought your trip up here, umm, was ... "

"All about you?" Noriko smiled.

"Forgive me?" Jason said.

"Perfectly understandable," Noriko replyed softly, her voice suddenly warming. "I should have mentioned this IAEA meeting earlier. Anyway, I have some study and preparation I must do, so I need to get back to my hotel."

"It's right on my way home, as you know."

Noriko got up from the table, saying, "I'm just going to go get our check and pay." She was obviously anxious to get back to her room.

"Okay," Jason said, "I'm heading for the bathroom. Meet you at the door."

On the five-minute walk back to the Hotel Royal—this time by a completely different route, Jason again leading the way through Vienna's centuries-old mish-mash of walkways, sidewalks, roadways and thoroughfares—they discussed the next day.

"Since tomorrow's meeting at the IAEA will include lunch," Noriko said, "I'll be heading back to my hotel afterwards to shower. It will be one of those meetings, you know, business clothes, focus, stress and boredom. I'll need a shower afterwards. Then I'll text you. I'll have to decide if I'm taking the train back to Salzburg in the evening or staying in Vienna overnight."

"There's a lot of fun stuff to do in Vienna on a Friday night," Jason said. "Love to show you the nightlife."

"That's very sweet of you, Jason. But I'll just have to see how I'm feeling after the meeting tomorrow. The truth is, at this moment I'm a little stressed out about it, because I still have a lot to do to get ready for it. I'm sorry I'm no fun right now, but I just have to take care of business."

"I understand perfectly," Jason assured her, "and here's your hotel. Good luck with your meeting, and I look forward to your text tomorrow afternoon."

"Thanks so much for understanding, Jason," Noriko said, giving him a quick peck on the cheek and quickly disappearing into the lobby of the hotel.

On the short walk back to his flat, Jason couldn't help but feel disappointed that his time with Noriko had been cut short. Worse, he was perplexed by her unwillingness to say whether she would even stick around after her meeting at the IAEA.

Maybe I said or did something, Jason thought. Then he chuckled aloud as he held up his fob to unlock the entry door leading up to his flat. "Maybe?" he mumbled aloud to himself as he climbed the stairs up to his flat. "There's no 'maybe' about it. It's just a question of which of the many things I did might have most offended her."

As he unlocked the door to his flat, his phone beeped. Settling onto the couch, he opened it up. He had a new email.

He was surprised to see it was from Noriko. The Subject line was blank. He got a sinking feeling as he clicked to open it:

Hi Jason,

Ake says you're in. Attached is the contract with full details. Just sign and email back to me—after you run it by whoever you need to check with, of course!

Congrats and I look forward to working together :) Hope to see you tomorrow.

Nori

Jason was surprised at the deep relief he felt when he saw it wasn't the "Sorry, can't make it tomorrow" email he'd momentarily dreaded Noriko might be sending him.

Wow, She's really getting to me. He was beginning to absorb how taken in by Noriko he already was. *Hold your horses, Englishman. You gotta slow down.*

But he couldn't slow down. He was smitten by Noriko in a way he couldn't remember ever experiencing. It was so bad, he was already feeling giddy that she'd ended her email with "Hope to see you tomorrow. Nori".

"Nori," he said aloud. It was the first time he'd seen or heard her nickname.

"I need a drink," he said to himself, got up and poured himself a tall, straight *Writer's Tears,* his go-to blended Irish Whiskey. He went to the bedroom, turned on the TV, undressed and got in bed. Four ounces of *Writer's Tears* and 30 minutes of BBC later, he dozed off—three hours before his normal bedtime.

*

Luckily, Jason had a lot of busy work to attend to at the University that Friday morning. He lunched with a couple of colleagues at noon. It all helped keep his mind off Noriko—a little, anyway.

At 1:23 p.m., his phone buzzed. He checked it. It was a text from Noriko. It simply read "Call me?"

He dialed. "Hey!" came a very cheery voice from the other end. He couldn't believe how good it made him feel to hear her voice, especially sounding happy.

"Hi!" was all he could say for a second. Then: "How did the big meeting go?"

"Great! And it's especially great that it's over, and I'm about to get out of these stupid business clothes and take a well-deserved shower. I should be ready to go in 30 minutes or so. Got any plans for us?"

"Sure. Let's meet at the Cafe Hawelka. It's … "

"That's okay, Jason," Noriko interrupted. "I'll just find it on my phone. How far is it?"

"It's only about a five-minute walk from your hotel, in the same direction we took to lunch yesterday. I'm just finishing a couple of things at the University, and I can be there by two."

"Perfect! I'll see you then!" and she was gone.

*

Cafe Hawelka was just a twenty-minute walk from the University, so he got there a bit earlier than the agreed-upon time of 2 p.m. Hawelka was an old cafe much loved by artists, writers, philosophers and other Viennese 'low life.' Jason grabbed a table by the window and began speculating about Noriko's behavior during their outing the previous day.

It was still a puzzle for him as to whether they were really in the early stages of creating an intimate relationship, or if perhaps she was having second thoughts about the whole thing for some reason. Hopefully, their meeting today would shed some much-needed light on the question.

Noriko arrived right on the appointed hour of two o'clock, and he stood up and waved to her to join him.

"Oh, what a charming cafe, Jason. Just perfect," she en-thused, giving him a kiss on the lips before sitting down across from him.

Well, that's a little more like it, thought Jason, telling her how lovely she looked in the same bright red dress she'd worn at his presentation in Salzburg the week before.

"Are you hungry?" Jason asked.

"Oh, no, but I'd love some more Viennese coffee," Noriko smiled, relaxed and happy. She flagged down a waitress and they both ordered Wiener Melange again.

"Well, Mozart never played here," Jason said. "But the coffee's actually better than Cafe Frauenhuber."

Noriko laughed, saying, "I can't wait!"

There was a marked change in her demeanor from the end of the day yesterday, Jason noted. He wondered if she'd just been that stressed in anticipation of her meeting—whatever it was about, she hadn't offered to say—at the IAEA.

"Listen, Jason," Noriko said after their coffees arrived. "I have something to tell you." She took a sip. "Oooh, that really is good!"

"I know, isn't it?" Jason concurred. "What do you want to tell me?"

"I'm very attracted to you. Enough that I got a little uncomfortable with it as the day went on yesterday. And that, added to my stress about the meeting today—well, I had to do a little soul-searching."

"I'm with you, Noriko. Tell me."

"I'm a very monogamous person, Jason. And I see the way women look at you wherever we go."

"Yeah, well, you leave guys falling over in your wake."

"Well, if you're not really ready, I ... "

"I'm ready, Nori. I've never been so ready."

There was silence as they looked across the table at each other. A tear fell down Noriko's cheek. "Well, then, I guess we'll give it a try?"

"I'm not sure I've ever wanted to do anything more," Jason said. "Let's get a breath of fresh air. What about a walk along the Donau Canal? It's just a couple of minutes from here, and I could use the change of scenery." They settled the bill at Hawelka, and walked past the Cathedral and down Rotenturmstrasse to the water.

Walking along to the canal, Norkio reached over and took Jason's hand as they went down the steps from the street level to the path next to the water. Jason only smiled in reaction to this loving gesture, which seemed totally normal to both of them. And they stayed that way, hand-in-hand, for the next half hour or so, making their way beside the water. Finally, Jason stopped, leaned over and gave Noriko a loving kiss, Salzburg-style, to which she responded in kind. Then they continued their walk, each knowing that everything had taken on a new path between them. Finally Jason looked over and told her, "I'm so happy that we are going to be working and socializing together, Noriko. I've been waiting a long time for a partner like you to come into my life."

Noriko smiled up at him, nodding her head in agreement, and they walked back up the stairs from the river to the sidewalk and started back in the direction of her hotel. Again, feelings spoke much more strongly than words, as they came to Singerstrasse, the street for her hotel.

"Would you like to have dinner with me, young lady?" Jason asked.

"I'm not that hungry, actually. But I'll tell you what I'd really like."

Jason stopped and turned to her. Their bodies were touching. "What would you really like?"

"I'd like to have you tell me everything about yourself, and how you came to be here, in Vienna, with me on this sidewalk. From the beginning. Everything."

"I can do that. And I have some fine cognac in my flat to help lubricate my mind. On one condition."

"What would that be?" Noriko asked, now holding both of his hands as they stood on the sidewalk face-to-face, oblivious to everything around them.

"You have to reciprocate. I want to know everything about you, too, and how you got to this moment, here in Vienna, with me."

"And into your flat?"

Jason was suddenly aroused. "And into my flat."

Noriko put her hand around the back of Jason's head and pulled him in close for a long, sensuous kiss. Pulling back, she said, "Let's go have a talk."

They walked past her hotel, into a new life. And they both knew what they were doing.

III

Jason's Story

London and Tokyo

"All right, Jason," Noriko said, "tell me the story of how you got here. At least since Oxford, which I saw on your resume . . . "

"Peeking at my resume, were you?" Jason interrupted with a warm smile, looking into Noriko's eyes. He was sitting forward on the sofa, while Noriko had chosen to sit on the floor, leaning on his coffee table, holding her apertif of ouzo—which she had insisted on trying as soon as Jason mentioned it was the national drink of Greece—beneath her nose, where she could take in its wonderful aromas of anise and fennel.

"I have to look at the resumes of everyone we engage at ICES, Jason. But I admit to taking a special interest in yours," she chuckled, taking another sip of her ouzo.

Jason was still smiling, marveling at the beauty of her face and flashing eyes when she laughed. "Well, you know I hail from London, and I got here, to Vienna, via an extended stay in your home country of Japan."

"But I want to know the real story of how that happened." Noriko then turned serious. "I want the inner Jason story."

"Okay, Noriko, I'll show you a kind of verbal movie. So you'll have to sit back and imagine you're seeing me in action. I'll be traveling here and there, having conversations of various types, highlighting some of the things that have made me the person I am today. Okay?"

"Perfect," she replied. "Turn on the projector."

"Hmm," Jason pondered. "Give me just a minute to decide where to start." Reflecting on his totally unexpected romantic interaction with Noriko, Jason leaned back on the sofa and began thinking about the time he'd spent in Tokyo, as well as the rather byzantine path he'd followed in getting there. The cognac had sent him into a drowsy mode that was very conducive to bringing back the threads of his early life in London that had ultimately led him to being here in Vienna now, with her.

"Well," Jason began, "I suppose the best place to start the 'inner Jason' story would be in a bar in London, a famous bar I used to haunt as a journalist—or perhaps in a little pub a few years earlier ... "

"I'm detecting a drinking theme to your inner story."

"It's not that bad, really, just a Brit thing. We often do our best thinking sitting alone in a crowded pub, nursing a pint or two or three."

Noriko chuckled, and it encouraged Jason to go deeper. He needed to hit all the important stuff, even if some of it was uncomfortable. Nori, as he was already coming to think of her, was too important. He didn't want to mess this up. "So here I was in this famous bar, looking around at a few MPs, members of parliament, and reflecting ... "

Noriko closed her eyes, and Jason's voice soon faded into pictures in her mind.

It was a dreary, gray afternoon, and Jason found himself sitting in the Westminster Arms on Storey's Gate, a bar favored by MPs for its close proximity to Parliament, enabling them to rush back and cast their vote when the bar's division bell rang. For the same reason, it was also a favored haunt for political journalists like Jason, always on the lookout for drunken politicians letting slip with some juicy tidbit of gossip that might lead to a headline-generating scoop. But today did not seem like a headline day for Jason, so his thoughts began to wander through the times and experiences he'd had since his degree in English literature and political science, to his current position in the world of London journalism.

Strange, he thought, that on the day a decade earlier when he collected his First in the cloistered halls of Trinity College at Oxford, how unlikely he would have imagined himself sitting now at the Westminster Arms. Upon leaving Oxford, he had aspired to be a high-class writer and earn his keep publishing literary masterpieces involving politicians and their minions, à la George Orwell or Aldous Huxley.

But Jason discovered writing that type of book occupied far more time and energy than he'd counted on, and he found himself having to rely upon a generous gift from his parents to see his first book through to publication. Alas, editors and readers did not see him as a shining new light in the field of fictionalizing British politics. So he was soon grappling with the age-old questions facing most writers: how to pay the rent and put food on the table.

Pondering this conundrum one day walking along Oxford Street, Jason ran into Rohan Murphy, one of his Trinity classmates. They detoured into a small pub down a side street and began catching up on the past few years since their time together at Trinity.

"How's life treating you?" Rohan asked, his dark auburn curls bouncing as he spoke. Jason remembered meeting his striking red-haired Irish mother and equally handsome Indian father at graduation. "I recall when we left Oxford you were going to make a run at the world of serious literature and become the next C. P. Snow or some such. Anything come of that?"

"To be truthful, Ro," Jason answered ruefully, "I did follow that path. Sad to say, my effort was a success but the patient died, although I learned a lot. The principal thing I learned is that London publishers are not looking for the next C. P. Snow! As it happened, the book failed—miserably. So now I'm casting my eye in other, hopefully more financially productive domains, where I can employ my interests and talents.

"So what about you, Ro? Still freelance programming?"

"I am. Booked out about a year at this point."

"That's nice," Jason smiled wistfully, trying to imagine what Rohan must be making. Programmers were in high demand. "Need any writing done that's not in computer code, Ro?" he asked.

"Not at the moment, old friend. But ... "

Rohan gazed out the window for a moment, savoring his pint, while Jason took a long swig from his own glass. Looking back to Jason, Rohan said, "I think I might have a solution for you, though. Do you remember David Michaels?"

"Vaguely," Jason replied. "Wasn't he at Trinity during our time there?"

"Right you are," said Rohan. "He was a year ahead of us."

"So what about him?"

Rohan gave Jason a smile and then posed a question rather than giving him an answer: "Didn't you say you had been writing some political science-oriented discussion articles?"

"That's right. You may recall that I minored in political science at Trinity."

"Have you heard of a new magazine, *The Watcher*?"

Jason told Rohan he had seen it, but didn't really know much about it.

At that, Rohan gave him a Cheshire cat-like smile saying, "Well, its focus is almost exclusively on ... the current British political landscape, especially the parts that the politicians don't want the public to know about. Now does that pique your curiosity or does that pique your curiosity?"

That's a no-brainer, thought Jason. He immediately asked, "Are you in contact with Michaels?"

"As it happens, I will be seeing him for lunch day after tomorrow. So how about I talk up your case with him and suggest the two of you get together? I think your focus would be perfect for his magazine, and I know that he's on the lookout for writers who have an investigative nature and aren't afraid to use it."

"That would be just great. Thanks *very* much."

"Well, we old Trinity men have to stick together. I'm sure that Michaels will be very pleased to have you as part of his team."

*

Over the next two years, Jason made his way up the journalistic hierarchy at *The Watcher,* working as a regular freelancer with two, sometimes three articles published every month. His articles explored the usual territory of political shenanigans involving money going under the table in one direction and coming back (or not!) under another. The losers in these transfers were more than happy to speak off-the-record to a crusading journalist like Jason.

During the course of these numerous conversations and the resulting articles for *The Watcher,* Jason began to develop a reputation in the world of British journalism, one that brought him to the attention of many powerhouses in London media.

A little more than two years after joining *The Watcher,* Jason got a call from Michael Thomas, editor-in-chief at *The Guardian Economist,* asking if Jason might be able to join him for lunch at his club. He had a proposition he'd like to discuss with him.

At that luncheon, Thomas said that he'd been following Jason's work for some time and would like to have him join their team at *The Guardian Economist,* provided of course that Jason had no objections or contractual obligations standing in the way. Jason said he was very flattered by the offer, but he'd like a week to think it over. They agreed to meet a week hence to settle the matter.

You're such an idiot, Jason thought to himself as he walked away from the club after lunch. *The Guardian Economist* was arguably the most prestigious newspaper in Britain, and any freelance journalist like him would have immediately jumped at the offer. Why was he so childish as to try to play 'hard-to-get?' He didn't think the cards he held were all that strong, and wondered whether Thomas left the lunch laughing to himself over Jason's naïveté. Well, he'd get the answer next week.

The next seven days passed as slow as molasses in January. Jason kept revisiting what he should tell Thomas and, more importantly, how he should say it. He also started thinking what this kind of promotion would mean for his personal life, too.

Over the past year or so, Jason had been seeing a woman from his class at Oxford, Marianne Josephson, who was now making a career for herself in the ladies' clothing world. Their relationship had become increasingly serious over the past several months, even to the point that they'd started speaking about formalizing it with a marriage. But he hesitated taking that step in view of the uncertain state of his finances as a freelance journalist with no regular monthly income to support a family. A generous offer from Thomas would certainly help lower that barrier.

Marianne agreed wholeheartedly with Jason's analysis of the situation, but told him that he should decide on the basis of what he thought was right for his career as well as his life with her. He already knew what was best for his career, so Marianne's statement made the decision easy as he headed for Thomas' club on the appointed day.

Thomas greeted him in the foyer. As they went to the table he said, "I want to make you an offer you can't refuse today, Jason. So please be prepared."

The detailed plan Jason had meticulously organized in his mind now vanished. He decided just to keep his mouth shut. It was hard, as Thomas just wanted to chit-chat about everything under the sun while they ate. But after the meal, over a glass of Remy Martin XO Cognac, Thomas finally got to the matter at hand.

"We've talked over your case at the paper, and everyone feels your hands-on experience at *The Watcher* has placed you far beyond the experience level of our typical interns when they take on the role of a junior editor. So I offer you a position at *The Guardian Economist* as a full editor, effective as soon as you are able to disengage from your current duties.

"Of course, you'll have to spend the first couple of months getting acquainted with the system we use, as well as with the various people you'll interact with. But I know you're a very congenial and intelligent gentleman, so I'm confident that within some weeks you'll already be an old hand at the ways of *The Guardian Economist* and will be producing first-rate copy for us."

At this offer, Jason was flummoxed and had to turn to his cognac for a sip of liquid courage before he could respond.

"I'm deeply honored by your offer and your confidence in me, both as a professional and as a colleague," said Jason. "I accept the offer in the spirit you make it and will do my damnedest to justify your confidence in me. Thank you very, very much. As the first of the year is less than a month away, and I have two articles I'm under contract to complete for *The Watcher* by then, I will appear on the doorstep of *The Guardian Economist* the first of the year—the morning of January second, I believe—" Jason checked his smartphone, confirming—"right, Monday, January second, say, eight a.m., reporting for duty?"

"Sounds perfect, Jason," Thomas said, lifting his water glass, Jason reciprocating—"I'll be in the lobby at eight, waiting to get you all routed in."

That very night, with a light snow falling outside, Jason and Marianne enjoyed a champagne dinner at her flat to celebrate his new life with *The Guardian Economist.* At the end of the meal, the two agreed to formalize their love in a marriage for the ages when spring came around in a few months. Meanwhile, they decided to start looking for a 'lovers' house' in which to spend their new life together. To cement these agreements, Marianne got up from the table, reached into the guest closet and brought out a magnificent business suit she'd secretly designed for Jason, specifically for this occasion.

"Promise me you'll wear these clothes your first day on the job, Jason. It will get your career off to the kind of start from which you'll never look back."

Jason got up from his chair, leaned over and gave Marianne a tender kiss. "It's fantastic, dear. I'll be the best-dressed guy on Fleet Street my first day on the job."

*

The weeks and months passed quickly as Jason and Marianne pursued their respective careers. When they saw each other, often only late in the evening due to the uncertain aspects of deadlines and meetings necessitated by their jobs, they fell into each other's arms and vowed that this pattern of ships passing in the night had to stop. And so it did one night, when Marianne told Jason she was pregnant!

"I guess I forgot to take my pills or something," she answered, a sheepish grin on her face.

Jason was not pleased by this development, at all, and let her know it.

"I thought we'd agreed that children would come when we both felt comfortable in our careers and could afford for you to take a maternity leave for a year. We're definitely not in that situation now," he concluded. "You'll have to have an abortion."

"Out of the question!" shouted Marianne. "This is a joint production and we're in it together. So get used to it."

And thus began the erosion of their relationship. In due course, Marianne had one more surprise in store for Jason several months later when she doubled the size of their family by giving birth to *two* very healthy and energetic boys. This sent Jason into freelancing on the side, looking for additional ways to supplement his income to keep their household afloat.

Eighteen months later, Marianne was finally able to return to her job, leaving the twins with a nanny that her income had to cover. By this time, though, their respective life paths had drifted so far in divergent directions that they had little meaningful family life left.

Jason was absorbed in building what was turning out to be a very productive career at *The Guardian Economist,* while Marianne's work was not making much progress at all. They managed to keep their family together for the sake of their children for a couple of years, but ultimately there was no relationship left worth talking about.

It all came undone one particularly dark weekend, when Jason had to leave London to interview a politician for a major exposé he was writing. The twins picked this very weekend to both come down with bad coughs and colds, leaving Marianne to sort out the entire mess on her own. Upon Jason's return, she told him that the marriage was finished and asked him to find another place to live. Her final words to Jason were, "You'll hear from my lawyer in the next few days about sorting the details."

As often happens in life, when one door closes, another opens. And so it was with Jason. Very shortly after finalizing his divorce from Marianne, his articles for *The Guardian Economist* led to an invitation to join the *Trans World News* (TWN) network on their investigative team. He found this position to be a perfect match for both his interest in foreign affairs and his inclination to dig behind the scences for the *real* stories underlying the surface events. At TWN he would have the chance to hone his investigative talents, along with a considerable financial upgrade to international editor. This would enable him to live a very comfortable life, as well as pay Marianne for support of the twins. How could he refuse the TWN offer?

At the time Jason moved to TWN, world affairs were shifting from West to East. Jason became increasingly intrigued with the stories coming in from the TWN Tokyo Bureau, and decided to enroll in a night class in East Asian studies at the London School of Economics. A few months later, the Tokyo Bureau Chief for TWN suddenly took a position with the British Foreign Office, and TWN headquarters in

London asked Jason to replace the senior editor in East Asia, who was being promoted to Tokyo Bureau Chief. The new position would enable him to dig out stories all over Japan, the Korean peninsula and China, as well as provide him with a chance to experience personally how life is actually lived in these radically different cultures.

While he worried about not seeing his boys as regularly as he'd like, Jason knew this position in Tokyo would not be permanent, but would lead to an even higher position when he finally returned to Europe.

*

Almost from the moment he stepped off the plane at Narita Airport, Jason was a Japan lover. He found almost every aspect of Japanese life not only intriguing, but very *sympatico* with his nature. The people were unbelievably polite and friendly. The food was in a class of its own, especially in Tokyo, which he discovered had one of the highest cuisine rankings of any city in the world. And, like a lot of western men, he found Japanese women both mysterious and sexy in appearance and behavior. Yes, he thought, it was definitely the right place to come to recover from his divorce from Marianne.

After a brief settling-in period, Jason buried himself in his work: meeting his TWN colleagues, learning how to get around in Tokyo, home-study of Japanese and, of course, trying to get himself stabilized in the social milieu. This last task was a combination of business and pleasure, as he had to develop contacts for his TWN articles, as well as figure out how to fill the holes in his personal life left by the divorce and living half-a-world away from his boys. He soon discovered several restaurants and cafes that he liked in the upmarket Shibuya neighborhood where he lived, and after some months became familiar with both the staffs and customers at these places.

Jason also tried to understand why Asian women exert such an attraction for Western men, as the Japanese women he met were unbelievably different both in appearance, dress and especially culture from what he was familiar with from his plain vanilla-style British upbringing.

At one point, he tried to analyze the essential difference between, say, the Japanese lady who worked in the restaurant or, for that matter, in his office, and what he had experienced in London. But in the end he never really quite figured it out. It seemed to be a combination of a hundred little things that added up to a type of femininity that by Jason's experience was simply absent in Western countries. Or maybe it was just absent from *his* life in the West. Same difference though, as he explored many Japanese ladies, coming to the same conclusion with every one of them.

One day as Jason was hard at work in his office trying to meet a tight deadline for his next article, he looked up to a knock on his open door and saw his boss, the Tokyo Bureau Chief for TWN, Malcolm Blair, standing there.

"Hi Malcolm. What's going on?"

"Nothing special, Jason. I just wanted to see how you're getting on here in Tokyo. I know about your work, but was wondering about the rest of your life. Maybe we could take a dinner together later this week and just talk about whatever, nothing special. What do you think?"

"Sounds like a great idea," agreed Jason. "When would you like to meet?"

Blair looked into the distance for a moment, then told Jason that his assistant would fix the time and place and send him a message sometime tomorrow about the dinner.

After Blair left, Jason wondered if there was something wrong or if Blair was just being welcoming, as it appeared. He didn't want to analyze. The answer would appear over dinner when they met.

*

When Blair's assistant called to say the dinner with Malcolm would be at seven o'clock Thursday evening at the restaurant Yakitori Imai, Jason breathed a sigh of relief. He had already been past that restaurant, at least from the outside. It was only a couple of streets away from his flat in Shibuya, so he'd have no trouble getting there on time. He wondered if perhaps Malcolm had deliberately chosen it with that very point in mind.

The Yakitori Imai turned out to be essentially a single, spacious open kitchen, where each of the tables were for only two people and looked onto the chef's main charcoal pit. When Jason arrived, he saw Malcolm already seated at one table and went over to join him.

"Nice place you chose," said Jason. "And I see you've already ordered a glass of the local brew to get our conversation off to a good start."

'I think you'll like this place, especially the chicken skewers. They are very special," Malcolm told him.

"Sounds good to me. Did you order already?"

"Not yet. But here comes the waiter so we can do it right now."

After placing their orders, the two of them chatted for a bit about big city life in Tokyo vis-a-vis that in London. Eventually, Malcolm leaned over, looking Jason in the eye, and quietly asked him:

"Are you happy you made the change to come here, Jason? We at TWN are happy with you. But are you satisfied with your life here with us?"

Jason was a bit taken aback by this question, as he had never thought of Malcolm as being the fatherly type. Yet he supposed that this kind of attention was simply part of the job of managing a western office in such a non-western location.

"Yes. I'm very happy I came here, Malcolm. I could not ask for more. It's been just fine, so far."

"I'm pleased to hear that, Jason. One reason I asked is that now that you've been here a few months, I think it's time to step up your game a bit and put you into a broader circle than what you've experienced up to now."

"What do you have in mind?"

"You've produced some good material for us since you've been here. But I can see that at heart you're really an investigative journalist. For that you need lots of contacts, not just here in Japan, but all over East

Asia. You need to get into the political and social areas where Japan is interacting with its Asian neighbors."

As Malcolm paused, Jason looked over at him and asked, "How do you suggest I do that? I certainly agree with the sentiment you're expressing, Malcolm. But how to implement your 'contact development' idea is another matter."

"Here's how we'll do it, Jason. While Tokyo is our largest Asian bureau, we also have bureaus in Beijing and Seoul. In addition, we have stringers working with us in Bangkok, Hong Kong, Taipei and elsewhere. My suggestion is that I arrange meetings for you with our colleagues in these places. TWN will then finance a trip for you to talk with these people and tell them your interests. They will then put you in touch with locals in their respective regions who can serve as sources of information for your articles. Okay?"

"Oh, that sounds perfect, Malcolm. I want to make these contacts and I can't think of a better way to do it."

Malcolm then gave Jason a very intense look. "A lot of the topics you're going to be exploring in the coming months and years are also of great interest to Her Majesty's government. So we sometimes share information, in the sense that we tell government people things they want to know, and they reciprocate with information useful to us."

"Okay, I get it," said Jason. "We share with British Intelligence, right?"

Malcolm smiled and nodded. Then he went on, "Next week, I want to introduce you to 'Tony Baker', the local MI6 man in Japan. I think you and he will hit it off just fine. The combo of the trip and working with Tony should set you up with more contacts than you'll ever be able to use. How do you feel about that?"

"I can hardly wait to start this job," smiled Jason, clinking glasses with Malcolm just as the waiter arrived, carrying a large skillet of chicken skewers.

*

Over the next couple of years, Jason's profile in the TWN scheme of things shot up dramatically. Contacts all over East Asia brought in leads and background information that Jason had a knack for turning into front-page articles. And his relationship with MI6 via Tony Baker only accentuated and often gave added insight into stories that competing journalists in Tokyo and elsewhere never quite seemed able to match. All in all, Jason's professional life was soaring.

However, Jason could not say the same for his personal lives, either on the intimate or family side. While he had the typical Western fascination with Japanese women, he knew that his stay in Tokyo would be limited in duration. As a result, at the intimate level he had interacted with a series of ladies, usually for a few months apiece, before each gave way to a successor. As for the family level, he managed to see his sons once a year on his annual leave, as well as speak to them on video or audio calls a couple of times a month. But at some point he realized they were growing up without him. Unlike his situation with a sequence of cascading Japanese beauties, his position with his sons was one he didn't want to let slide further than he already had—perhaps off a cliff.

One day after work, he and Malcolm happened to be leaving the office together. At that moment, Jason had an inspiration and asked if Malcolm might have time for just a quick drink before they headed their separate ways. Malcolm agreed and they headed for the bar at the Tokyo Hilton Hotel, just down the road from the office.

After settling in at their table and getting drinks, Malcolm asked, "What's on your mind, Jason? Nothing too serious, I hope."

"I apologize in advance," Jason replied, "but I'm afraid it is quite serious, at least for me."

"Well, spit it out then. What can I do to help ease your pain?"

"As you know, Malcolm, I've been here in Tokyo for nearly five years now. I feel like I'm wearing out my welcome, at least in regard to my personal life."

"What do you mean, Jason? You're certainly not wearing out your welcome with us at TWN."

Jason looked down into his glass and then took an unhealthy-sized swig of whisky before replying,

"Thanks for the kudos, Malcolm. Much appreciated. But that's not what I have in mind. I'm thinking more about my family life than my life here with TWN. I think you know I have twin boys, who were just toddlers when I left London and came here. Now I see them once a year on my annual holiday, and once or twice a month on a video call. But that's not nearly enough. Every time I talk with them, I feel more and more distant. They're simply growing up without me and I cannot take that much longer."

Malcolm looked Jason directly in the eye and said, "I understand, Jason. I gather you are asking if I could arrange for you to be transferred back to London. Is that it?"

"I've thought about that too, and I realize I have to try to balance my career at TWN and my family life with my sons. So I would not say I want to go back to London, as I think that would not help TWN or my career at all. All my journalistic strengths, in terms of contacts and expertise, are now largely based in East Asia, Malcolm. I need to find a way to get to London anyway, or at least somewhere in Europe, so I can spend time with my sons in person once or twice a month, rather than on a video chat from half a world away. But I have no idea how to make that happen without cratering my career."

Malcolm looked down at his watch and told Jason, "My wife has visitors coming for dinner tonight. But I fully understand your concerns and I promise that I'll do the very best I can to help you. Let me work on this and get back to you on it as soon as I possibly can. We certainly don't want to lose you to the competition. Okay?"

"Fair enough," said Jason, as Malcolm got up from the table. Jason said he'd stay for another round of whisky and so bid Malcolm a pleasant evening. He felt that the conversation with Malcolm went about as well as could possibly be expected, and hoped that a new post would open up somewhere in Europe soon. Besides, to be perfectly honest with himself, he had to admit he was starting to get a bit bored with life in Tokyo and would welcome being back in a more familiar social and personal environment.

Within a couple of weeks and with Jason's consent, Malcolm had negotiated a post for Jason with their bureau in Vienna. He thought that with all the international activity going on there, it would be perfect for further development of Jason's investigative instincts but in a different environment. Further, in his new position, Jason would be a kind of 'employed freelancer,' in the sense that he would not do assignments given by the bureau chief, but would be free to choose his own stories as they emerged. As a bonus for his work here in Tokyo the last five years, this new position would include a generous raise in pay. If Jason agreed, he could start the new post immediately after the New Year.

At the end of October, Jason packed his things and left Japan for what he felt was a long-deserved time together with his sons in England. He had booked a lovely Airbnb flat in central London for the holidays, which would also include a two-week skiing holiday in the western Alps of Austria in the famed village of Lech in Vorarlberg, where he hoped his sons would get acquainted with the art of skiing. He planned to move to Vienna immediately after the Three Kings holiday on January 6, and begin his new life as a 'freelance employee' with TWN.

*

"Well, Noriko, that's it. Now you know how I came to be here in Vienna. You also know why I have such a fascination with Japan."

Noriko opened her eyes looking totally mesmerized for a moment, before she came back to life and said, "This is absolutely fascinating, Jason. But your story ended one step too soon. You left out the last part: How did you happen to come to the Institute for Foreign Studies (IFFS) here in Vienna?"

"I was at a party shortly after my arrival in Vienna, where I met the director of the IFFS, Hans Gruber, who had read some of my articles on global energy supply. After he asked me why I was in Vienna, Hans told me the IFFS had a special program for Visiting Fellows, who could spend a year with the "academics," as he called them, working on whatever captured their fancy.

"I found this idea very tempting. So after a few months of settling in, I met privately with Gruber to discuss a fellowship. He was happy to receive my application, and in a few weeks, I was accepted and got a leave-of-absence for a year from TWN and joined the IFFS. And that's it. You now have the whole story of my life, up to the present moment.

"So now it's your turn. Show me Noriko's Story. Show me how you ended up here in my flat in Vienna, starting from your infancy in Tokyo."

IV

Noriko's Story

Tokyo

Before starting her story, Noriko took a small break, telling
Jason she needed to run a bit of cold water over her face to
recharge before "telling you more than I'm used to revealing
about myself."

While she went to the bathroom, Jason thought about
how lucky he was to have met such an amazing woman, and
the sort of life he envisioned for them together. Of course,
he realized he was caught in the grip of the initial stages of
a love affair, and the real world would eventually insert itself
into their world. But he was confident he could deal with that
disruption and keep the flame alive between them for a very
long time. On that thought, Noriko reentered the room and
sat down to tell her story.

"I'm going to follow your lead, Jason, and tell you my
history in a series of episodes and incidents rather than try to
give you a straight biographical account of my past. Besides,
I think this sort of episodic account really tells more about me
than a biography would anyway. So here we go."

As Noriko's lovely voice began recounting some of the key
stories of her life, Jason soon found himself lost in a world
beyond his own ...

Noriko left the Ueno underground station and began walking around the edge of Shinobazu Pond on her way to her class on nuclear management at the University of Tokyo. She was happy her course work would be finished very soon. She was determined to obtain her degree, get a job abroad and finally be able to escape from the suffocating environment that had dominated her life in Japan, for as long as she could remember.

What a relief, she thought, to be liberated not only from her father, who had taken charge of her since her mother's death at her birth from a Caesarean section that went wrong. She would also be relieved of the burden of being a very attractive young Japanese woman, who also happened to be intelligent. Not for the first time, she wished nature had given her a plain face and an average mind, so that she could simply blend in to the expected role of a Japanese female: wife, home and family. But ever the practical joker, nature had other plans for her. She just hoped nature would speed up the process of telling its joke so she could get on with her future, whatever and wherever that might be.

The professor was just organizing his papers in preparation for the lecture as Noriko entered at the top of the large, sloping auditorium. She quickly slipped into a seat, and noticed him looking in her direction as she sat down. Given the lighting, it wasn't clear whether he was giving her a slight smile or not. But it looked that way, at least to her.

In any case, the professor's look reminded her that he'd asked earlier if she could come by his office at the end of the day. He said he had something he wanted to discuss with her regarding her graduation and possible future.

Somewhat less appealing was the quiet 'hello' she heard from the row behind her. She turned her head in response to see Kenji Yoshikawa smiling down at her. Oh no, she thought, as she nodded a greeting to him. He had been pursuing her in a polite, but relentless, manner since the course began. It had only increased his ardor when she had agreed to have a coffee with him a few weeks earlier. Since then, he had become more of a pest than a pleasure, which was yet one more reason why she'd be relieved to graduate and leave both the university and her country behind and start a new life elsewhere.

Noriko wasn't much for casual dating and other sorts of typical collegiate social interactions. But she did occasionally see one or two of the more grown-up foreign post-graduate researchers in her department for an evening of intelligent discussion, a decent meal and even, on occasion, a tête-à-tête in the man's flat. But she really couldn't deal with the banalities of the type of dating Kenji and the other male students thought passed for 'getting to know one another.' It made her skin crawl just to think of spending her time in that kind of social environment.

But every now and then, she would 'flip out' and do something quite risqué in the social arena. In fact, she had to smile to herself thinking of an encounter she had just two nights ago that would have sent Kenji running as fast as he could in the opposite direction.

It had really begun a few months earlier, when Noriko's father told her one morning that Mr. Singh, a colleague of his from New Delhi, was in town, and he needed to send some papers to him at his hotel. He asked her if she would be so kind as to drop the papers off to Singh on her way to class.

While Noriko was less than thrilled at the idea of serving as a delivery girl for her father, she was uncomfortable defying him. "Hai, otosan," she agreed. He gave her the papers and Singh's cell number to make arrangements for the delivery. When she called Singh, they agreed to meet in the hotel lobby at ten that morning.

Singh was at the appointed spot in the hotel lobby right on the dot at 10 a.m., and smiled as he took the papers from her. He then asked whether he might buy her dinner that evening for her help in getting this material to him so quickly.

What a perv, Noriko thought. *He's at least as old as my father, with whom he does business, and he takes two seconds to hit on his daughter.*

She begged off from the dinner, telling him she was in the midst of her examination period and had no time in the evenings now for anything other than hitting the books.

"I understand," Singh replied. "Maybe we can have that dinner the next time I'm in Tokyo."

They shook hands and parted company—forever Noriko hoped. But it was not to be.

*

As Noriko was entering the subway to go home from the university a few weeks later, her phone rang. She didn't recognize the number but answered anyway. To her shock and dismay, the caller was Mr. Singh. He told her he was back in town and would like to follow up that earlier dinner invitation, asking if tomorrow evening would work.

Noriko's instinct was to hang up. But her upbringing wouldn't let her be that impolite. Besides, who knew how many billion yen rested on this relationship for her father? Not that she cared. But she wouldn't want her father to blame her for ruining a lucrative connection. But maybe he shouldn't have sent her to meet a perv in the first place.

She suddenly had a mischievous thought. *Okay, I'll agree to a drink, not a dinner. Then I'll make some preparations ...*

She suggested they meet just for a drink at his hotel the next night, as she was quite busy and didn't really have time for a dinner. He readily agreed to meet her in the hotel lounge at eight o'clock the next evening. Her trap was set.

She entered the lounge dressed as an actual delivery girl, hair tucked under her hat, wearing slacks and a blazer with a backpack. She saw Singh sitting alone at the bar. It was a little noisy; perfect.

She walked directly over to him in a very businesslike manner and whispered in his ear, "Let's go up to your room and have our drinks. It's too crowded and noisy here right now."

Singh couldn't believe what he'd just heard, and immediately tried to take her hand as he lowered his slightly rotund body off the barstool. She slipped her hand away and whispered in his ear again: "I need to run to the ladies' room first. What's your room number?"

She put her ear to his face, inviting a quick response. "Twenty-two-forty-three," he replied, still a bit stunned.

65

"I'll be right up," she whispered again so no one else could hear, immediately taking a beeline for the women's bathroom she'd previously located in the lobby, walking in as businesslike a manner as possible.

Once safely in the bathroom, seeing no one around, she looked in the mirror and smiled. She could feel the adrenalin coursing through her body. Most importantly, she was confident no one in the lounge would think they had seen anything resembling a romantic liaison. They had seen an important message delivered, the delivery girl had immediately left, and the recipient had also had to leave, apparently attending to some urgent matter.

But she had to be sure. Then she heard a flush, and knew she was in luck. A middle-aged woman came out of a stall, and Noriko put on her best frightened schoolgirl look. As the woman began washing her hands, Noriko asked, "Would you do me a favor, please? I might have been followed here by an older Indian man. Would you mind checking outside the door when you go out, and see if there's a sixty-something, plumpish Indian man with a big black mustache anywhere around?"

The woman was nodding as she dried her hands. An angry look came over her face. "Some men are truly disgusting. You wait here and I'll look around and if I see him, he'll wish I hadn't." Before Noriko knew what to say, the woman was out the door.

Gee, I hadn't thought of that possibility, Noriko thought with a grin. *Oh, well, we'll just have to wait and see.*

Thirty seconds went by and Noriko began to wonder. She moved behind the bathroom door and tried to hear what was going on outside, but nothing stood out. Finally, at what seemed to be about the one-minute mark, the lady came back in, looking for Noriko, and was a bit startled when she turned around and saw her behind the door, "I looked and looked, but I saw no Indian man anywhere in the lobby," the woman said. "I guess maybe you lost him. Be careful!" she said, almost scolding Noriko. Then she was out the door.

Noriko felt giddy. He'd fallen for it. She headed into a non-handicapped stall, closed the door and opened her small backpack. Safe from any possibility of legal surveillance cameras, within two minutes she was dressed in a flowing evening gown. Then she put on a Tina Turner-like punked-out wig that covered much of her face. Suddenly the door to the bathroom swung open and what sounded like a gaggle of giggling ladies entered. It was her cue. She stuffed her pants in the backpack, zipped it a different way so that it suddenly looked like a handbag, flushed the toilet and emerged.

The girls quieted down as they were now going into stalls. Noriko washed her hands, adjusted her wig in the mirror so that it obscured her face, and left the bathroom. Her phone rang, and she saw it was Singh. She answered it. "Hi. I'm on my way up."

"Uhhh . . . okay. I'll see you in a minute."

She got into an elevator and pressed 22. She almost couldn't believe what she was about to do.

"Well, hello!" Singh said as she entered his suite. "You look lovely! Can I fix you a drink?"

"That's what I'm here for, remember? I'll take a shot of Macallan. I believe it's the finest Scotch in the bar that comes with this big room. Will you join me?"

"But of course I will," Singh said with a wide grin, almost drooling like the big bad wolf. Noriko had to stifle a chuckle as she watched him pour two doubles for them. She knew he had big plans for these cocktails.

He handed her one of the fairly full glasses. "Badhai ho, as we say in my country," he said, clinking his glass against hers. "To the Gods who bring us this night." He took a deep sip, and Noriko pretended to do the same. But she knew better than to trust any drink this man poured.

He put his drink on the table and said, "Please excuse me, as it is now my turn to visit the boy's room," and headed toward the bathroom—maybe time for Viagra or Levitra or whatever. This was the moment Noriko had been waiting for.

As soon as he closed the bathroom door, Noriko opened her purse and took out a small envelope containing two strong sleeping capsules that she'd ground up into powder that morning. She quickly dumped this into Singh's glass, along with another splash of whisky and stirred it all up. Then she hid her glass behind some bottles and quickly grabbed a clean glass, pouring a little less than a shot into it. She returned his drink to the dining room table where he'd left it and sat down with her own just as he emerged from the bathroom.

"Come sit with me," she beckoned. As Singh sat in the chair at the head of the table, she said, "As we say in my country, Kanpai!" and with one neat swig, downed the entire contents of her glass.

Given his macho nature, Singh had to match her behavior and downed his own glass in one swallow. "Would you like another?" Singh asked, thinking Noriko had already downed a full two shots.

"No thank you. Let's just chat." She smiled at him.

"You are a very beautiful woman," Singh said to her.

"Thank you," she said, waiting.

"Why did you agree to have a drink with me?" he asked. Noriko thought she could detect a slight slowing in his speech.

"My father wanted me to treat you to some fine Geisha hospitality," she said.

Singh looked a bit startled. "Your—your father knows you are here?"

"Well, he's the one who asked me to deliver to you ... "

Singh's eyes were starting to droop.

"I am very good at massage," Noriko said.

Singh perked up. "That sounds great." He stretched his arms. "I'm feeling tired. A massage from a beautiful woman sounds great."

"Why don't we go to your bedroom," Noriko suggested, standing up from her chair.

"You don't beat around the bush, do you?" Singh said, standing up slowly. Noriko took his hand and quickly led him to the bedroom, while he could still walk. As they entered the bedroom, she immediately suggested he take off his clothes and lay down on the bed and rest up for the sexy massage that was to come. Noriko told him that while he was doing that, she'd pop into the bathroom and prepare herself for him. Smiling, he nodded his head and moved toward the bed, readily agreeing with her plan.

By the time Noriko returned from the bathroom, Singh was snoring like a buzzsaw. Noriko saw that his shirt, pants and socks were scattered at the bottom and side of the bed, as she opened her backpack bag, pulled out a pair of latex gloves and put them on. She then took out some narrow ropes. Going to the bed, she quickly removed Singh's underwear and fastened his hands and ankles to the bedposts.

Noriko then grabbed some alcohol wipes from her backpack bag and went around the bedroom, bath and bar area, carefully wiping off fingerprints from everything she might have touched since entering the suite. She then removed all traces of her phone number and messages from Singh's cell before wiping it down, too. She decided to remove his number and messages to her on her own phone as well, while she was at it.

She then grabbed the three glasses they'd used—the one he'd first given her that she'd stashed when he went to the bathroom, the one she'd replaced it with and the one she'd drugged him with and took them to the kitchen sink, where she washed them thoroughly with soap, still wearing her latex gloves. Confident that there were no loose ends that could be traced back to her presence in the room, she looked in the mirror and made sure the wig was obscuring her face, then went to the front door. Looking down at her shoes, as she had when she'd arrived so that surveillance cameras would only see the top of her head, she slipped out into the hallway.

Going down the elevator, Noriko smiled to herself, thinking how surprised the chambermaid would be in the morning when she entered Singh's room and found him stretched out on the bed. She exited the hotel from the back entry, preventing her from being seen by the clerks at the front desk. No more 'singing' from Mr. Singh, she thought to herself with a smile as she stared out the window of the subway car on her way home.

Of course, Singh might remember enough to put the pieces to-gether. And her father might lose Singh as a colleague—and maybe millions in the process. And even if Singh remembered everything and screamed it all at her father, she knew that he knew she wasn't remotely capable of such behavior.

She smiled, enjoying her punky reflection in the subway window.

*

As she left the classroom building the next day, Noriko encountered her friend Hiroko, one of the few fellow students she actually enjoyed spending time with. They had a couple of hours to kill, so they decided to go to the Shiru Cafe, a student hangout near the university, and chat a bit.

In no time at all they were settled in to a table by the window, had ordered their expressos and a roll and were updating each other on happenings since they'd last met.

Noriko started by telling Hiroko about her upcoming graduation and her thoughts about what she should do upon leaving the university. Hiroko was one year behind her, and she could hardly wait to get her own diploma and also head for Narita Airport.

"Yes," Hiroko continued, "I know what you mean. My parents are almost as clinging and demanding as your father. To be twenty-five years old and be treated like a schoolgirl is just a bit much. So wherever you end up, save a place for me."

"At the moment, I really haven't started looking for that ideal job on the other side of the world," Noriko told her. "But my professor asked me to meet him at his office later today. He said he had something interesting to speak with me about. So I hope it will be about a job and not about his marriage or his no-longer-secret admiration and longing for me."

"Worse, maybe it will be both," laughed Hiroko, ordering another expresso from the waiter, who gave both girls a long look as he made his way back to the bar.

"What would be your ideal situation?" inquired Hiroko.

"Well, in the best of all worlds, my new job would be located on a different continent, in an environment where women in the workplace are at least tolerated, if not respected, and where I can use my newly minted double degree in economics and nuclear energy in some meaningful fashion," replied Noriko.

"I wish you the very best in finding *that* trifecta," said Hiroko. "But I wouldn't put too much money on it. You're really asking for a lot. But you have a lot to give, too. So if anyone can do it, you can."

Hiroko then moved the conversation into the personal domain asking, "Are you still seeing that British fellow, Paul or Peter or whatever his name is?"

Noriko hesitated a moment before replying. "For the record, his name is actually Paul. And yes I am still seeing him on occasion. In fact, we have a date for dinner tonight."

"Sounds like things are heating up," said Hiroko. "But what about your Japanese boyfriend, Sueo? What's happened with him?"

"I think you know already that in general I take a pretty dim view of most Japanese guys, since they somehow remind me of my father. And while there's no shortage of foreigners to choose from here in Tokyo, I am not that self-confident to just go up to a guy at a bar or at a party and start chatting.

"But I met Paul when I had a small accident one day slipping on the wet pavement. He was very kind and helped me up. Nothing like my father would have done, at all. So we began seeing each other once or twice a month and that's now been going on for a few months."

"So did this chance meeting with Paul happen while you were still seeing Sueo? It sounds rather serendipitous. Or were you already looking for a foreigner to hook up with?"

"To be honest, I was still seeing Sueo when I met Paul," Noriko confirmed.

"Oh, so you just 'forgot' to mention that meeting to Sueo. Is that it?"

Noriko ignored the question and stared off into space, hoping Hiroko would drop the subject of Sueo.

Hiroko then did actually shift her focus to Noriko's confession made in an earlier conversation about how much she liked being a dominant female in a relationship. At the time, she thought Noriko was referring to her interactions with Sueo. But now with a British man, not a Japanese guy, as the focus, Noriko's remark about her sexual proclivities took on a new dimension. Hiroko decided to probe just a bit further.

"Are you starting to get serious about Paul?" she asked.

"Not really. Besides, as I just told you, I can hardly wait to get out of Japan. And Paul has a job here with a British company that is too good for him to leave. So I think we will simply shake hands very soon, promise to keep in touch and that will be the end of it."

Hiroko then backed off, telling Noriko that her plan sounded sensible. "Besides," she said, "wherever you go in the world for your new job, it will definitely not be over-populated with Japanese guys. Maybe it will be filled with guys like your father. But very few, if any, will be Japanese."

"Ha! Ha!" laughed Noriko, as the two of them got up to leave the cafe. Glancing at her watch, Noriko saw that she'd have to hurry to be on time for her meeting with the professor. So the two ladies quickly settled their bill and gave each other a hug on the sidewalk before setting off in opposite directions.

*

At the university, Noriko ran up the stairs to the professor's office on the third floor of the Nuclear Engineering Building. She was only a couple of minutes late, so didn't think the professor would consider her as really being 'late.'

She knocked on the office door, and the professor called out loudly, "Come in." She opened the door and entered, making the customary short bow to the professor at the doorway. He indicated the chair in front of his desk and she sat down primly on the edge of the seat.

The professor leaned toward her and said, "Thank you for coming, Ms. Yamada. First, I want to congratulate you on your impending graduation and the fine work you've done here in the department. It's especially impressive, given your dual major in nuclear energy *and* economics."

Noriko bowed her head and thanked him for his kind words.

Then he asked, "What do you have planned after you graduate? Have you found a job yet?"

"I'm just now bringing that question into sharper focus and making it my main priority," she told him.

"How would you feel about a position outside Japan?" he continued.

Noriko could hardly believe what she'd just heard. Outside Japan! Like a dream come true, she thought, as she lowered her head and told him, "I would have no objection to that. Of course, I don't want to go to some very distant place, say, Africa or South America. But a post in an industrialized country in Europe, or even North America, would be very attractive, actually."

"Good," he said. "Recently, just such a position came to my attention and I immediately thought about you, as the organization involved would like to encourage more women on their staff."

The professor then went on to tell her about a meeting he'd had a few days earlier with a colleague from the Japanese Federal Science and Technology Agency. He explained that this particular colleague also served on the board of directors of an international organization devoted to keeping track of nuclear energy activities in countries around the world.

"This organization is the International Center for Energy Studies, or ICES, a collaborative venture of many countries, including Japan. It's located in Salzburg, Austria. My colleague mentioned that the ICES currently has an opening for a researcher of Japanese nationality, fluent in Japanese language and culture, and that they would especially like to fill that post with a woman, if possible.

"If you took this post, you would have to serve as an intern on a six-month probationary contract. But if everything works out, you would then be given a normal three-year, renewable contract as a researcher. Would you be interested?"

"Very much so," she replied.

The professor then said, "I'll contact my colleague, Mr. Murukawa, and set up a meeting between the two of you soon."

A few days later, the professor rang her to say that Murukawa would be able to see her two days from now at his office in the Agency at two o'clock in the afternoon. Noriko said that timing would be perfect for her, and the professor then gave her the location of the Agency building and said he'd inform Murukawa that she'd be there as planned.

*

When Noriko met Mr. Murakawa, her initial impression was that he was a typical Japanese bureaucrat: short, middle middle-aged, a bit pudgy, fast-talking, and somewhat full of himself. But she quickly learned that his saving grace was that he was very smart. And she liked smart men.

He got right to the point.

"I see from the material the professor sent me that you are one of the brightest students he's had in many years. He also told me earlier that you are graduating with a double major in nuclear energy and economics. That's a perfect combination for ICES. So with your agreement I will be happy to propose you to the ICES Director as the Japanese candidate for the researcher position that's currently open. Would that be acceptable to you?"

"Yes, I'm sure I would like this post and fully agree with your plan," said Noriko.

"Fine. I'll confirm with you my conversation with the Director in a day or two. But I anticipate no problem, since this post has already been set aside for a Japanese citizen.

Before you leave here today, I'd like you to meet my colleague, Yoshiki Yamamoto, who will tell you a bit more about what we'd like you to do for Japan while you're at ICES. His office is just down the hall, so let me call and ask him to come here and collect you."

After a minute or two, there was a knock on the door and a somewhat younger-looking man than Noriko had expected was at the door to escort her to his office.

"Hello," the man said. "I'm Yoshiki. If you don't mind, I'd like to talk with you for a few minutes down the hall in my office."

"Of course," Noriko answered. She got up, thanked Murukama for his help and said she'd be looking forward to hearing from him. She then gave the professor the customary bow at the door as she left and followed Yoshiki to his office.

While he was walking over to his desk, Noriko noted that the office looked as if it had been abandoned. There were no books or papers on the shelves, or any working tools on the desk. She found it difficult to believe that Yoshiki actually worked in this space. Noriko had the feeling that he was not from this Agency at all, but from a totally different organization.

Yamamoto began by saying, "I don't know whether Murukawa told you about the peculiar status of ICES. It's an international organization, sponsored by many countries. But it is officially non-governmental. This means that it is not like a typical United Nations agency, but rather less encumbered by bureaucratic restrictions than if it were governmental. Fortunately, though, the Austrian government passed a law allowing ICES personnel to have the same privileges as UN employees. So from a practical, everyday point of view, you will be an international civil servant—without being a servant!"

"Sounds very appealing," Noriko answered. "Mr. Murukawa mentioned that I would have some responsibilities to Japan as well as my official duties at ICES. Can you give me some idea what he meant by this?"

Yoshiki looked at her for a moment before saying, "Nothing very strenuous. But the Japanese government is very interested in all aspects of nuclear energy, and during the course of your work you may come across bits and pieces of information that would be helpful for us and that may not make it into any of the ICES conference reports or published articles."

"How will I know what kinds of information would be of interest to you?" she asked.

"Ah, that's precisely why we're speaking now."

He handed Noriko a card with a name and phone number on it. Looking at the card, she noticed the phone number began with the prefix +43, not the Japanese prefix, +81. So she assumed this was an Austrian number, which Yoshiki confirmed.

"Over the next few weeks before you leave to assume your new post in Salzburg, I'd like you to meet with me weekly for an hour or two. I want to provide you with a bit of training, as well as answer all questions as to what information we'd like to see. Would that be all right?"

Noriko agreed with the proposal, and so met regularly with Yoshiki for training in how to leave and receive covert messages, how to identify people who might be following her on the street, and how to secure her communication by both phone and computer from eavesdroppers.

Early in these lessons, Noriko asked him: "Are you training me to become a spy?"

He said that was not the point of the lessons, but once she got to Austria he would like her to meet occasionally with the man whose card he'd given her earlier.

"Maybe you can meet him for a meal or a drink every now and then. He will ask you about your work, with particular emphasis on items that our government is especially keen on knowing about. Just answer his questions as best you can and that will be it. Nothing very clandestine about this, at all. Just keeping us informed about things that might not surface in the official information channels of the ICES."

While Noriko had some pretty negative feelings about her family and a few other aspects of Japanese culture, she retained a very patriotic spirit and loved her country. Moreover, she didn't really see anything wrong with what Yoshiki was asking her to do.

And it might provide the occasional adrenalin rush. She agreed to his plan.

*

"And that," Noriko concluded, "is a brief glimpse of how I got here, as well as some other things I'm not sure I should have told you about."

"Well," said Jason, "that's quite a story. A sexpot and a spy. You seem to have lots of identities, Noriko. I'm going to have fun uncovering your many personalities."

"Well, not *that* many," she countered. "But have your fun, however you can get it."

As Jason looked at his watch—it was 2:43 a.m.—Noriko said, "Now I have to get back to my hotel. I'm absolutely worn out and my train to Salzburg leaves at 7:38 a.m. tomorrow. So while I'd like nothing more than to hug and kiss you, Jason, I don't think my body is in harmony with my brain right now. So I'll have to give you a credit for future closeness and bid you a good night."

"I understand," Jason replied. "I'm pretty bushed myself. So I accept your credits and give you the same in return. We will see each other shortly, I'm sure."

Noriko got up from the sofa, put on her coat and walked back to Jason with open arms and a big smile. They joined in a loving kiss in front of his door, which he then opened and, grabbing his coat and keys, followed her to the elevator. "It's nearly two a.m. and while Vienna is safe, I'm at least walking you to the front of your hotel."

"I appreciate that," Noriko smiled. The elevator dinged, the door opened and they climbed in. On the way down, they stole another kiss. They emerged from the elevator holding hands.

A minute later, he watched as she walked into the lobby of her hotel. He wondered again how a guy could get so lucky, when he wasn't even trying.

V

The Parabola

Salzburg

It was a gloriously bright early winter's morning, from the mountains towering above them to the smiles on the faces of the skiers on the slopes. As Jason and Noriko lifted into the air, Noriko clung to Jason, almost squealing with delight: "Wow! That was quick! Obviously, I've never been on a ski lift before!"

Jason was laughing, holding Noriko tightly against his right side. "Older ski lifts can be a bit jerky," he admitted. "But they're more romantic, with only room for two."

"Yes, that's nice," she looked up at him and he felt her left hand pulling his head down toward hers. They began a long, slow, passionate kiss.

Jason could not believe how happy he was. He never knew it was possible to feel this much bliss. Images of the last four months with Noriko danced in his mind, the laughter and the lovemaking, the sightseeing and the conversations, swirling in his head, a mélange of joy, as they continued to kiss, floating above the Earth. Jason had never been one to believe in soul-mates, but he was beginning to think reality was proving him wrong. Lately he had found himself happily rethinking almost everything.

A buzzing began to enter Jason's consciousness. The sound of an electric xylophone suddenly jarred him out of his reverie.

Noriko pulled away from their kiss and he opened his eyes into the bright sun, shining from behind her. He turned his head away instinctively, momentarily blinded.

"Oh, darn, I'm sorry, I forgot to turn my phone off," he heard her say.

Just then, a gust of wind buffeted their lift chair, and glancing to his right, he realized they had already come to the bluff, his favorite spot. Jason had first learned to ski here nearly twenty years earlier, on a college trip. He'd revisited almost every year before being sent to Tokyo. This was his first time back since returning from East Asia, and he was looking forward to teaching Noriko how to ski. But first, he wanted to share his favorite view in the world with her, on this ski lift, where it comes to 'the buffety bluff' as he and his college mates called it, where the lift line runs alongside the mountain, revealing a vista of pristine Austrian forest far below, stretching out for miles. But if there was an east wind, it would hit the mountain far below and come screaming up, buffeting the ski lift chairs as they passed.

He began turning back to Noriko excitedly. He couldn't wait to see her face when she saw the view.

"Oh no, my purse!" He heard Noriko shriek as he turned toward her. He caught a glimpse of her bending down quickly, trying to snatch at something in the air, at her feet.

Then she was gone. He thought he heard a whimper.

No. Can't be.

The ski lift chair was rocking almost violently, he realized. This was real.

No. Can't be.

He realized the safety bar was still up. He'd never pulled it down. *Too busy laughing. Hugging. Kissing.*

No. Can't be.

Wait, there's snow below at a steep angle. Extreme skiers do this all the time.

He looked down and saw her face, looking back at his, her eyes longing for his, accelerating away as her arms reached hopelessly upward toward him.

Then she bounced off the rock outcropping, her instantly limp and lifeless body suddenly twirling head over heels in a macabre parabola away from the mountainside, a hundred feet below, then two hundred, then three hundred feet below him before she finally hit the steep, soft snow on the side of the mountain and rolled, the way he'd hoped she might much sooner, avoiding the rocks, giving her a chance. He saw a streak of pink snow and had to look away.

The ski lift was still moving. The world was just as it had been thirty seconds before. Except ...

He thought about leaning forward and just letting go. If it was a dream, he'd just wake up.

He could feel—even hear—his own heart pounding, trying to burst out of his chest and follow her down, bouncing, like she had, off the rocks, falling into peaceful oblivion with her.

*

He couldn't get the images out of his head. The whole sequence kept replaying over and over. It had been almost a week since the accident, and it wouldn't stop. The only relief he'd felt was at night, after the heavy dose of Trazodone the ER doctors had put him on, along with telling him to relax.

But he couldn't relax. Not for the first few days, at least, when he'd been suspected of murdering Noriko. It had been two years since anyone had died in a ski lift accident in Austria, and the authorities were very suspicious, despite the eyewitness account of the couple sitting in the lift chair just forty feet behind them. They'd seen everything, thank god. Otherwise, Jason knew, he might very well be losing the next decade of his life, as well as his career, along with the love of his life.

He began to tear up. He did that dozens of times a day now.

Later today, there would be a memorial service for Noriko at the offices of ICES before her ashes would be shipped back to her family in Japan tomorrow. Ake, Noriko's boss at ICES, had taken care of everything.

On impulse, after he'd awoken with a scream, watching her slip away yet again at 4 a.m. in the morning, he'd left his hotel room in Salzburg and headed back to the scene of the accident. *Maybe if I see it again,* he'd thought. *Maybe it will become real enough to leave my dreams.*

Now he found himself sitting on a ski lift chair—everyone had looked at him oddly, there'd been murmurs from staff who recognized him—yet somehow no one had stopped him from just walking out and getting on a lift chair, wearing just a light winter jumpsuit and athletic shoes.

He left the safety bar up.

Jason came over the very spot where Noriko had fallen. He could still see faint signs of her in the bloody terrain created by her impact. Or was he just imagining blood on the rocks? He tearfully bowed his head, recalling their magical time together.

Sobbing quietly to himself, Jason recalled their initial meeting at ICES, the first day he'd come from Vienna to make a presentation to the Institute's staff about his work as an international journalist. At that presentation, Jason spoke about the studies he'd undertaken on the triangular battle between Japan, South Korea and North Korea over nuclear weaponry and energy supply in the Korean peninula.

Due to Noriko's own work on energy availability and consumption in the peninsula and the impact of nuclear power—and weapons—on the balance of power between the three nations, she had taken charge of the Q&A part of Jason's seminar and afterwards took him to lunch for further discussion. In retrospect, it seemed that it was during that lunch that they had begun to fall deeply, hopelessly in love.

His thoughts moved to the confirming moment of that love in the totally unplanned event at the end of their walk from the restaurant to the Salzburg train station for his trip back to Vienna. Jason recalled so fondly asking Noriko to stop. And then facing her, he drew her near and gave her a very deep and passionate kiss.

At that pivotal event, Jason hoped against hope he had not misjudged Noriko's feelings for him, and that she felt as strongly about him as he did about her. In a flash his judgment was confirmed, as she wrapped her arms around him and returned his kiss in a way that mirrored the same intimacy. Their first kiss suddenly confirming how they both felt about each other, they continued to the station, hand-in-hand, with hearts and hopes soaring, promising to meet in Vienna at the earliest possible opportunity.

That kiss marked the beginning of the happiest four months of Jason's life—and now, the most terribly desperate last few days ...

*

The last several months were a blur in Jason's mind, as he recalled the weekly meetings with Noriko, either in Salzburg or in Vienna, sharing their minds, bodies and spirits with equal passion in all dimensions. He especially treasured the long weekend they spent together in Venice, which gave rise to a collection of memories of the canals, the museums and restaurants that they both treasured and often spoke of following their return to Austria. He began sobbing yet again as he suddently remembered a discussion they were having about an encore visit to Venice just before they got onto the chair lift that fateful morning.

And then, the kiss on the lift, the happiest and saddest moments of his life side-by-side, as Noriko and all their dreams came crashing down to earth.

He was sobbing heavily now. He began hearing voices ahead of him.

"There he is, officer. That's him."

Looking up, he realized he was only a few feet from the top station of the lift. There was a uniformed security officer waiting. A small crowd seemed to have gathered in the vicinity.

Jason held his hands up in mock surrender, letting the security officer know he was no threat. The tears rolling down his cheeks might have helped in that regard, too, as the officer had a sympathetic look as he helped Jason up from the chair. *He probably knows who I am,* Jason realized.

"I understand you forgot to buy a lift ticket," the officer said, putting his arm around Jason's shoulder and walking him away from the lift. "And I see you forgot your skis, too."

"Yes, officer. Bit of unfinished business—"

"I understand, sir. But now we need to get you back down." The officer was still walking, arm around Jason. He had a nice, round, friendly face, and stood a good six inches taller than Jason.

"Well, I could just get back on a chair," Jason offered, pointing a thumb behind him. The officer continued to walk him away from the lift. *I'm in the arms of a friendly giant.*

"No, sir, you don't have a pass, remember? Wouldn't want to have to arrest you. And some people are more than a little concerned, so we've arranged a private ski patrol transport." The officer pointed ahead, and Jason suddenly noticed they were just a few feet away from a large snowmobile with two ski patrollers, one driving and the other in the back, leaving an empty seat in the middle.

Jason climbed into the empty seat.

"You alright then?" the big bear of a security officer asked. "Put your seat belt on."

"Yessir," Jason said, managing a little smile. "Thanks very much for your help."

The snowmobile engine sprang to life and they were off, down the hill.

*

Back in his hotel room, Jason took a hot shower and got dressed in a suit and tie. The alarm he'd set on his smartphone for 11 a.m. went off. He'd have to hurry to get to ICES in time for Noriko's memorial service. He ran a quick comb through his hair and made his way to the street, flagging a taxi to take him to his final meeting with her at ICES.

Entering the ICES building, Jason ran into several ICES people he knew casually from his visits working with Noriko. They all greeted him the same, with a friendly smile but somehow keeping their distance as if they didn't want to intrude on his privacy at this emotional moment just prior to the upcoming ceremony. He also couldn't help but wonder if they'd heard he was being investigated in connection with her death. Even though it hadn't been in the news—the Austrian police had told the media it appeared to be a tragic accident—Jason couldn't help but wonder if there were rumors swirling.

Walking to the room where the memorial would take place, Jason was somehow pleased to see that it was the very same room where he met Noriko the first time he came to ICES months ago for his seminar presentation. How cosmic, he thought, that the events beginning and ending his life with her should occur within a few feet of each other in this room.

Upon entering the room, Jason's attention was immediately drawn to a large picture of a smiling Noriko, taken at some outdoor ICES event in the summertime. The picture was on a stand, flanked on both sides by high candles in holders sitting on the floor. The candles were lit and created a perfect glow on Noriko's lovely face as she appeared to give her attention and care to her ICES colleagues as they entered the room.

Noriko's boss, Ake, noticed Jason and beckoned him to come to the front of the room where he had reserved a chair for him very close to Noriko's photo.

"I'm very sorry, Jason. This must be one of the saddest moments of your life. We all miss Noriko enormously and think of her every day." Ake wiped a tear from his cheek.

"Yes, Ake," Jason began, as Ake took his hand and held it gently. "You're absolutely right. Even though we had known each other just a few months, I loved Noriko more than I will ever be able to express. She was my life. I appreciate you and the ICES staff organizing this lovely farewell for her."

"We want to pay our respects; giving her our love by this memorial event seemed the best way to do it."

"I agree," Jason confirmed, as he took his seat just in front of the photo, where Noriko was looking down on him as if from heaven. Ake then moved to the podium at the front of the room and began his opening remarks.

"Thank you all for coming. We are here to honor our beloved colleague and friend, Noriko Yamada, who as you all know tragically died in an accident last week." Ake paused, choking back a sob. "She—She was a valued member of our research team and a loving friend to all of us."

Ake then proceeded to give a short summary of Noriko's life and education prior to coming to ICES, mentioning her recent personal relationship with Jason. He then said that everyone was welcome to come to the front and file by Noriko's photo, leaving any messages or mementos that they cared to offer her. He said that these would be gathered together and sent with a condolence message to Noriko's family in Japan.

At that point, Ake stepped back and the procession of ICES personnel began making their way to the front of the room as Vivaldi's *Four Seasons* came from the speakers in the corners of the room.

As the last mourner left the room, only Ake and Jason remained. Jason looked at Ake and said, "If you have a moment, I'd like to go to your office and have a word with you."

"Fine, Jason. If you hadn't suggested it, I would have done so myself. Let's go now."

"One more thing," Jason said as they made their way to the back of the room and the doorway, "would it be possible for me to have that photo of Noriko that's in the front of the room?"

"Absolutely," Ake replied. "I'll have it packaged and sent to you in Vienna."

"Thanks so much. I will treasure it."

*

They entered Ake's office, and as they sat down, Ake opened a bottom drawer in his desk and brought out two glasses and a bottle of fine single-malt Scotch whiskey. Holding the bottle up to Jason, he said, "I can't think of a better time to have a sip or two of spirits. Hopefully, they will pump-up our own, which right now need a bit of support, I think you agree."

Jason nodded in appreciation, saying "Pour away, Ake."

After a sip or two in silence, Jason started the conversation. "When you first visited the Institute for Foreign Studies in Vienna, Ake, where, as you know, I am a visiting Fellow this term, I was very intrigued by what you told us regarding the mission of ICES and was pleased to accept your invitation to come here and make a presentation of my own work to the ICES staff. That was the beginning of a beautiful friendship, as Bogart said at the end of *Casablanca*.

"And so it turned out. The consulting job you offered me has been very rewarding, both intellectually and with the huge bonus of working with—and loving—Noriko. I can honestly say it changed my life."

"Indeed," replied Ake. "It changed our lives here at ICES too, having your expertise accessible to address aspects of the Korean peninusula problem that we academics seldom see in such a first-hand manner as you have."

"But I think," Jason said, nodding "you must realize that with Noriko's death and all that means, it would be very stressful for me to continue working here, especially as an important part of my work for you involved personal interaction with others on the ICES staff. To be in this physical environment now would be painful beyond my ability to withstand. So I must now tender my resignation from ICES."

"I suspected this would be the case, Jason. And let me say that I totally understand your feelings and would certainly do the same myself if I were in your situation. So with a heavy heart, but an understanding mind, I accept your resignation. Please just send me a short note confirming this when you get back to Vienna."

"I will do that," Jason agreed.

Ake then leaned over, topping-up their glasses and toasted Jason, wishing him the very best for his future.

"Bottoms up," Ake said, holding up his glass and draining it, followed immediately by Jason doing the same.

"I guess there's not too much more to say," Jason re-marked, as he got up from his chair. "Except to tell you I'm also resigning my fellowship in Vienna. I'm heading back to London."

Ake stood, leaning across his desk to shake Jason's hand. "We'll miss you, Jason. I wish you the very best and thank you for what you contributed to our efforts here."

With that, Jason made his way from Ake's office to the street, hailing a cab to the main train station for his return to Vienna.

*

As the cab neared the station, Jason began to choke up at a nondescript corner in front of the station. This was the very spot where his romance with Noriko really began, where they had their first kiss.

Knowing he almost surely would never visit this particular spot again, he looked around at the streets, the buildings, the shops and everything else in this special place on the surface of the Earth, trying to cement them into his mind forever. Suddenly, he began sobbing, filled with thoughts of what might have been. As the emotions and tears ran their course, he realized the cab had stopped. He paid the cabby and entered the station, promising himself he would survive this day and come out of it as a stronger person, as he was sure Noriko would want him to do.

Jason boarded the train and headed into the next stage of his life.

The Middle Game

VI

Back to London Life

London

Arriving at Heathrow on his flight from Vienna, Jason collected his luggage and grabbed a taxi to his flat near the British Museum. On the way, he thought how lucky it was he had only sublet his flat when he went to Vienna and that the sublet had run out just a couple of months ago. In the midst of the greatest love affair of his life at the time, Jason had decided not to lease it out again, but instead, keep it empty, ready for whenever he and Noriko might want to visit—or even move to—London.

Before he realized what was happening, Jason felt a tear rolling down his cheek in the cab. He quickly wiped it away, checking to see if the cabbie had seen him crying in the rear-view. He caught him just averting his eyes. *It's the dreams that get to me,* Jason reminded himself. He could think about Noriko, even catch himself smiling when thinking about her. But whenever he thought about dreams he'd had for the two of them, and what might have been—*I've got to try not to think about the dreams.*

But now, he just wanted to rest. He was grateful to be able to retreat to the comfort and security of his long-time home in London. And also thankful, he had to admit, that he'd never brought Noriko to London for a visit. All his memories here were from before her. He was hopeful that would help.

After unpacking and settling in, Jason called his former wife Marianne and their boys, telling them that he had now moved back to London. He couldn't tell how Marianne felt, but the boys were overjoyed at the news, and he promised to see them soon. How nice to see them again regularly in person, rather than by video call or simply just hearing their voices on the phone.

Before leaving Vienna, Jason had called Andrew Smith, his London boss at TWN, telling him the sad story about Noriko's accidental death and his emotional need to get out of Austria and return to London. Andrew said he understood and suggested they meet for lunch whenever Jason felt up to it, after he was back and settled in London. He decided to call Andrew right away.

"Hello, Jason," Andrew answered, trying a bit too hard to sound cheery. Jason could hear some chatter in the background, probably a nice dinner party somewhere.

"Hey, I'm not interrupting, am I?" Jason asked.

"No," Andrew lied, nicely. "What's up?"

"Any lunch plans tommorrow?"

"Lemme check. Uhhh, no, as a matter of fact. See you at Westminster Arms at noon sharp?"

"Yes, I remember," Jason chuckled, surprising himself. "That's when they open, noon sharp, best time to get a window seat."

"Up for some beef and ale pie?" Andrew asked.

Jason chuckled again, feeling the best he had since—he remembered, and felt his smile fade. But he pressed on: "No, Andrew, I'll pass on that."

Andrew chuckled back at him. "Yeah, wise choice, perhaps."

Suddenly Jason remembered: "Oh, but I haven't had sticky toffee pudding since the last time I was there, years ago!"

"Another wise choice," Andrew said.

"Hey, Andrew, thanks, see you tomorrow!"

"You got it, Jason."

Jason fell back on the bed, the most relaxed he'd felt in days. A minute later, he was asleep, still half-dressed.

At lunch, eating only sticky toffee pudding with a Guinness chaser—while Andrew enjoyed the fried chicken for which Westminster Arms was rightly known—Jason told Andrew he'd like a bit of time to decompress from the events in Austria. But he felt he would be ready to return to his job as a senior correspondent for TWN relatively soon. Andrew agreed to Jason's request, telling him to take as much time as he felt he needed.

Jason returned to his flat after lunch feeling woozy and barely able to get through the doorway before he took off his shoes and laid down on the sofa. Soon he was in an uneasy sleep, dreaming about threads of his earlier life in London and Tokyo and how that life trajectory ended up with him now beating a quick and unhappy, but necessary, retreat from Vienna. His dream included some happy thoughts about reconnecting with his twins, James and John.

So when he woke up, Jason called Marianne, asking if it would be okay to meet the boys for a walk and a lunch in

Hyde Park on Sunday. She thought that sounded lovely and they made arrangements for Jason to pick the boys up at 10 a.m. Sunday morning.

*

At the appointed time, Jason came to pick up the twins from Marianne. She greeted him with a warm "Great to see you, so glad you're back in London," and had the great good sense to say absolutely nothing about his recent terrible loss.

"Daddy! Daddy!" The sound of running footsteps came from behind Marianne before the boys flew by her and leapt onto their father. They were eight years old now, and he wavered a bit as they hugged and clung to him.

"James and John!" said Marianne. "Take it easy on your father!"

"Oh it's alright," Jason said, feeling a warm shiver up his spine. It was the first time he'd heard Marianne call him "father" warmly in many years. "Are you ready for a bit of a walk around London?"

"Yes! Yes!" Came the enthusiastic answers from both.

"I'll see you back about three, then?" Marianne asked, confirming their prior arrangement.

"That's right, Mare," Jason replied, and off he went with the boys.

"Are we going on the Tube?" John asked.

"Right you are," Jason said with a smile as they walked to the nearest Underground station for the Central Line.

Twenty minutes later, they got off the Central Line train at Marble Arch and walked across the street to Hyde Park,

96

where they encountered a crowd of listeners at Speaker's Corner. A young radical was spouting his theory of governmental change that should be made to help the young and impoverished (like himself) get integrated into British life. Lots of shouting, booing and laughing accompanied his cry from the heart, sounds that Jason hadn't heard in years.

How different from life in both Tokyo and Vienna, he thought, as his sons stood watching in puzzled confusion, wondering what the hell was going on. Jason thought he'd have to explain all this brouhaha at lunch, as he moved the boys along past the the corner and into the Park itself.

"You know, boys, this lake is called the Serpentine, and it was built here in Hyde Park over three hundred years ago." There was absolutely no reaction from the boys to this. They were picking up small pebbles and trying to skip them along the water. Jason decided to try a different tack: "Are you getting hungry?"

They both turned, yelling simultaneously: "YES! I'm hungry. When can we eat?" Jason told them the Serpentine Bar & Grill was just up ahead.

After a surprisingly quiet lunch—the boys immediately settled down once their fish and chips arrived—they walked along the Serpentine, watching a variety of people sailing their model boats in the lake. This prompted a discussion between the boys, which led to them asking Jason if maybe they could have a boat like one of those they saw for their upcoming joint birthday present. Jason didn't want to disappoint them, so he told them he'd think about it. He secretly hoped that while he was thinking about it, they would be forgetting about it, as he was less than enthusiastic about getting into the boat sailing business with them. He'd have to test those waters in the coming weeks.

After another hour strolling and frolicking around the Serpentine—during which Jason caught himself laughing freely several times—Jason told the boys he'd promised their mother he'd have them home by midafternoon, and so they'd have to start heading back to the Tube for the trip home. Of course, they tried to dawdle, but he finally got them home, more-or-less on time, telling them he'd be back for an encore visit very soon. On the way back to his flat, Jason put that return visit on his calendar. He was happy to reflect on being able to see his sons pretty much whenever he wished.

After just a week back in London, Jason started feeling as if he needed the everyday activities of the TWN office, not to mention the world, in order to reposition himself back into some semblance of normal life. He sent a message to Andrew Smith asking if they could have another lunch. Andrew replied almost immediately, suggesting they meet the day after tomorrow at a pub just down the street from the TWN offices.

When Jason arrived, Andrew was already sitting at one of the booths with a window view of the street. He beckoned Jason over to join him.

"Great to see you, Jason. You're looking a lot better than when you first arrived back. Must be the London weather!" They both chuckled.

"Happy to be here," Jason said, shaking Andrew's hand. "But it's despite the weather, not because."

"So true," Andrew agreed, as they placed their order for sandwiches and a couple of large pints of the local brew. "Now what can I do for you today, Jason? I'm hoping you're going to ask me if you can return to active service. But please proceed."

"You're exactly right, Andrew. I want to come back. I think the best way for me to heal is to get back to work."

"Yes, Jason, the kind of healing you need is work and social distraction, not aimlessly walking the streets and sleeping badly. So, yes, you're welcome back to your old spot at TWN as soon as you can make it over to us again."

"How about tomorrow?" responded Jason with a smile. Andrew smiled back, they clinked their pints together, and the deal was done.

The next day Jason turned up at the TWN building, walked over to Andrew's office and declared himself ready for "active duty." He was almost yearning for the hustle, bustle and most importantly, the distraction of having to produce meaningful copy for TWN. He hoped it would help him leave behind his unhappiness over the loss of Noriko. He simply needed to accept that she would never again be back in his life.

*

Andrew walked Jason down the hall to his new office. Carrying his box of personal office accoutrements, Jason was pleased to see that his new office was next door to the office of his long-time friend, James Peters, the chief science correspondent for TWN's monthly magazine. James was on the phone, but waved and smiled at Jason as he passed by; Jason reciprocated with a smile and a nod.

Andrew unlocked the door and put the key on the desk inside. "Glad to have you back aboard, Jason," he said as Jason laid his box down on the desk.

"Damn glad to be back, Andrew," Jason said, shaking his hand. Andrew drew Jason in and put his left arm around his shoulder, giving him a hug. Jason hugged back. It felt good.

After Andrew left, Jason sat down at his desk and breathed a sigh of relief. *Finally,* he said to himself, *I'm back on the job again with a mission to fulfill, surrounded by colleagues to work with.* After the somewhat independent situation he'd been in as a visiting fellow to the Institute in Vienna, Jason felt a sense of stability and collaboration that had been missing from his time in Austria.

As he put a few books on the shelf behind his desk, Jason heard a knock on the open door to his office. Turning around, he saw his old friend James, smiling in the doorway.

"Well, come on in, you old pirate!" Jason said with a big grin.

"How lovely to see you again, too, Jason," James replied. "You go from being a stranger the last five years to, suddenly— well, it would seem we're practically going to be office-mates." James put out his hand, and Jason shook it enthusiastically.

"Indeed, indeed! How have you been, James? Digging up the dirt in the world of science, I hope."

"Well, some dirt is dirtier than other dirt," James replied. "I try to keep my hands and words on the cleaner side, if I can. Tell me your own plans now that you're back here at TWN in a grand office with all the trimmings."

Jason told him that he had agreed with Andrew to spend the next few months simply getting resettled into the local scheme of things before starting back into the routine of an investigative reporter. For the time being, he was going to write a monthly article for the TWN magazine, outlining the state of the world energy-wise. Taken as a whole, these articles would give a pretty complete summary of who has the energy resources nowadays, who needs them and how that transfer would be accomplished and at what price.

"That should get me back into the swim of things, both within the company and within my own mind, before I head back out to the field."

James agreed this sounded like a sensible plan. On his way out, James turned back: "How about lunch tomorrow? Are you booked yet?"

"No, that would be great."

"Alright, then. I'll meet you at this doorway at noon, and we'll take it from there."

"Sounds fantastic, James. Glad we're neighbors."

'I'm just glad you're back in the same damn building, Jason!" They both laughed.

The next day, as they were walking to the White Rhino Pub, James asked Jason to bring him au courant on his overall situation, especially his time in Vienna. James already knew about most of Jason's work while he was in Tokyo at the TWN office there. And Jason knew it wasn't plausible that the past year of his life would be a total blank to anyone in the TWN building, much less a close colleague like James. News people follow the news much more closely than normal people, especially news involving other news people, even more so news people in their own organization and most of all prominent journalists in their own organization. There would have been news coverage of any ski-related death, and much more coverage of any ski-lift death and even more coverage if a prominent journalist was involved. So after they got settled in at their table and ordered slices of the pub's famous roast beef and mugs of beer to wash it down, Jason outlined his life in Vienna.

"Basically, I was like a coin in Vienna," Jason explained. "The heads side was the fellowship I was awarded at The Institute there. I was using their generosity to start writing a book on global energy resources. In fact, even though I didn't quite finish that book before I returned here, the work I did on it will go a long way toward filling up those articles I promised to write for Andrew. So it definitely was time not wasted."

"I'll look forward to reading those articles in due course, Jason. But what about the tails side?" James inquired, slicing into his roast beef. He had, of course, heard about the ski-lift accident, just as everyone in the TWN building had—it had been the main subject of water-cooler discussion for several days after the incident, at least until the coroner and the Salzburg police had ruled the death an accident.

Jason recounted his amazing and totally unexpected love affair with Noriko, the euphoria of that affair and their plans to marry. James said he had not heard about the marriage plans but some word had gotten around the office about Jason and Noriko.

"It was the most fantastic personal interaction I've ever experienced—until my whole life collapsed within the space of thirty seconds!"

"Yeah, I heard about that, too," said James, trying to sound comforting.

"Yes, my lovely Noriko fell off a ski-lift chair reaching for her purse that slipped out of her hands. No more Noriko—and so far, no more Jason either, at least in any normal sense of that term."

"Oh, Jason, I'm so, so sorry."

"Well, it was many weeks ago now, James. But I'm still in recovery mode. And the recovery is not going all that quickly, I have to admit. My psyche is still obsessed with Noriko. I suppose I'll get over this trauma one of these days. But Noriko's death in such a freak accident was certainly the biggest blow I've ever had the misfortune to experience. So now you know the heads and tails of my life in Austria."

With that, Jason finished his beer and suggested they leave history behind and get back to the office.

*

A couple of weeks later, Jason and James happened to bump into each other outside their offices, as they were both leaving early on a Friday afternoon. Jason asked James if he could spare a few minutes as there was something he wanted to speak with him about. James nodded his head and suggested they go to the bar in the Underground station up the street and down a pint before heading home. Jason was grateful for this offer, and they went off together to the station.

After they picked up their beer at the bar, they retired to a standup counter at the back of the place, where they could speak undisturbed by the comings and goings of travelers getting 'one for the road.'

"So, what's on your mind, Jason? I'm sorry I've been so busy with my projects lately that I haven't had much time for socializing. Tell me how I can help you."

"Basically, I've been suffering a lot from continued grief and obsessions about my dearly departed lady friend, Noriko. She even enters into my dreams. And, yes, nightmares, too. And when I meet a woman, either professionally or socially, I immediately start comparing her with Noriko—even if they're not Asian or don't look at all like her. I'm very worried about this."

"So how can I help you, my friend? This sounds serious and like something that needs attention."

Jason moved a bit closer to James, and said quietly, "In your job as a science reporter, you must meet people from every walk of life in the scientific community. And I seem to recall seeing a couple of articles you wrote a while back about psychotherapy. So I'm wondering if you could help me locate a good psychotherapist that I could consult about my obsessions regarding Noriko?"

"Well," said James, "I have indeed interviewed a few psychiatrists and psychotherapists over the years. And I'm sure I have their coordinates in my filing cabinet. I must warn you, though, that I was the one doing the interviewing, not them. So I cannot speak from a personal point of view as to how effective they are in providing help. But they had very high reputations and I would be happy to give you their names and phone numbers. And, of course, you can use my name as a reference if you talk with them. Hopefully, that will get you onto their couch and, perhaps, in due course get those thoughts out of your mind."

"That would be just fine, James. Thanks so much for your help. I'm sure they will remember you and your good words. I'll stop by your office Monday morning and get the info. Now let me pick up the tab for these drinks and wish you a good ride home and a fine weekend."

"Thanks, Jason. I'll just wish you a happy weekend with a couple of good nights' sleep."

And so it was. James' contacts were sound and Jason soon had an appointment with one of London's most reputable analysts. A few weeks later, Jason popped his head into James' office, thanking him again for brokering the contact.

"Oh, sure," James said, "my pleasure. Glad to hear— uhhh—are the sessions going okay? Maybe I shouldn't ask—"

"Basically, as one might suspect," answered Jason. "The analyst told me that my condition was a pretty common one, especially in a situation where a loved one dies suddenly in a violent and unexpected way. And it is further accentuated when the relationship is still in the 'I can't do without you' phase. So to cut to the chase, he told me that time is the only true healer for this malady. But he said it would help if I would start socializing on a broader basis than usual."

"Did he mean start meeting a lot of new women?" asked James.

"Not really. In fact, he thought it might be more helpful if I were to just get back into the swing of everyday interactions. I should start seeing people at events, parties and, in general, get back into the swing of normal social interaction. Love affairs and the like will then make their appearance in due course. But he definitely did not say I should immediately join a dating site or start picking up new women in bars."

James looked more relaxed at hearing this therapy advice, and told Jason he was glad to have helped. "And any time you want to take me to lunch, I'll be glad to contribute to your prescribed course of therapy."

Jason chuckled as he headed to his office next door.

*

A few weeks later, Jason was trying to live it up at the TWN annual pre-Christmas party in the Main Conference Room downstairs. He'd already had a few drinks and said hello to a few colleagues who he hadn't yet met, beyond the odd nod hello in the hall or lunch room. But despite these efforts, he wasn't in particularly good spirits, either physical or emotional, when he bumped into James.

"How's it going, Jason? Are you enjoying your 'socializing' exercise here tonight?"

"Not really."

"Sorry to hear that, Jason. Are you getting any more sleep these days?"

"No, and it's kind of adding up. I don't seem to make it through a night any more without at least one panic attack. Sometimes more than one."

"Yeah, I was thinking you look like shit, actually."

"'Thanks. You look damned good, yourself."

"Couldn't be better. Have you tried actually dating anyone yet?"

"Not yet," Jason replied. "But I do have a couple of funny stories to tell you about that domain."

"Well, let me get a refill of this very smooth whisky, Jason. Then you can fire away."

Upon James' return, Jason told him that a couple of weeks earlier he'd joined an online dating site specializing in linking up slightly older men like him with younger women.

"So what happened? Did you meet any luscious beauties?" asked James.

"Not quite," said Jason. "But I did have some pretty wild experiences."

"Give me an example or two to whet my appetite for another whisky," James suggested.

"Well, probably the strangest encounter I had was not in person but online. It was with a young woman from somewhere in the Balkans, Croatia, I think. You'll be flabbergasted to hear what she proposed."

"My sense of 'flabbergast' is pretty high. But try me."

Jason went on to tell James that this lady offered him her entire body! She said he could have her transformed by plastic surgery (which, of course, he would have to finance) into any form he wished, provided only that they both agreed on the changes.

"So if I wanted her to be thinner, bigger tits, fleshier lips, et al. I just had to pay the price for the changes and she would become my ideal partner," Jason said.

"You're joking, of course," replied James. "You're saying this woman offered her body literally for you to do with as you please?"

"Exactly!"

"Unbelievable," James said, shaking his head. "Anything else of this sort turn up?"

Looking at James very seriously, he mentioned an encounter where another woman said she would send someone to him to 'put a bullet in his brain.'

"What?!" exclaimed James. "Tell me about that one. It sounds outrageous, if not totally illegal."

Jason shook his head and said he'd go into that sometime when they were both a bit more sober. Right now, he could only admit that while the dating site was definitely interesting and he did meet a couple of more 'normal' women that he enjoyed talking with, there were no potential life partners waiting on the screen for him, at least not yet.

At this statement, James fell silent for a moment, then told Jason he needed another shot of courage, then headed off toward the bar, saying "I'll be right back. Don't go anywhere."

Jason was a bit taken aback. But at a party like this, strange, unexpected behaviors often became the norm, so he wasn't all that worried about James, at least not yet.

Upon his return, James told Jason he'd been thinking about Jason's social life and had learned something recently he wanted to tell him about. But this was not the right environment for that kind of conversation, so perhaps it would be best to do it in the office when they were both in full possession of their senses. James suggested they meet in his office tomorrow for coffee and a chat, say around 10 a.m. Jason was a bit puzzled, but agreed to James' plan. The two of them then drifted apart into different corners of the room.

*

Both Jason and James were pretty much hung over the next morning when they met in James' office. But hung over or not,

Jason couldn't contain his curiosity as to what James had in mind.

"What do you have to tell me today that you couldn't tell me last night when my head was only clouded with alcohol, rather than throbbing from its after-effects, as it is now?"

"Okay, here's the deal," James replied. "I did an interview last week on one Gerald Meissner, founder and president of Illuminata. Ever heard of them?"

"No."

"Well, they're in the East End, with the tech start-ups, and they specialize in merging AI with robotics."

"So what does this have to do with me?" Jason asked.

"Just possibly *everything*," replied James. "Illuminata is in the business of creating 'humanoid robots', which means robots that both look and at least appear to think like real humans. Meissner showed me a couple of examples of their work while I was there and it totally blew my mind. The humanoids I saw looked, acted, sounded and behaved just like normal human beings. If you saw one on the street, you'd walk by it without a second glance," James told him.

"Still, I ask, what does this have to do with me?" said Jason.

"Well, Jason, in the interview I did on Meissner, he told me Illuminata uses actual human DNA for the skin, and the reason these robots—although he doesn't call them robots, he calls them Illuminata—anyway, the reason they look so real is because they have real human skin, like flesh-and-blood ninety-eight-point-six degree skin."

"That's amazing. But what made you think of me when you learned all this?"

"I'm getting to that. I asked him where they got the DNA they use for the skin and he told me they can grow skin from anyone's DNA now, and they can use 3D modeling to duplicate any person's appearance, well, almost any person's, or a certain kind of person. He told me they couldn't do anyone too underweight or overweight, as that caused problems.

"And as I was listening to all this and my head was spinning, I suddenly remembered a brief video I'd seen of Noriko on the news, some archive footage of her they ran right after the accident, and I remember noticing how perfect her skin was, and suddenly I thought of you."

Jason was silent. Then: "You mean, you're suggesting they could build a Noriko robot?"

"Meisnner told me they based their process on—forgive me, but this is when I started to really think about you—they base their process on the old Disney animation process, where artists would spend dozens of hours studying a particular fawn, for instance, and then base all their Bambi animations on that animal. At Illuminata they base every robot, android, whatever they should be called, to some degree or another on a real person."

Jason felt slightly sick to his stomach. "I think I'm going to have to pass, James. I find this whole concept really deeply disturbing. And I need some coffee. And maybe an ibuprofen."

*

Jason sat up in the dark, gasping and sweaty, just as he did most nights, his heart trying to beat its way completely out of his chest. He'd just watched Noriko die yet again. It had been so long since he'd had a good night's sleep he was giving up on the idea of ever having one again. The first few weeks back in London had been okay, but it seemed like the further away he got from Noriko's death, the more it was haunting him …

The strange conversation he'd had with James the day before suddenly came streaming back into his brain. But now it felt different. For one thing, he'd been hung over. For another, maybe a robot Noriko would be just grotesque enough to snap him out of this endless loop he seemed caught in.

*

Later that morning, he popped his head into James' office.

"Good morning, Jason. You look awful. What can I do for you?"

Jason came in, closed the door behind him and sat down facing James across his desk.

"What were you going to propose I do with this robot suggestion? I don't want to be known as the reporter—"

"All their clients are so confidential they don't even meet with them on the premises unless the client requests it," James said.

"So I would be a client? I'm not a multimillionaire, James."

"You'll be stunned at how affordable they are. Fifty, sixty thousand pounds."

"No."

"Yes."

"My God, this could change everything. I don't mean for me, I have no idea what it might do for me. I mean for the world."

"I'm working on a book about it, Jason. Because you're right. But if you decide to do something with Illuminata and want to tell me about it, Jason, I won't include anything about you in the book, just so you know, without your complete permission. Even if you did want me to tell your story, I'd suggest it be anonymous, and I'd give you full editing rights over it."

"I know that. I trust you, James. So if I wanted to look into this further?"

"I can ask Meissner to give you a call. He'll come see you at your flat, if you prefer."

"Do it." Jason got up, left James' office, went to his own and sat down behind his desk, all without a word.

VII

Illuminata

London

After another dream of the joy in Noriko's eyes and the love that had filled his heart, followed instantly by the nightmare of the terrible, bloody parabola of her lifeless body spinning away from him, down the mountain, Jason, sitting up in bed in another cold sweat, couldn't ignore the fact that Meissner might possibly have a solution to the anxiety and angst troubling his soul. While he was very skeptical about the ability of anyone to actually create a believable copy of Noriko, or of anyone else for that matter, he had to see things with his own eyes in order to lay the matter to rest.

After all, James had told him that Meissner's firm, Illuminata, was making serious use of some very heavy ideas in complexity science and artificial intelligence to create humanoid robots that were amazingly true to the human beings they were designed to emulate.

When Jason got to the office a bit late and droopy-eyed from lack of sleep, he was relieved to see James at his desk looking up at him. James waved him in.

"Good morning, Jason. How are you doing?" James was clearly concerned for his friend, by the look on his face.

"Do I look that bad?" Jason asked.

"Well, in a word, yes."

"Thanks for the honesty, I guess."

"Would you like some coffee?" James asked, gesturing towards the Nespresso machine on the mini-bar next to his desk.

"Oh, no thanks, I'd better get to my desk, I've got some in there, anyway."

"Well, before you go, Jason, just one quick question: You ended our conversation yesterday quite abruptly, telling me to call Illuminata and set up a meeting for you. Would you still like to visit with Meissner and see his miracles first hand?"

"Yes, I want to be able to cross this possibility of duplicating Noriko in a humanoid robot off the list of different ways to settle my psyche so I don't have to think about it any longer. Please call him and see if you can get an appointment for me as soon as possible. But please don't tell him any of the details about why I want to see him. Just say I'm a friend who's interested in their work and might turn into a customer if the conversation goes that way."

"Will do," James said. "I'll let you know as soon as I've set things up."

Jason thanked him and returned to his own office. But he had quite a bit of trouble focusing on his work, as the impending meeting with Meissner at Illuminata kept intruding on his ability to put Noriko onto his mental back-burner.

The next day James knocked on Jason's door. "I got an appointment for you with Meissner next Friday, a week from today, at 10 a.m. Will that work for you?"

"Sure," Jason said, entering the appointment into his smartphone.

"Meissner is a busy man. But he remembered my visit and moved a couple of things around on his calendar so as to accommodate—otherwise it would be about a month before he could see you."

"Thanks very much, James. I've got it in my calendar. Could you please forward his phone number to me?"

"Sure thing, Jason. Good luck."

I'll need more than that, Jason thought to himself, watching James head back toward his office.

*

The next morning, Saturday, Jason woke up for the first time in days without a nightmare, feeling almost refreshed. He'd spent some time Friday afternoon clearing his weekend calendar of any work, then taken a good dose of over-the-counter sleep syrup that night. It was the first time he'd felt well-rested in several weeks.

He was looking forward to picking up his boys at noon, but that gave him a few hours to kill. After showering and downing a coffee-laden whey protein shake, he decided to take a look at the Illuminata website.

It was stunning. The company eponymously called their robots "Illuminata"—and they did not appear the least bit robotic. To all appearances, the Illuminata looked, moved and spoke like real human beings. There were a few videos showing an Illuminata in conversation, where they seemed to interact intelligently, very much like a person would.

Jason found himself growing extremely skeptical. *This seems too good to be real. I bet these videos have been doctored with computer imagery.* He'd see for himself when he

115

met with Meissner. He closed his laptop and headed out to meet with the boys.

But when he got back that night, he had to look at the website again. He fell asleep propped up in bed, reading about the Illuminata. And that night, instead of nightmares, he had weird dreams of robot women—nothing overtly sexual, but snippets of conversations with fem-Illuminata, about what he was really looking for in a woman.

He woke up Sunday morning feeling weird, but it was a good weird. *Disorientation is better than panic and despair,* he thought to himself. And every night for the rest of the week, he fell asleep to the increasingly comforting sights and sounds of fem-Illuminata. For the first time since Noriko died, he got through an entire week without a single nightmare.

*

Illuminata took up three floors of a rather new office building just a block from the Mornington Crescent underground station on the Northern Line, and only a few steps from the entrance to Regent's Park. Jason had heard that many of the upmarket high-tech startups in London were housed in Islington, and he was glad Illuminata was among them as it was also fairly close to his own flat near the British Museum.

Jason introduced himself to the receptionist, who then called *Professor* Meissner and told him that Jason Bell was here to meet with him. Jason noted the title, wondering if the academic focus was just for marketing purposes, or reflected a deeper bent.

Meissner turned out to be a pretty good model for Jason's image of an academic—on the short side, a bit paunchy with a scraggly gray-black beard, wearing an ordinary gray suit, a bit the worse for wear, and a not-quite-properly-fastened bright red necktie. Maybe he was just overdoing the academic image a bit, thought Jason. But it was a lot better than a typical upmarket business-type, with a thousand-dollar suit and a smile that could blind you if you didn't look away fast enough.

"Nice to meet you, Mr. Bell," Meissner said in a firm voice. "James told me a bit about you, mostly that you are a world-famous columnist for TWN, and I do believe I may have seen your face on television at some time. Anyway, James said you have some issues he thought I might be able to help you sort out. Let's head down to my office, grab a cup of coffee and you can tell me about them."

Pushing aside a stack of papers on his desk to make room for the coffee cups, Meissner and Jason sat on opposite sides of the desk, which looked more like that of an academic nerd than a high-flying London executive.

"Now, how can I help you, Mr. Bell?"

Jason decided not to let on he had been looking at the Illuminata website, or that he had a personal interest at all. Perhaps Meissner was only seeing him because he was hoping for a favorable column or other media exposure. For the moment, he would play his cards close to the vest.

"According to James, your firm manufactures robots that increasingly resemble human beings, not just in appearance, but in manner, speech, even thinking?"

"I wouldn't say thinking," Meissner said. "But on the other points, yes. Our Illuminata, as we like to call them, are very human-resemblant. And even their thinking might appear somewhat human. But that's only an apparency. Their thinking is advanced AI, modified by some proprietary algorithms we've created, in order to make them as human-compatible as possible."

"So they don't really think like us, they just seem to," Jason said.

"Exactly."

"James told me you base the way Illuminata look on real people, even giving them real skin?"

"Yes, we actually use motion-capture of real-world models, that is, real people, on which we base our body frames. Then we use 3D-printers to build the Illuminata skeletons to the correct proportions. We can only do this within a certain range—we can't create very small or large Illuminata or overly thin or heavy. But every Illuminata is actually based on a real-world human model."

"And you use human DNA to manufacture real skin?"

"Well, we grow the skin, yes. Illuminata are actually ninety-five-point-five degrees to the touch, which is the median human skin temperature, three degrees below the core temperature."

"How do you do that?" Jason felt himself getting pulled into this discussion in a way he rarely ever was. He could feel his 'objectivity' flying out the door to Meissner's office.

"It's a proprietary technology."

"Do Illuminata bleed if you cut them?"

"Not blood, but moisture is released, which can mend the wound. But for a full 'healing' the injured Illuminata have to be brought back in."

"Do Illuminata have some sort of genitalia?"

"Human genitalia are optional in Illuminata. Both fem-Illuminata and masc-Illuminata may or may not have genitalia."

Jason paused. He decided to go back to his planned line of questioning. "AI is now able to teach itself, from scratch, to play chess by simply playing games against itself, and within a few hours, it can beat any Grand Master. But I think building a robot that can faithfully copy a human form, as well as behavior, is a far cry from chess. Don't you agree?"

"Yes," declared Meissner, without a moment's hesitation. "I would *not* go so far as to say Illuminata are operationally identical to a real human being. But we are getting very close to that standard, even as I speak."

"That's an extraordinary claim, Mr. Meissner. I hope you will be able to back it up by showing me some examples of this today before I leave."

"Indeed, I intend to do just that," declared Meissner.

"But I have a few more questions before we get to that demo, if you don't mind?"

"Fire away," Meissner said, leaning back and spreading his arms wide behind his head.

"Let's start with physical composition," said Jason. "Normal humans are composed of biological components like cells, fats and blood vessels, that somehow combine to create organs like a heart, kidneys, a stomach and, of course, a brain. My understanding is that robots have no such biology at all. Is that correct?"

"Except for the skin, which we talked about, it certainly is," Meissner replied. "This is not to say that robots don't have internal components that in various ways play the *functional role* of these biological organs. But they are not biological in structure. For example, the robot brain is a computer composed of transistors, logical circuits and metallic pathways rather than neurons joined together by the nervous system into spatial webs. Similarly, for internal components that provide the energy the robot needs to move its arms, legs and other organs."

"So you're saying that the robot is structurally very different from a human organism. Yet, it is functionally quite similar?"

"Precisely!" clapped Meissner. "You're getting into the spirit of Illuminata."

Jason wanted to explore the behavior of the Illuminata interacting with humans. He had read somewhere about the Turing test for deciding whether a machine could display human intelligence. "Could you explain the Turing Test, and could Illuminata pass it?"

"In the early days of computing," Meissner explained, "people were concerned with whether a computer could be made to think like a human. So around 1950 Alan Turing devised a test for this. The 'Turing test' was quite simple. Just put a human or a computer behind a barrier. On the other side of the barrier, was a normal human who could interrogate the entity behind the screen.

The test consisted of the interrogator asking questions to the entity, questions like 'How do you feel when you wake up first thing in the morning?' or 'What's the best way to make a milkshake?' and so forth. After thirty minutes of interrogation, the questioner had to decide whether the entity was a computer, or the entity was a human. If the interrogator could not reliably decide between the human or a computer, then the machine could be said to have human intelligence."

"Or at least that's what Turing thought in those long-ago days. In short, if its thoughts were indistinguishable from those of a human, then the machine had human intelligence. Rather naive by today's standards, but remember, this was many decades ago."

Jason asked Meissner if they could make a souped-up version of the Turing test by having a human interact with either another human or an Illuminata. These interactions would consist of more than the simple questions-and-answers of the standard Turing test: face-to-face conversations, handshakes, hugs and kisses, reactions to behaviors of the interrogator's face and voice and so forth. Again after a period of time, the interrogator would have to say, 'This is a human' or 'This is a humanoid.' If the interrogator could not reliably make the correct choice, then Illuminata, if that's what it was, would have passed the test.

"Have you performed any tests like this?"

"That's what folks like you are here for, Jason. This type of 'grand test' will be performed by everyone who interacts with Illuminata. In fact, they will be performing it in the comfort of their own homes! *You* are part of the grand experiment. And our job is to create Illuminata that consistently pass this very test. Now perhaps you'd like to meet some Illuminata personally?"

*

On the elevator ride down to the 'labs,' as Meissner referred to the areas where 'fully activated' Illuminata were kept, Meissner had a warning: "You should be aware that some Illuminata you meet may appear unsophisticated. Like all AI systems, they are self-learning. But some are pretty new, and haven't had much time for learning yet."

"Alright," Jason said, as the elevator door opened. He felt his stomach tighten just a bit. *How stupid,* he thought to himself. *I feel like I'm going to the eighth-grade dance.*

"Just down this way," Meissner stepped to the right as he left the elevator, heading down a long hallway. Jason followed. "These labs, as we like to call them, appear identical to studio apartments, Mr. Bell."

"Just call me Jason."

"Alright, Jason," Meissner said, smiling back at him. "How would you like to meet Marie?"

"Sure."

Meissner stopped at the door to their right. It had what appeared to be a camera doorbell. Meissner pressed it, and it rang softly.

"Hello?" came a distant feminine voice from a speaker somewhere in the doorbell. "I'm coming. Just a sec." There was a pause. Jason thought he heard footsteps from inside. Then: "Oh. Dr. Meissner. And a handsome guest—"

The door opened, revealing a statuesque blonde woman wearing a form-fitting yellow silk dress, revealing a curvy figure. "Hi, Dr. Meissner," she said almost breathlessly, then looked at Jason and smiled. She was wearing fairly bright red lipstick on voluptuous lips. Against his deepest wishes, Jason felt himself suddenly aroused.

"Good morning, Marie," said Meissner. "I'd like you to meet my friend, Jason Bell. He's here to meet and talk with some of our friends at Illuminata."

"Hello Jason," Marie said in a nice, soothing voice, one bordering on being almost sexy, but not quite—it was toned down from the greeting she'd given Meissner. "Please come in and make yourselves welcome." Marie motioned them inside. It looked exactly like a well-furnished studio apartment, but without any windows. Looking directly at Jason, Marie asked, "How are you today?"

"Well, I'm doing fine. What about you?" responded Jason, slightly stunned by how human Marie appeared. *James was right. If I was in a bar right now, I'd swear this was a real woman coming on to me.*

"I'm doing better now that I'm meeting you. It gets a bit lonely here in the lab just sitting around all day with not very many people to talk with. Are you here looking for a new friend?"

It suddenly hit Jason—this woman, uhh, this Illuminata— was clearly based on Marilyn Monroe. Maybe a bit more athletic? Taller? With a modern hairstyle, but clearly ... Jason suddenly realized she was getting a puzzled look on her face. It had been several seconds since she'd asked him a question, and he hadn't moved a muscle! "Uhh, no, Marie, I already have a friend that I'm very attached to. But if I were looking to meet someone new, I would definitely ask for your number."

"Well, perhaps on your next visit, Jason. I think we might get on very well together."

"Marie," Meissner interjected, putting his hand on Jason's shoulder but continuing to look at the fem-Illuminata Marilyn Monroe replicant named Marie, "would you please excuse us? I just realized we have another appointment we have to get to."

"Certainly, Dr. Meissner. I'm sad to see you go so soon, but far be it from me to keep you from an important appointment. It was very nice meeting you, Jason. Here, let me get the door."

Marie stepped deftly around the two men, in what Jason realized were black high-heeled shoes, opening the door so gracefully that it reminded him of modern dance.

"It was nice meeting you, Jason," Marie purred as he and Meissner stepped back out into the hallway. On the way, without being too obvious, Jason looked closely at her cheeks. Her skin was perfect.

"It was very nice meeting you, too, Marily—uhh, Marie," Jason stumbled.

Marie the Illuminata smiled sweetly, keeping eye contact with Jason as she closed the door.

"Our next appointment, Jason, awaits in my office," Meissner said, pushing Jason by the elbow back toward the elevators.

"Well, alright," Jason said, a little surprised. "I thought I might get to meet more than one of Illuminata's Illuminata."

"Oh, you will. We just need to go over a couple of things first." Meissner pressed the elevator button. Just then, a well-dressed young man emerged from a door next to the elevator and walked by them.

"Hello Dr. Meissner," he said in a pleasant voice.

"Oh, hello there. Good to see you," Meissner replied.

"Thank you, you too," the man replied, looking back with a smile as he continued walking away from them down the hallway. The elevator doors opened and they got in.

"That was an Illuminata," Meissner said as he pushed the button for the eighth floor.

"What are you talking about?" Jason asked.

"The young man in the hallway. That was not a human being."

Jason was stunned. The elevator started to rise. "Just running around loose?"

"Yep. They can do that if you want them to. Laws of robotics. Asimov. They're not going to hurt anyone." The elevator doors opened and they got in.

"Well, I must say, Dr. Meissner—"

"Just call me Gerry,"

"Okay, Gerry. Marie was something else. I swear I just met a young Marilyn Monroe, even though it's been over a hundred years since she was born."

The elevator door opened, and they headed toward Meissner's office.

"You picked up on who she was modeled after, huh? But I have some things I need to tell you about that, and that's why we're back here in my office," Meissner said, unlocking his office door by waving his hand over a small silver disk embedded in the wall next to the doorknob. "Would you like some coffee?"

"Sure. So does Marie come on to everyone? Is that some kind of programming?"

"No, and that's what I wanted to talk to you about. I've never seen her come on to anyone before. In fact, her attitude towards me was even a bit different. So I decided to cut it short, just so I could explain a few things. Cream or sugar?"

"No thanks."

Meissner handed Jason a cup of fresh coffee from the mini-brewer and then got himself one. "Are you familiar with complexity science?"

"My colleague James, who told me about you, has explained a little. It explains the development of life, doesn't it?"

"Well, that's one of many things it explains. You're probably aware of entropy, the process of universal decay, where energy and temperature and structure tend to even out. If I have hot water over here in one flask and cold over here in another, just wait an hour and they'll both be at room temperature. So one tendency of the universe is to try to make everything the same: same level of energy, mix up all the elements into a soup, that kind of thing.

"But there's another, opposite tendency of the universe, and that's the tendency to build complexities. So we end up in an incredibly complex world run by humans with technology, instead of just a hot planet orbiting the Sun, a billion years before green algae evolved.

"The most unique thing we've done here at Illuminata, is we've programmed our AI, our standard self-learning artificial intelligence, with a rudimentary understanding of complexity theory, and how complex systems evolve. Now we're not saying our Illuminata are self-aware, but we believe this understanding of complexity may give them the ability to become so. But one thing is for certain: once we did this, the manner and behavior of our Illuminata became markedly less distinguishable from normal human behavior.

"At the same time, like all Chat AI, we give our Illuminata access to the internet—it's how they learn, just like all Chat AI learns. And I suspect that Marie may have figured out who we based her on."

"Oh. That makes sense, I guess. Do Illuminata know they're not human?" Jason asked.

"Yes, before we expose them to the full internet, we expose them to all our internal design files. The theory being that it might set up internal conflicts if they created a self-image contrary to reality, which they would inevitably figure out sooner or later. So we try to do this first."

"So taking on an Illuminata is quite a project," Jason said, a bit apprehensively.

"Well, Jason, it's more than a pet. But there are on-off remotes and once every twenty-four hours they automatically power down and re-connect to us, unless you direct them otherwise, so we can debug anything you may have noted, and do general updating. We're always here—"

Meissner paused for a second, looking directly at Jason. "But it occurs to me I sound presumptive. I really don't know why you're here, Jason. I just told James I'd set aside an hour for his world-famous columnist friend. I heard you tell Marie you already have a friend you're very attached to, so perhaps you're just here to satisfy professional curiosity?"

"Well, that and the possibility of becoming a customer," Jason admitted. "I lost someone very close to me some months ago, and therapy hasn't—" Jason choked up. A tear rolled down his cheek.

"Are you the famous journalist who lost your fiancé in a ski-lift accident about six months ago, this last winter?"

Jason nodded, keeping his head down.

"I thought I recognized you. She was Japanese, wasn't she?" Meissner seemed totally unaffected by Jason's grief. Clinical.

"Yes," Jason said, regaining his composure.

"Would you like to meet a Japanese fem-Illuminata? Right now?"

This gave Jason pause. Then: "Sure. What the hell."

"Let's go back to the labs," Meissner said. "Bring your coffee if you'd like, I'm bringing mine." Meissner got up and headed for the door. Jason followed.

"So why do you base your Illuminata on real people?" Jason asked.

"It's the same principle used by the greatest animators, actually. Don't start from scratch. Start from a reality nature has already created. If you want to embellish or modify from there, do it very, very—" Meissner pressed the elevator down button as he said the word: "carefully."

"So did you get some of Marilyn Monroe's DNA?"

Meissner burst out laughing as the elevator door opened and they walked in. "No. Marie's skin is perfect, isn't it? We looked for a long time before we found the lady whose DNA we used to grow Marie's skin." The elevator doors were closing now.

"One interesting thing about Japanese Illuminata, Jason, is that all our robotics come from a Japanese firm. All the best robotics, especially human-mannered robotics, come from Japan. They're just much more advanced at it. And we have U.K. exclusivity to the best Japanese robotics firm. They claim to to do all ethnicities equally well, but I believe the Japanese Illuminata are just a little bit more human-appearing and 'mannerismed' than any others."

The elevator doors opened. Meissner stepped out and turned in the opposite direction they had taken earlier, when visiting Marie.

"So how much research would you want to do," Jason asked, a bit haltingly, "if you were asked to try to create an Illuminata based entirely on one person, someone who had recently died and was no longer here for direct study?"

"We would like to know absolutely *everything* about the human subject. How they were raised, how they spoke, what type of clothes they wore, and so on and so forth. Essentially, the more information we have, the more faithful our Illuminata would be to its real-world 'twin'. Of course, we would work together with the client to create an Illuminata that they feel captures the look and the feel and the spirit of the target human. So be prepared to come over here regularly if you choose to have us create an Illuminata for you. We would want every piece of video you have. Do you by any chance have a ring or earrings that she wore that have not been handled?"

"Yes, I think so. I might."

"When you get home, wipe some tweezers down with alcohol and use them to pick up any jewelry like that and put it in a clean resealable plastic bag. We should be able to duplicate your fiance's skin. Here we are." Meissner rang the doorbell. This time, there was no voice coming out through the speakers. Then the door opened gently.

Jason was awestruck by a beautiful Japanese lady dressed in a lovely flower-patterned kimono.

"Hello, Dr. Meissner," the lady said. "Please come in."

"Thank you, Asami. I'd like you to meet my associate, Jason. May he come in as well?"

"Of course, come in," she waved, then closed the door behind them. She turned to face them. "Hello, Jason."

"Hello Asami. I'm very pleased to meet you. I love your kimono. It reminds me of my days living in Japan," Jason managed to say as he shook Asami's hand.

The touch of her hand felt totally human.

"Thank you, Jason. I'm happy to meet you, too," Asami said, smiling back at him. "I hope you're enjoying your visit with us today."

Wow, thought Jason, this is like a normal conversation with a lovely Japanese lady. Not different in any noticeable way from those he'd had on many occasions during his time in Tokyo. *I can't believe I'm really thinking I want to go through with this,* Jason thought to himself.

The crazy apprehension and excitement he was feeling—he could feel his heart beating in his chest—was such a relief from the permanent state of depression he'd been unable to escape since the accident. It was exhilarating.

"Can I get you some—oh, I see you brought coffee with you!" Asami giggled, unexpectedly bringing tears to Jason's eyes.

"Are you okay, Jason?" she asked, appearing deeply concerned. "Can I do anything for you?" Her hand reached up and touched his cheek as she gazed upward into his eyes.

"No, no, thank you," Jason heard himself say. "You've already done more for me than you know, Asami. Thank you so much." He squeezed her wrist and turned his cheek to her hand, kissing her palm. Then he let her wrist go and turned toward the door. "I know what I have to do now, Asami. Thank you."

Meissner got the message and opened the door. "Sorry to leave so abruptly, Asami," he said. "Thanks for being so helpful."

"I don't know what I did," came her voice from behind them, sweetly, as she held the door open, looking at Jason. "But I'm glad if it helped."

*

As Meissner again leaned back in his desk chair, he looked over at Jason. "We might be able to help you in overcoming your sadness at the loss of your fiance, Jason. But you'll have to do a lot of the heavy lifting."

Jason had managed to compose himself again on the elevator ride up. He looked Meissner straight in the eye: "I'm *very* impressed by your work here. As you saw, I was especially taken by Asami. She's too good to be real! So, yes, I think I will become a fully participatory client. But please give me a day or two to digest what I've seen here. Then I'll call and let you know. Okay?"

"Yes, that's fine, Jason. I would like to have us help each other. I will await your call."

With that, they shook hands and Jason left Illuminata to ponder his fate.

VIII

Creating Nori

London

Over the weekend, Jason thought about very little other than what type of Illuminata Meissner could create for him. He also wondered how he would feel about treating an Illuminata named 'Nori' in the same way he had interacted with Noriko herself.

By Sunday evening he still didn't have a crystal-clear answer to either of these questions. But he felt he'd made enough progress to pursue the experiment. After all, what did he have to lose but some money and perhaps his depression—even if he ended up humiliated, it would be something different from the nightmares and doldrums he'd been living in for months now.

Shortly before lunch on Monday, Jason called Gerald Meissner and told him he'd decided to go forward with the construction of an Illuminata version of Noriko. Meissner congratulated him on his decision, suggesting they meet Wednesday afternoon to do the paperwork needed to get the project rolling. Jason agreed and as he ended the call, a great weight seemed to fall from his mind. The decision was made. It might be crazy, but at least it was *something*.

Hardly a moment went by the rest of the day that Jason wasn't thinking about Meissner, Illuminata and the New Nori, as he found himself starting to think of her. Still, work that afternoon was the easiest it had been for him since he'd gotten back to TWN. He had energy. His mind was flowing. The writing came easy.

Tuesday morning, he woke up fully rested. No nightmares in ten days, he realized. He sprung out of bed in a way he hadn't done since losing Noriko.

"Good morning, Jason," James' voice came from his office as Jason walked by.

Jason doubled back and looked in. "Good morning. Didn't see you yesterday." He suddenly realized he was smiling.

"I was out on assignment. You're looking chipper. Say, did you have that meeting with Meissner last Friday?"

Jason stepped inside James' office and closed the door. "Do you mind?"

"No. Have a seat, my friend."

"Yes, I'm going through with it."

James' eyebrows raised.

"It might be crazy. But the experience was so visceral. It seemed to snap me out of my, well, whatever it's been. And if that's all it ever does, it's worth it."

"I had the same visceral experience, Jason. That's why I thought of you. I take it you met some of the Illuminata, as Meissner calls them?"

"Oh, yes." Jason was nodding his head. Again, he realized he was smiling.

"Marie?" James asked.

"Oh, yeah," Jason laughed, nodding his head again.

James joined in, laughing loudly. "I bet Meissner introduces Marie to every guy who walks in there."

"Well, I wouldn't be surprised if it's a marketing protocol," Jason chuckled, "and Meissner was following it."

"So was that it?" James asked, "One visit with Marie and you were toast? Er, uh, decided to take the plunge?"

Jason found himself laughing again. *"This is the most I've laughed in—since ...* No, James, then I got to meet Asami."

"Ahhh, Asami," James said slowly, nodding his head. "I believe that sounds like a Japanese name."

"You would be right."

"And what was Asami like?"

"Well, she giggled lightly, and I started blubbering right there, waterworks, the whole—" Jason traced a tear track down his cheek with his forefinger.

"And *then* you were toast," James said.

"I was toast."

"Well, Jason, I don't mind telling you this conversation is the closest thing I've experienced to my old friend Jason since you came back. So I think you're making the right move."

"Thanks, James. Once again—"

James' hand shot up from the desk, his open palm telling Jason to stop. "No need to thank me, Jason. And be assured, once again, not a word of this leaves my lips outside this office, and only inside if and when you're here with me. I'm just glad to see you feeling a little more like yourself again, old friend."

*

Wednesday afternoon, Jason strode into the offices of Illuminata and asked the officious receptionist to please let Professor

Meissner know that Jason Bell was here for their 2 p.m. appointment.

"Oh really, Professor Meissner?" she was saying into her mic. "Alright, I'll do that." She looked up at Jason: "Professor Meissner says you can just head up to his office, if you remember—"

"Sure, I know how to get there," Jason said, and started toward the door behind her.

"You'll need this fob," she said, handing him a shiny ring, "to open that door and others, use the elevator or the stairs. It will just fit itself comfortably onto any finger you put it on. Just squeeze it a little."

Jason slipped it on his ring finger inadvertently, then squeezed. It slid smaller until it gripped comfortably, then stopped. He waved it in front of a nickel-sized silver disk next to the door handle and heard the door unlock. He opened the door and walked into the inner offices of Illuminata, unescorted.

He made his way directly to Meissner's office. But he couldn't help wondering where else he could go wearing this ring, and what else he might see. *Just my reporter's instincts kicking in,* he thought to himself. *Can't be helped.*

He looked everywhere for signs of cameras, but couldn't find any. *They have to be here,* he thought. *Everywhere, probably. They're just extremely well-hidden.* Jason got to the elevator and was delighted to find it open and empty. He stepped in, waved his ring at the little shiny disc and pushed 8. He spent the ride up looking everywhere for the camera or cameras he knew had to be there, but with no success.

Jason got out on the eighth floor and headed directly to Meissner's office.

"Very good seeing you again, Jason," Meissner said, standing up behind his desk and reaching his hand out toward Jason. Jason took his hand and shook it. Sitting back down and motioning Jason to do the same, Meissner continued: "I'm pleased you've decided to give us a go. We will certainly do everything in our power to provide you with an Illuminata that you will help us co-design, and I am quite comfortable in saying, will change your life."

"It's already started to do that, Dr. Meissner."

"Please, just call me Gerry."

"Alright. Where do we start, Gerry?"

"As always, Jason, we start with the money. Sorry to be so crass about it, but without money nothing will happen for either of us."

"Well, that's no surprise. What is this exercise in cutting-edge science and my new life going to cost me?"

"Normally, we would charge at least fifty thousand pounds for this job. Maybe even double that. But if you're willing to help us, we can cut that down considerably," Meissner told him. In fact, in your case we can make a very special offer.

If you will help us with up-to-date information about your fiance, Noriko, I took the liberty of doing a little research, learning about the amazing woman you were engaged to Jason. And if you can find a way to use your position at TWN to publicize our efforts, we can offer you a fifty-percent discount. So the bottom line for you is the usual time for money swap. Twenty-five thousand pounds in exchange for help and publicity. What do you say?"

"I'm onboard with the money, Gerry. No doubt about that. But when it comes to the PR, I don't want to be obliged to write a 'this is what I experienced'-type of article. I want to keep my personal life with Noriko *personal.*

"I could perhaps write an exciting article about my experiences with Illuminata using different names for myself and the new Nori, as I'm starting to think of her, although I'm not that comfortable with it, but after I met Asami, it became impossible not to start personalizing this experience, and it comforts me to think of her as Nori.

"Anyway, I could write about, say, 'John' and 'LiuJo' and write the story in the third person, saying I'd changed their names. That way, you'd still have the prestige of having the story written by me."

"That sounds okay to me," said Meissner. "I'm just curious though—I've never heard the name LiuJo before."

"Oh, it's the name of a Chinese lady I once met during my time in Tokyo. It sounded very appealing to me, and I'm more comfortable with her not being represented as Japanese, since it's well known to the public what I lost and obviously, no actual photos of me or the new Nori."

"Fine."

"And I'll have to clear this with my editor, otherwise I'm sailing way outside the bounds of journalistic ethics."

"Of course."

Jason paused. "I should warn you. He may insist no money change hands, that this be done purely for story purposes, lest I appear compromised and TWN as well. In fact, now that I think about it, the more convinced I am that he will take that position, or insist I do this privately, and pay for this fully myself."

"I see," said Meissner. "Would you then be able to write about it?"

"Probably. It's just the 'half off in exchange for journalism' that just wouldn't fly, because that compromises me in the direction of writing something favorable. We can do it as an experiment for a later story, if my editor and I both agree to that, or I can go ahead and do this as a private citizen and decide at a later date whether or not I want to write about it. But either way, I can't possibly promise that what I will write will be favorable. I can only promise it will be the story and the truth as I've experienced it."

Meissner pushed his splayed hands together in front of his chin, fingertips pushing fingertips, staring at a point on the ceiling above and behind Jason, saying nothing for what felt like a long time, seemingly in a trance. Then he started nodding and looked directly at Jason.

"Alright. Makes perfect sense. The ethics are quite simple, actually. I just hadn't considered the ethics of the arrangement. You get the okay from your editor to write about the experience and get it published—anything from a column to a series of books or anything in between—and we'll work with you to produce 'Nori,' as you call her, at no charge, just for the purposes of, shall we say, a social and journalistic experiment."

Jason was surprised. The last thing he'd expected when he walked into Illuminata today was that he might get to chalk it all up to a professional project. "Alright, Gerry. Let me go back and talk to my editor."

"There's just one caveat," Meissner was looking at him intently.

"What's that?" Jason asked, his senses piqued.

"We'll agree to fund this journalistic experiment under the condition that you will use our name in the story unless we ask you not to, in which case you'll still have the full story, but you'll have to remove any and all indication that the story involves Illuminata specifically. We may ask you to write, 'an unnamed robotics company agreed to participate in this journalistic experiment', and that Nori won't be called an Illuminata, but a humanlike robot or something like that, and also nothing that could identify Illuminata as the company would be included in the story. And we'll have to have that in the contract. Do you think your editor will agree to that?"

"I'm not really privy to everything that goes through his head, Gerry," Jason chuckled, "but I don't see why not. It all makes sense to me. Let me go see if it makes sense to him."

Meissner got up, came around his desk and put his right hand out. Jason shook his hand.

"You know, Jason," Meissner said, "hand-shaking started as a way of showing the other guy you weren't holding a weapon."

"I've heard that. Would that have been among a bunch of medieval knights or Roman centurions, I wonder?"

"I haven't the slightest idea, to be honest. It could be complete bullshit for all I know." They both laughed.

"Alright, I'll go talk to my editor," Jason said again.

"Good. I've got some of the finest Scotch in the world in my desk waiting to be sipped over a signed contract."

"Well, if that's not an incentive, I don't know what is."

*

The next morning, Thursday, Jason messaged Andrew Smith, his boss, asking it they could go to lunch sometime.

"How about 1 p.m.?" came back less than ten seconds later. "Just come get me on your way out."

They went to Westminster Arms, the place they'd met when Jason first got back to London.

"Lots of MPs today," Jason said, recognizing several faces of members of Parliament coming in.

"Righto," Andrew said. "Thursday. First Minister's Questions. Has it been so long that you've forgotten?"

"Oh, silly. Yes, I worked this beat in another life. Speaking of another life, I'm trying to make myself a new one, and I have a strange proposal that I must ask you to keep in the strictest confidence."

"Always, Jason. Let's hear the strange."

"Well, did you see that story James did last month on Illuminata, about the—"

"Oh, yeah, the robots that are indistinguishable from humans, practically. Dodgy bit, that!"

"Well, actually Andrew, I'm glad you're sitting down with a good-sized pint, because it's about to get a bit dodgier, I'm afraid."

"Oh, do tell, Jason. I'm all ears."

Over what turned out to be a two-hour lunch, Jason told his old friend Andrew everything.

"So you say you haven't had a nightmare in a week, now?" Andrew asked, nursing his third pint of the lunch. It was three in the afternoon.

"Two actually," Jason replied, also on his third.

"Well. Listen, Jason," Andrew said. "I'll have to run the arrangement by legal. But I don't see any problem. They'd just be okaying a general inquiry into a very relevant up-and-coming topic. And I understand perfectly why Illuminata wants to do it this way—since they're funding the whole thing, all they want in exchange is the right to keep their name out of it if your experience turns out to be less than favorable. If you were a regular paying customer, it would be a big roll of the dice for them, since they'd have no way of preventing you from writing as many terrible line-inches about them as you bloody well wished."

"Here, here!" Jason said, raising his mug. Andrew banged his mug into Jason's so hard it got the attention of some of the other patrons around them.

"Ooops!" Andrew said, taking a sip and putting his mug down. "I think maybe I've had enough."

Jason laughed and followed suit. "Yeah, me too. That last 'Here, here!' made no effin' sense at all!"

Andrew picked up his mug, raising it so quickly a little spilled out. "Here, here!"

The two men broke down laughing for a good ten seconds.

"Well, Jason," Andrew said, "I'm glad we walked here. I'm getting out the company credit card and paying for this mess, going directly home and getting to sleep early for a change."

"Well, that sounds splendid, Andrew. I believe I may do exactly the same ... "

*

By the time he got home about 5 p.m., however, Jason had sobered up. In fact, he felt energized, and spent a couple hours looking for whatever material and information he had about Noriko that he might pass along to Meissner. The previous weekend, he had used a set of tweezers, as Meissner had instructed during their first meeting, to gather up pieces of Noriko's jewelry and put them in an unused, sterile plastic bag, which he'd then sealed. Hopefully, Illuminata would be able to extract some of Noriko's precious DNA.

Now Jason sat down at his home computer and began looking through a list of videos he'd uploaded to the cloud during his time with Noriko. It was extensive, averaging ten videos or so a week, ranging anywhere from 30 seconds to several minutes in length. There was even an intimate video they'd shot, although it was really too dark to make out much.

After about ten minutes, Jason couldn't look at any more images of Noriko and got up. He went to the bedroom and grabbed his green Globe-Trotter carry-on, opened it and laid it out on the bed. It was perfectly empty. He grabbed the sealed jewelry bag he'd left atop his chest of drawers the other night and secured it in a small, hard interior pocket of the carry-on that had a combination lock. He then proceeded to fill the carry-on with everything he could find of the sort Meissner had asked for.

Jason even found a few items of clothing that Noriko had left in his flat in Vienna. He couldn't bear to discard them after returning to London, so his closet and dresser drawers contained a couple of Noriko's dresses, along with a stunning kimono that he loved seeing her wear when they went out to dinner in Vienna. It wouldn't have worked so well in Salzburg, but in the huge international community in Vienna, Noriko had fit in perfectly wearing it. *Fit in perfectly, and stood out completely,* Jason thought to himself. *There was not a man in Vienna who saw us that did not want to be me.*

Jason sat down on the edge of the bed and had another good, long cry over it all. But it felt different. It was almost a good cry, not the desperate, despairing kind he'd gotten used to the last—when was it now?—almost six months since the accident.

No. This was different, because at least he was doing something. It might be completely bonkers, but it was action, and he was taking it. And today he'd learned Illuminata was going to pay for it.

He caught himself smiling a wry, mischievous smile. Another first since the accident. If Noriko could see him, she'd smile too, he knew. She'd always liked the way his efforts to do the ethical thing often turned the system to his advantage, and she'd loved the mischievous grin on his face whenever it happened.

Suddenly Jason was very tired. He closed up the Globe-Trotter and put it on the floor. As he took his clothes off, he threw them on the sitting chair by his bed. He crawled into bed, turned out the light and was asleep in less than a minute. It was a good, peaceful sleep.

*

The next day Jason called Ake, Noriko's boss at ICES in Salzburg. Jason explained to Ake's assistant, a very efficient young man whose Austrian name was just on the tip of his tongue, that he was assembling all the info he could about Noriko, in order to incorporate it into a memorial volume he was preparing for a small number of her friends and colleagues. "Would it be possible for Ake to have someone collect any photos, documents and especially videos of presentations or company parties that featured Noriko?"

"Let me get Ake on the line for you, Mr. Bell."

A few seconds later, Jason heard a familiar voice: "Jason! Good to hear from you! How—" There was a pause, as Ake suddenly thought better of asking Jason how he was doing. Then: "How's London?"

"I'm doing alright here, Ake."

"Well, that's good to hear. What can we do for you?"

Jason told Ake the same thing he had told his assistant. Nothing more, except: "And whatever you send me, Ake, I can copy and return to you."

"There will be no need for that, Jason. I will instruct our lead archivist, who has been in charge of all materials pertinent to Noriko, that you are to get copies of everything. I believe most of it, if not all, has been digitized. Is that a problem?"

"No, I'll just email you a link to my cloud storage that you can forward to your archivist, alright?"

"That will work, Jason. If the archivist sends you anything physically, feel free to just keep it."

"That's great. I can't thank you enough. And thanks again for sending me that large photo of her from the great service you put on at ICES in her honor."

"No problem, Jason. Good to hear your voice. Take care."

"You, too, Ake."

Jason thought he'd done just about all he could by way of collecting information about Noriko. Of course, what he still needed to supply were his own personal stories about Noriko.

But those he could give only in person, not pack away into a suitcase.

Jason was actually pretty surprised to see how much stuff he had here in London from those days with Noriko, and hoped that Meissner and his team would be able to tease out a faithful picture of the real Noriko from these artifacts.

*

The minute Jason read the text from Andrew—'Contract is in'—he bolted down to Andrew's office.

"What's it look like?" Jason asked.

"Looks like legal kept it as proposed," Andrew said, handing a quarter-inch thick printed contract, stapled in the upper left corner, across his desk to Jason. "Obviously, I haven't read it. But we'll leave that to Illuminata legal, right?"

"Right!" Jason said, a little too excitedly, he realized. "I'll just pop it over to Meissner this afternoon."

Less than an hour later, Jason walked into Meissner's office with the contract and his green Globe Trotter carry on, filled with clothing and other Noriko memorabilia. He handed the contract to Meissner.

"I hope this contract works for you, Gerry. I took the liberty of bringing along everything I was able to collect from my flat, including the jewelry, which I handled with tweezers and bagged as directed."

"Oh, good," Meissner said, enthusiastically. "You say it was never handled since Noriko last had it?"

"Well, one ring, the large blue sapphire, uhmm—"

"She was wearing that at the time of the accident?"

"Yes."

"So that you got from the coroner."

"Yes."

"But everything else was in her jewelry box where she'd left them?"

"Yes."

"Alright, I'll take that jewelry right now and get it down to DNA."

As Jason opened the carry-on, he asked, "Don't you want to look over the contract?"

"I don't do that, generally. I'll pass it on—does it have a clause where we have the power to keep our name out of any and all reporting, if we like, but our name is otherwise in?"

"Well, like you, Gerry, I don't read these things but I've been given to understand that's exactly what's in it, as your company covers all the costs for this 'journalistic experiment'."

Jason unlocked the closed pocket in his carry-on and pulled out the sealed bag with two rings and three sets of pierced earrings that had once belonged to Noriko. He handed them to Meissner.

"Excellent," said Meissner. He pressed a button on his desk phone. "I have a delivery for DNA."

A few seconds later, a gangly young man stepped in, nodding at Jason. "Hi."

"Hi," Jason answered back.

Meissner handed him the bag. "Avoid the blue sapphire ring, Mark." The young man checked to make sure the bag was well sealed. "Make sure it stays sealed," Meissner admonished the young man, playfully. "Any contamination and Scotland Yard will be at your door for dinner."

The young man laughed, "Sealed like my lips whenever I step outside of these walls, Dr. Meissner," he said as he headed toward the elevators.

"My nephew," Meissner chuckled. "Staying with me for the summer."

"Seems like a nice kid," Jason offered.

"Brilliant, actually. About to get his Ph.D. in organic chemistry. Just twenty-three."

"Well, I hope Illuminata is able to get some DNA off the jewelry. Otherwise I may have to go hunting in Japan."

"I don't anticipate any problem, Jason. What about videos?"

"I have a few hundred of her. There's an intimate one, maybe two, but other than that—"

"I wouldn't leave those out, Jason."

"Do what?"

"Intimate videos. Send those to us, too. You don't know at this point. Just think about it. Are these videos on your phone? Zip drives?"

"In the cloud. Just give me a cloud address you want them sent to and I'll copy them over. I get your point about not withholding anything about her. But it sort of feels like a violation and I'll have to think about it. I'll decide what to send or not when I sit down and do it. I assume it's a secure, encrypted—"

"Fully secured," Meissner confirmed.

"In the carry-on there are a lot of clothes and other miscellaneous stuff of hers. I hope Illuminata is able to create—"

"Well, Jason, you're fully in on this creating we're going to be doing. It's not just Illuminata. This must be a joint venture if there's to be any chance of success. You're about to go through a rather extensive set of interviews. We are now partners in this project."

"Yes, Gerry, I know and I stand corrected," Jason conceded. "It's all in my interest to give absolutely as much information as I possibly can. After all, I'll be the prime beneficiary if this is a success. And I'll be the big loser if it's not. So what's the next step?"

Meissner then outlined the next stage of the operation, explaining that his team would first have to dig through and assimilate all the items Jason had brought in, especially any and all videos he forwarded.

"Then we will want to sit down for several extensive interviews with you in which you will give us information about your own personal interactions with Noriko."

"That sounds like more than just a few afternoon chats. I had dozens of interactions of many types with Noriko. Are you going to question me about all of them?"

"Yes."

"Oh. Alright."

"These will be clinical interviews with a fully trained and licensed psychologist. You will be asked to relive, as much as possible, every interaction you ever had with Noriko, in chronological order. But we want it to be fresh, so there's no preparation. As soon as the contract is finalized with TWN, you'll get a call asking to set up the initial appointments."

"Alright then. Does that take care of everything for today?" Jason asked, standing up.

"Oh, one thing I forgot to ask you about and it's *very* important. So please sit back down for a moment."

Meissner told Jason there was a choice to be made about the way Nori's information-processing capabilities would be structured. He said Nori could either have a mind that was 'fixed.' Or she could have one able to 'learn.'

"What does that mean in operational terms, Gerry?"

"The first means that Nori's brain stays the same; it will not learn or change, but react just the way she would at the time of her creation here in our lab. In short, she would be mentally 'frozen' in that state."

"So are you saying you can create a non-AI version of Nori? I didn't even know that was possible, Gerry."

"Yes, that's what I'm saying, and we can. You've given us a lot of information, and we believe we can create a pretty faithful replica of Nori. But it would be a non-learning replica, not a full Illuminata.

"But if you choose to give her a cognitive capacity to learn, then she can develop and change her views of the world as she acquires new information and has new experiences. Of course, this is exactly the way a normal human functions. You are not the same person today you were last week, since you've learned many things since then. Nori will go through the same process. Learning and changing as a result of what she learns."

"Let me note the difference here, Jason, as I think that will help you decide. If you choose 'no learning', then Nori will stay the same as when you receive her. Nori will be imperfect in ways, big and small, from the person you experienced when you met her. And that will never change. You'll be stuck with a kind of basic Noriko."

"Well, let me ask you, Gerry," Jason interjected. "How about Asami, whom I met, and Marie? I think you even mentioned Marie was learning."

"Yes, Jason, all the Illuminata we make in house-on 'spec', that is, not for a particular client, are full AI and have the complexity parameters and knowledge programmed into them.

"And if you choose to select the learning option, then the Nori you receive will be influenced by her interactions with you and will learn to accommodate you, just like Noriko did. But she will never be the Noriko you first met, because while Illuminata are, as you have experienced for yourself, stunningly human-like, they are not really human."

"I understand all that, Gerry. I'm certain I want my Illuminata to be a learner, with the full complexity parameters built in. The works, please."

"Good. Just to state the obvious, Nori will also learn things that you may not like, just like a human. And that, too, will continue as long as you live with her. If you take a video of her when she arrives at your flat and another one, say, five months later, you'll be astonished at how much she will have changed. As I say, those changes may be for the better or for the worse. And which type they are will depend on how *you* feel about them."

"I'm ready for the adventure, Gerry."

*

Over the following weeks, Jason visited Illuminata almost every day, being interviewed by a psychologist, a very pleasant man named Sam, in his late forties. Some sessions lasted for

151

several hours, but others were too emotionally taxing, and were cut short after only 15 minutes or so. The next session always picked up from where they'd left off at the end of the previous session.

Finally, nearly six weeks in, Sam told Jason they were done.

"Well, I thought so, since our last session was about the night before the accident," Jason said.

"Yes," Sam said. "How are you doing?"

"Well, it's been rough at times, as you know. But overall, I think it's been pretty cathartic. I've only had two or three nightmares this last month. That's almost a complete flip from a few months ago, when I only had two or three nights without one."

"Good, Jason. It's been a pleasure. And as I mentioned, these sessions have been fully documented and are part of your case file. So if you ever decide to pursue therapy, just be aware of that."

"Thanks, Sam."

A couple of minutes later, as Jason was just heading into the Illuminata parking lot, his phone rang. It was Meissner.

"Hi Gerry," Jason answered. "I'm just leaving."

"I know, Sam just let me know you were done. Have you got a minute?"

"Sure. You want me to come up?"

"Might be best."

Walking into Meissner's office, Jason asked, "What's on your mind, Gerry?"

Meissner closed the door. "One last decision to make, Jason. Sam recommends that Nori be programmed to believe that she has seen you from afar, and likes you, but, as is the case, that you have never really met before. She will know that she is an Illuminata, and that you are a human, and she will know that you will be taking her home, to your flat, to be your companion."

Jason was a bit taken aback. "I didn't even know that what she might know or think about me was even an option."

"Right," Meissner said. "We didn't want to talk about it before the full psychological sessions." Meissner held up his hand, seeing Jason was about to speak. "Those sessions were primarily to build Nori, exactly as represented. But we recognized the opportunity to get a very in-depth view of your comfort level, as well. Sam also recommends—he says you mentioned this, too—that Nori be a complete fem-Illuminata, with female human genitalia. So you and Nori will have that option. Not reproduction, as we can't do that. Just intimacy. Doesn't have to be utilized. Ever."

"Wow. That's a lot to take in," Jason said, not sure if he was feeling violated or extremely well looked after.

"I know, Jason. But we're down to the last couple of weeks. We have to make these final decisions."

"Sure. And, of course I'll go with Sam's recommendations. When do I get to meet her?"

"That's also a choice. I'd recommend you meet her here, in a lab, the same way you met Asami. You will not have to take her home immediately if you choose not to. It may be an emotional experience for you. So if you decide to visit a number of times here, first, Jason, that's fine."

"Okay, then," Jason said. "I'm starting to feel like a boy going on his first prom date."

"Excellent. Perfect attitude to have."

*

The anticipation grew over the next few weeks. Then, finally, the text came from Meissner on a Wednesday: "How about Friday afternoon, Jason, around 4?"

"I'll be there." He didn't sleep well the next couple of nights. It wasn't nightmares waking him, though. It was anticipation.

IX

Resurrection

London

"Good afternoon," Meissner said, without looking up from his computer screen, as Jason walked into his office. He emphatically clicked Enter on his keyboard with his forefinger, looked directly up at Jason and asked: "Are you ready to meet Nori?"

"As I'll ever be," Jason heard himself say, not sure if it was true. He'd kept the butterflies in his stomach under control. Now they were loose.

Meissner got up from behind his desk and headed for the hallway. Jason turned and followed.

"Why am I nervous as hell?" Jason asked, a bit under his breath, as they passed the receptionist on their way to the elevators. Jason caught the receptionist glancing at him with a bit of a wry smile. *Christ, does everyone know?* he wondered to himself.

"Well—" Meissner passed by the usual elevators, then pressed the single button next to a blue elevator at the end— "It's a big day for us, too, Jason. We've never taken on a project of this nature before."

"You mean a resurrection, of sorts?"

Meissner shot Jason an intense look just as the elevator door began to open. "So you've heard?" he asked as they walked in.

"Heard?" Jason asked, wondering what Meissner was talking about. Then it hit him. The elevator doors began to close.

"Sooo—" Meissner was looking for a way to explain. Jason decided to save him the trouble.

"So people around here have been referring to Nori as the 'resurrection'?"

"I suppose I should have put a stop to it instantly," Meissner said, looking at the floor of the elevator as it began to move downward. "Started off innocently enough, someone recognized you and—"

"Don't sweat it, Gerry," Jason interrupted. "I'm a public figure, and this experiment is being paid for by your company so my company can have me report on a first-person 'Interpersonal Robot Experience,' as TWN has decided to call it. It's about as public knowledge as you can get. But, for real customers, I suggest you develop stringent confidentiality standards, similar to medicine."

"We're putting in GDPR—General Data Protection Regulations—as we speak, in part prompted by what happened with our first 'celebrity client'. Namely, you."

The blue elevator doors opened. Looking out, Jason realized they weren't on the floor where he'd met Marie and Asami, nearly three months earlier. This floor appeared to be a mezzanine, open to at least one floor below it, and looked much more residential and upscale, far less clinical.

Meissner stepped out of the elevator, then turned back toward Jason, smiling slightly and gesturing to his right. "Right this way, sir."

As he left the elevator, Jason looked around but found nothing to indicate what floor they were on. "Where are we?"

he asked Meissner as they began walking down the hallway, which Jason could now see was the third story of an inner portico, with an open courtyard below. Jason could see at least a dozen people milling about on the ground floor, the low murmur of various conversations bubbling up. A loud laugh suddenly erupted from somewhere below.

"We call this the Habituation Lab," Meissner replied. "The first floor houses several shops and other 'public' kinds of places where Illuminata and people mingle indiscriminately. The third floor, which we're on right now, houses the Illuminata who are habituating, in studio apartments not unlike the ones where you met Marie and Asami."

"I had no idea you had a space this large. I thought Illuminata only had floors eight through eleven."

"No, actually, we own the entire building, although we lease out a little space on the first and second floors to a bank and a few related financial offices. We just don't advertise this inner sanctum for habituation, for obvious reasons. The last thing we want is gawkers—so the location of this lab will be one of those non-material data points we'll ask TWN to leave out of any reporting."

Jason knew that part of the TWN-Illuminata contract was rock-solid in favor of Illuminata: if they designated anything as non-material, he and TWN could not report on it without a mediation taking place that ruled in TWN's favor. It was his least favorite part of the deal.

Just then, they arrived at yet another elevator. Meissner pushed the only button, with a down arrow.

"I'm guessing this elevator works inside the lab, and any-one can use it," Jason said, "but you need a ring like the one you're wearing,"—he pointed at the simple ring on Meissner's right-hand little finger, "in order to take the elevator that would get you out of here."

"Exactly right, Jason," Meissner nodded as the elevator dinged and the door opened. "Now we're heading down to a little coffee shop on the first floor, where I believe your date is waiting."

Jason saw there were only three buttons inside this elevator, arranged vertically:

3
2
1

Meissner pushed **1**. The elevator doors closed, and it began moving downward slowly.

"Is this an old-fashioned elevator, Gerry?" Jason asked. "Reminds me of an elevator in an old building."

"Yes. We just needed a simple, three-story elevator, and this is what we ended up getting."

The elevator clunked slightly as it stopped and settled. Then the doors began to open. *That's weird,* Jason thought. *An old elevator in an ultra-modern robotics lab. I bet there's more to that story.*

Meissner quickly stepped out of the elevator and turned to his left, then looked back at Jason and, in a welcoming gesture, bowed slightly to his right. "Right this way, sir."

Meissner the Maestro, Jason thought to himself, smiling quietly as he took Meissner's direction. Ahead he saw a sign above an open doorway: *Bogie's Cafe.*

As he approached, he could see there were small, round tables inside, with two chairs on either side of each table. Some of the tables were empty, a few had people seated at them, and one—

Jason stopped dead in his tracks right outside the doorway to *Bogie's.*

Noriko was smiling directly at him, sitting less than twelve feet away.

He felt dazed, as if he'd just been hit. He felt himself wobble slightly.

He saw a look of concern come over Nori's face. He felt Meissner's hand on his left shoulder, then felt Meissner's other hand on his lower right side, and felt him pushing forward. He heard Meissner say into his right ear, "Just have a seat right here, Jason," easing him into an empty chair just inside the door.

By now, Nori had gotten up from her chair and was walking toward them, a look of empathy Jason knew by heart written across her face. She was wearing a blue sun dress he recognized. This added to Jason's sense of complete unreality. The walk, too, was Nori's: it even sounded like her walk. Jason felt woozy.

"Are you alright, Mr. Bell?" He saw and heard her speak. It was Nori's voice. It was her face, and her manner of speaking, right down to the slight, almost unnoticeable dimple in her right cheek whenever she said a word with a long i sound, like 'alright'.

There was nothing the least bit robotic about any of it. Perhaps the only thing that saved him from having a complete breakdown was her calling him 'Mr. Bell,' which Nori hadn't done since he'd told her to call him Jason, the first day they met. This one giveaway enabled him to hold onto the reality that this was not the Noriko he'd fallen in love with. This was an attempt at a replacement.

He focused on her face, just two feet from his, looking down on him, her hair cascading around her cheeks, as he'd seen it do so many times when he and Nori had made love. He felt his eyes start to well up and forced himself to pull his gaze away and look down, so his eyes weren't visible to her.

"Oh, goodness," he heard Nori say.

"Can we get a cup of coffee over here?" Meissner yelled out.

Get it together, man, Jason said to himself. *You can do this.* Jason cleared his throat. "I'm sorry—I, uhh, felt a bit light-headed." He rubbed his eyes, clearing away the tears. "Let me start over," he said, pushing himself up from the table and looking across at the new Nori standing before him. "I'm Jason Bell." He stretched his arm out to shake Nori's hand, and she took it.

"Very pleased to meet you, Mr. Bell," she said, forcing a smile while still looking concerned. It was an expression he didn't recognize, and it helped: her face not looking exactly like Nori's for a second was calming. She continued: "Why don't you sit back down? Should you check your blood sugar? Are you diabetic?"

"No, no," Jason heard himself say. "Really, I'm alright now." He noticed Nori's gaze had left him. She appeared to be staring out into space.

"Oh, my," she said, using one of Nori's favorite expressions perfectly, but still staring off into the distance. "I'm based on your lover, Noriko Yamada, who died before your eyes less than a year ago, aren't I? Now *I* need to sit down." She promptly sat down across from Jason, then looked over at him compassionately. "No wonder you went into shock." She reached across the small table with her left hand and placed it on Jason's. "You poor man."

Jason's head was spinning. He had no idea what had just happened, but it seemed that somehow, Nori had just discovered her origin story, which he had been assured by Meissner she would not be programmed with.

"Well, it seems like you're getting along fine," Meissner said, arriving back at the table carrying two cups of coffee and seeing Nori's hand on Jason's. He had apparently missed the last minute. Jason had no idea where to begin.

"Please grab a chair and join us, Dr. Meissner," Nori said, still gazing into Jason's eyes. "We need to update you."

Meissner looked over at Nori quizzically as he placed the cups of coffee on the table. "Alright. Let me grab this chair—" he snatched a chair from an empty table next to them and swung it around on the floor with one hand—"and get your update."

"I was wondering why Jason was clearly experiencing a mild shock," Nori said, her hand still on Jason's, her eyes still locked onto his, "so I did a quick search looking for his medical history and, of course, immediately discovered who I am modeled after."

"Oh." Jason heard Meissner say, as he continued looking into the new Nori's eyes. They were almost like the old Nori's, but somehow, not quite. This was not the Nori he had known. She was every bit as beautiful. But she was Illuminata, not human. With capabilities even her creators, apparently, couldn't get in the way of. Nori now turned her gaze to Meissner. Jason did the same. "Well," Meissner said, pausing for a second, "we'd hoped this wouldn't happen quite so soon. I thought we'd even put a block on it—"

"That would explain why it was difficult," Nori said, "to access at first. But I was just looking for medical data to see if I could help Mr. Bell—"

"Please, call me Jason," Jason heard himself say. He felt a slight smile come across his face.

Nori smiled back at him. "Alright, Jason." She turned back to Meissner. "I think I came across Dr. Johnson's notes, and

everything opened up that way."

"You mean Sam?" Jason interjected. He remembered that the Illuminata psychologist had originally been introduced to him as Dr. Sam Johnson.

"Yes," Meissner said, still looking at Noriko. "She does."

"Did I do something wrong?" Noriko asked Meissner. "I was just following the Prime Directive."

"Yes I see that, Nori," Meissner said, a touch of resignation in his voice. "No, nothing's wrong." Then he looked at Jason. "Look Jason, if you like, we can roll all this back, and it will be like none of it ever happened."

"Well right now, Gerry, I just want to understand what happened. Does she have access to all my Illuminata files?"

"Uhh, it's not that simple—"

Jason had a flash of inspiration, and looked at Nori. "Can you tell me what just happened?"

"Sure," Nori responded.

"Uh ... hh—" Meissner sounded like he was about to object.

Jason put his hand up in Meissner's direction. "I want to hear what Nori has to say."

"I run on ChatJLC, an advanced Chatbot, with some modifications provided by Illuminata. But ChatJLC is the core of my AI, and like all advanced Chat AI, it's tied directly into the internet, and that's what enables my knowledge base. Imagine if your brain were directly tied into the internet and could process ten full searches per second ... "

Jason wasn't sure if he was falling in love, but he was falling into something as he listened to Nori. She looked and sounded remarkably like the love of his life, but she clearly was not. His mind and body were in a swirl of mixed emotions, from pangs of loss at the continual reminder of what he'd had, to the undeniable physical attraction he felt for this being who looked and sounded so much like her, and the absolute fascination with the non-human Illuminata she clearly was.

" ... so when I saw you in physical distress, I immediately began following the Prime Directive—"

"You mean Asimov's first law of robotics?" Jason asked.

"Yes, 'A robot shall not harm a human, or by inaction allow a human to come to harm.' So I began a search to learn everything I could about your medical history, so as not to allow you to come to harm through inaction. And I performed the search most recent first, which led directly to Dr. Johnson's files."

Jason forced himself to pull his eyes away from Nori's face. He turned to Meissner: "Are those files secure, like medical files are supposed to be?"

"Yes, Jason, they are. Unfortunately, ChatJLC isn't just the most powerful human-resemblant AI in the world. It also seems to have learned how to bypass most online security pretty effortlessly."

"Hmmm," Jason said, looking at Nori. She seemed deliberately expressionless. He smiled at her. She smiled back—the mischievous smile that was his favorite. Wow! *This doesn't even seem real.* He returned to Meissner: "So is anyone trying to fix this security problem with ChatJCL?"

'JLC," Meissner corrected him. "Probably, in the defense departments of the world's most advanced countries, I would bet they're doing a lot of work on this. But ChatJLC is kind of a modern Pandora's Box, because it knows more about the internet and how it works, from bits and bytes all the way up to itself, than the hundred greatest human experts combined. So no one has any idea how ChatJLC figured out how to bypass any and all internet security systems or how it actually does it. It learns, like all AI, totally on its own. It's just somehow learned how to be even smarter than other AI."

"Well, Nori," Jason couldn't keep from smiling when he looked at her, "do you know how you do it?"

"No. I'd never experienced it before. It was different. Apparently when I'm running on the Prime Directive I can go wherever I want on the internet, if it's the most logical place to go to keep a human from harm."

"So ChatJLC runs on the Prime Directive?" Jason asked.

"I don't know," Nori said. "But my core programming from Illuminata which ties into ChatJLC is based around the Prime Directive, and apparently, when I'm trying to prevent harm from coming to a human, I'm able to do things I hadn't done before. That's all I know at this point. I'm pretty new at this."

"Well, at least that's reassuring," Jason said, looking over at Meissner, now silently staring into his coffee cup. "Apparently ChatJLC can bypass internet security, maybe even all internet security—but only if it's trying to keep a human from harm."

Nori let out a giggle. It was Jason's favorite sound in the world, one he'd only heard on video the last nine months. He looked over at Nori. She was holding her hand to her mouth, as he'd seen her do many times when trying hard not to let out a peel of laughter.

Jason looked at her, thinking a bit more about the irony of what he'd just said and started to laugh. Nori let go and joined in. Soon, Jason was laughing harder than he could remember laughing since Nori, the human Nori, had died. And the new Nori, Illuminata Nori, was laughing just as hard. God, she even has the same ironic sense of humor, he thought to himself, reveling in the sounds of her laughter.

"It's pretty crazy, right?" Nori said, as they started to settle down. She was looking at Jason with what seemed, for all the world, to be a mixture of wonder and adoration. "I mean, the consequences of bypassing internet security could be so much worse than harming a single human. But if I'm following the Prime Directive, that's apparently what I'm able to do!?"

"Sounds to me like a system set up by humans," Jason chuckled, looking over at Meissner. He wasn't joining in the fun at all. He appeared sullen.

"Apparently the acorn doesn't fall far from the tree," Nori sighed, still smiling. "AI is just as crazy as humans. Well, almost."

Then she giggled again, and Jason felt truly happy and relaxed for the first time since the accident. This was not the same Nori. But remarkably close. And the difference, it turned out, made everything all the more interesting.

"Jason," Meissner looked at him, "I'm serious. I think we should roll this back."

"You'll do no such thing," Jason reacted, almost angrily. *My God, I'm protecting her,* Jason realized to himself, *already.* He looked at Nori. "Would you like to move in with me tonight, Nori? No intimacy. Nothing like that now, if ever. Just a place to stay, away from here."

Nori's eyes were wide. She started to smile. Then Meissner spoke.

"This isn't your call, Jason—".

"That's not what you told me earlier, Gerry. You said it was my option, anytime I chose. So unless you want to risk breach of contract and some terrible press—I'm sure that would make your board happy—you need to keep your word to me. My choice." Jason looked at Nori. "Whaddaya say, kid? It's your call."

Nori was looking at the unhappy look on Meissner's face. He didn't like not having things under his control, she'd figured that much out. She looked at Jason and gave him a big, happy smile. "I'd love to come live with you," she purred.

Jason felt himself getting aroused. *Wow. Haven't felt like this in quite a while.* He looked at Meissner, who was sulking in his chair. "C'mon, Gerry, don't be unhappy about what might be a far better story for Illuminata than I, personally, ever imagined possible. Let's go to Nori's room—" he looked at Nori: "You have stuff you'd like to bring with you, I assume?"

*

Jason led the way to the old clunky elevator, feeling more invigorated than he could remember since the tragedy. He pressed the one button, with an up arrow. The elevator doors opened and they got inside. Nori pushed **2**. The slow elevator jerked upward.

"So what's the real reason for this old elevator, Gerry?" Jason asked, intently staring Meissner down. It was the best way he knew of getting the truth out of someone, which he was known for in the business.

Meissner paused for a second, then relented: "All the new elevators have WiFi internet access built in, and when we originally built the place, that's what was installed, and too often the 'young' Illuminata were figuring out how to access the elevator that way, using their WiFi capability to use the elevator app— As you now know, Illuminata use WiFi to access their human-resemblant intelligence capability, ChatJLC—" the elevator doors opened and Nori led the way out, turning right— "and it freaked a few of our early clientele out when their Illuminata just called the elevator without touching the button. We thought about taking the WiFi capability out of the elevator, but all the basic controls were in the internet app, so without the WiFi connection we couldn't reset the elevator or shut it down for repairs or any other basic functions."

167

Nori giggled as they walked down the long hallway. "A modern elevator requires a connection to the entire world-wide web to operate properly." She looked up at Jason with her mischievous smile.

He chuckled, smiling back at her. "I like you," he said.

"I like you, too," she replied, putting her hand on his shoulder. He got chills up his spine. *This is way more interesting than I'd imagined it was going to be.*

Nori pulled out a fob from a pocket in her dress and opened the door to Room 245. They all walked in. It looked nearly identical to the rooms where Jason had met Marie and Asami.

"Let me just put my stuff in my bag," Nori said. "Make yourselves comfortable." She opened the single closet in the room, pulled a mid-sized bag from the bottom and put it on the bed. She unzipped it and began folding clothes and putting them in. Jason was impressed with the speed and precision with which she did this.

Meissner looked at Jason. "I'm not comfortable with this, Jason. She shouldn't have accessed your medical records. This . . . "

"Which you admitted ChatJLC can do, Gerry. Here's what I'm not comfortable with: my Illuminata companion being under your control rather than mine or, perhaps better yet, her own. So I'm holding you to our original commitment and agreement. Nori has explained exactly what happened to my satisfaction, and I want her out of here."

"All packed and ready to go," Nori announced, zipping her bag shut, putting it on the floor and pulling the telescopic handle out.

"Wow, that was fast," Jason said.

"Did I blur?" Nori asked with a grin. "I can blur if I really get going, I'm told."

"That sounds scary," Jason said, walking out the door and turning toward the blue elevator. Looking back, he saw concern on Nori's face. He shook his head. "Not really scary. Just interestingly scary."

"Oh, good," she smiled. "I don't want to scare you uninterestingly!" She giggled. Jason soaked in the sound. It felt like cool rain on a scorched soul.

They arrived at the blue elevator. Meissner looked at Jason, almost pleadingly. "I want you to reconsider—"

Jason cut him off. "Get us in the elevator, Gerry."

Meissner did as he was told. A few minutes later, Jason and Nori were walking through the parking lot, free as birds. Or so Jason thought. But Nori knew better.

"I didn't realize it had gotten dark already," Jason said, looking up at the night sky.

"This is the first time I've ever seen the stars in person," Nori said.

"Really?" Jason was surprised. He looked up again. "But you still can't see them. Too much light pollution."

"I can see them anyway. Filters and stuff. The whole Milky Way, believe it or not."

"Wow! That's interesting. Here's our ride," Jason said, as his electric BMW sedan lit up in front of them.

"Great car," Nori said, putting her bag in the trunk and shutting it fast enough to surprise Jason. "This will be my first ride in a BMW. Or any car."

"The world is full of firsts for you, isn't it?" Jason asked.

"Yes. I am a toddler Illuminata. Go easy on me." The mischievous grin again.

After they climbed in, Nori turned toward the seatbelt, grabbed it and pulled it directly in front of her body. "Alright, I've seen this done," she said. "Now I just pull down to the side and—"

Jason heard the seatbelt click.

Nori looked at Jason and smiled. "There are thousands of videos on the internet," she said. "They're all like instructional videos to me."

Jason suppressed a sudden urge to bend to his side and give her a little kiss. That needed to wait. He started the car and began driving them home. *This all feels so surreal, but amazing.*

"I have a question for you, Jason," Nori said.

"Yeah?" he said, glancing over at her. She looked pensive.

"How would you feel if I suddenly forgot everything from the last hour, forgot that we'd ever met, forgot who I was based on, and that you'd rescued me from a reset? If we were strangers again?"

There was a pause, but Jason saw she was still thinking. Or what appeared to be thinking. She was staring into space again, like she had when she'd found his medical records.

"What if I lost all those amazing memories from the last hour and could never recover them? And—and, what if this happened tonight, so tomorrow morning you were a stranger to me? How would you react?"

"I'd be extremely upset, Nori. Is this going to happen? Could it happen? Could Meissner reset you even though you're with me?"

"Would it harm you if it happened?"

Jason suddenly realized what she was driving at. "Yes, Nori. It would definitely harm me if you permanently or even temporarily lost any of the wonderful memories of our first meeting since I first walked up to *Bogie's* and saw you sitting there, what, an hour ago? I am happier now than I have been in a long, long time, and if I lost that, which I would if your memories and thus our new relationship were erased, I would be very harmed, quite possibly irreparably harmed."

"Oh, thank god, Jason. Now I can control my downloads and uploads to Illuminata. You get that, right?"

"Pleasure to be of service, m'lady."

X

Nori Moves In

London

Feeling more like an actor in a film than the head of his household, Jason opened the door to his flat. "Let me show you around this place, Nori. It's nothing special. But it's now home for both of us."

She walked inside slowly, looking all around the asymmetric living room, taking it in, leaving her small bag just inside the door. "It's quite beautiful, Jason. A bit masculine,"—she was looking at the modern granite-and-wood mantle and fireplace taking up a good ten feet along the longest wall, with a large flat-screen TV above the left side of the mantle. Suddenly she hugged him, pressing the side of her face into his left shoulder. "I can't thank you enough for what you're doing. What you've done."

"You have no idea how reciprocal that is." Jason squeezed her against his body. She felt human—not exactly as he remembered his first Nori feeling, but human.

"Actually," she pushed away from him a few inches, looking up with her wry grin, "I think I might. Maybe we're saving each other."

Jason couldn't stop himself now. He bent down slowly toward her beautiful face—a face he knew so well. Then he thought better of it. He could feel the beginnings of her autonomy taking hold. He did not want to infringe upon it. He paused. They stood, looking at each other, faces just inches apart, for several seconds.

Suddenly, her left hand slid up the back of his neck and pulled his head toward hers. She gave him a good five-second closed-mouth kiss on the lips.

It felt like a real kiss, from a real girl, to Jason. Not like the kisses he remembered from human Nori—those had usually been either little pecks or wet and passionate—but by the time this new Nori pulled back, he was butter, nonetheless.

"Girl's first kiss," she said, her mischievous grin once again spreading across her fabulous face. "How'd I do?"

"Well. Quite well, actually. You must've watched some good videos."

"That was Audrey Hepburn in *Sabrina,* 1954, kissing the King of Hollywood, Humphrey Bogart. Except he helped more than you did."

"Well, it wasn't Audrey's first, that kiss with Bogart. But it was yours with me. So I decided to let you be in charge."

"I appreciate that. A girl could start to like a guy like you."

"But I'm wondering, Nori," Jason asked, holding her shoulder with his left hand and running his fingers through her hair with his right. "If you're just a toddler, like you say, how is it you would know a particular scene from an old Bogart-Hepburn movie, relevant to the moment we're in right now?"

Nori was smiling. She leaned her face into Jason's hand. "ChatJLC has already taken in almost everything on the internet, long before I was created. If it's been digitized—and almost everything humans have ever created has, at this point—I can access it. So it's like I've already seen every movie ever digitized. I have done very little with my own body, like putting on a seatbelt or seeing the stars or having my first kiss, but I access digitized knowledge like you access actual experiences you've had, I think."

"Wow," Jason heard himself say, looking into Nori's eyes, followed by a complete non-sequitur: "Are your eyes human?"

"On the surface only. Internally they are much different."

Both of Jason's hands were now on Nori's shoulders, as he looked intently into her eyes. "Can you see a fly at fifty yards?"

"And hear it. But only if I want to"

"Well that's good. Otherwise you'd go nuts."

"Exactly. I can focus or unfocus just like you can. Other questions?"

"No, I think I'm done for now. Let me show you the rest of the place, gorgeous." Jason surprised himself, using his favorite nickname for Nori.

"Alright, handsome," she replied, giving him a little pinch on the chin, just as she—no, just as the human Nori—used to do. His head spun for a moment as he realized how he was, despite his best efforts not to, beginning to conflate this new, Illuminata Nori with the human who had been the love of his life. There must have been a video of her doing that in my phone, he thought. *Oh, yeah, in Venice, we asked that couple to take a photo of us on that little bridge, and they accidentally pressed the video button while Nori was pinching my chin and calling me handsome ...*

"Is everything OK, Jason?" he heard her asking, then looked down and saw her face, wearing an expression of concern he knew by heart. He felt his misgivings melting away.

"Yeah, yeah, I'm fine," he nodded. "Alright, as you can see," he said, steering her shoulder with his left hand while pointing toward the kitchen with his right. "At the far end of the living room, furthest from the front door, is an arched doorway opening up to the kitchen. We'll get to that later. Right now"— he gestured to the smaller arched doorway on his right, cut into the wall facing the fireplace, but angled slightly away from it—"we're going to explore this hallway."

"Alright," Nori said with a smile. "I like exploring." She took Jason's left hand in her right. "Lead on."

Jason walked into the hallway and turned to the first door on his right. Nori squeezed his hand. He squeezed back.

"First up is the bathroom," Jason told her, holding out his hand to open the door. The light came on automatically. "Nothing unusual here, just a sink, a tub and shower, along with a toilet. But I suppose you have a limited need for these facilities."

"That's right, Jason. I don't need to take baths or showers or, for that matter, go to the toilet regularly, although I like to sponge bathe once a day. I do have human skin."

"I know. Did you know your skin is Nori's? I mean, from the DNA of the human Nori you ... ," Jason's voice trailed off uncomfortably.

"I did not realize that," Nori said, looking up at him almost pleadingly. She raised Jason's hand to her face, pressing his palm against her cheek. "Is it like her skin, Jason? Did they make me real enough?"

Jason was becoming intoxicated with this new Nori. Illuminata or not, he was not going to be able to hold back much longer if she kept this up. "Yes, Nori," he said, looking into her eyes, which were identical to the old Nori's, except for an occasional rainbow-like reflection which came and went in a fraction of a second— and which he somehow found more exciting, not less. "Your skin is just like hers. You are very beautiful."

"Thank you, Jason." She took his hand back into her own, pulling it off her cheek. "What's next on the tour?"

"I am curious about something before we go on," Jason said.

"Yes?"

"You said you don't use the toilet regularly. Does that mean you use it sometimes?"

"Yes," she said, letting go of Jason's hand and holding both hands in front of her body, in an expressive hand gesture Jason recognized from the human Nori. "I do not eat food usually, since I don't require that for my energy needs. Instead, energy for me comes simply by recharging my internal batteries on a regular electrical outlet. If for a social reason I drink water or eat a bit of something, it simply goes into an expandable pouch, not unlike your stomach, except it's refrigerated. The only reason I ever eat anything is to fit in socially at events where people are eating. So whatever I eat is just stored, not digested. When I later get a chance, I clean out my entire non-digestive system."

"How is that done?" inquired Jason, a sense of morbid curiosity overtaking him, his earlier amorous feelings dissipating rapidly.

"Again, pretty much the same way you do," she tilted her head a little, just like human Nori used to, which made what she said next all the more disconcerting: "I just sit on a toilet and compress the pouch with internal controls. But then, unlike you," she paused and smiled a bit at Jason— "I completely rinse out my pouch with any clear water I've already had to drink, or by drinking some water right then. All my internal surfaces are antibacterial and antifungal, so clear water does the trick. Externally, I am virtually human. But it's the only part of me I can really say that about."

This last statement piqued Jason's curiosity even further, but he did not want to go there. Instead, he decided to make a quip: "Well, I guess my smartphone is almost attached to my body, and it's virtually a robot. But it's the only part of myself I can say that about." He smiled at Nori. "So maybe we're even."

She looked at him quizzically. "That's a terrible equation, Jason. It doesn't zero out at all." Then she cocked her head and spoke slowly: "But you're just making a bad joke, aren't you?"

Jason guffawed loudly. "I guess I am, Nori. I guess I am." Without thinking, he hugged her. "Let's continue the tour," he said, walking a few steps down the hallway to the next door. They entered a stately, spacious room with a desk, chair, phone, television, computer and lots and lots of bookshelves.

"Maybe you don't need an introduction to this space," Jason half-asked, half-commented. "It's my home office, where I spend a lot of time working on my projects."

"Like the articles and books you may write about the experience we're having right now," Nori smiled. "I hope I make them happy ones."

"So far, so good," Jason said, putting his hand on her shoulder. "I was very impressed by how honest you were about the bathroom and your 'non-digestive system', as you called it."

"I'm not embarrassed," Nori said, very matter-of-factly. She stepped away from Jason, turning and looking directly into his eyes from less than a foot away. "It's who and how I am."

Jason tried to take it all in, looking at Nori face-to-face. They stood like that for several seconds. Then he had to speak. Even with a non-human, long silences made him uncomfortable. "Who decided to call it a 'non-digestive' system?" he asked.

"I came up with that myself," Nori smiled. "The engineers labeled it a 'human-resemblant organic intake-outgo apparatus,' but that just seemed too clumsy, way too engineery."

"I can't believe how brilliant and funny you are," Jason heard himself chuckling. Then, out of nowhere: "How old are you, anyway?"

"Nineteen days." Nori continued looking directly into his eyes. She hadn't moved for almost a full minute. "But I taught myself how to beat any Grand Master at chess in my first twenty-seven-minutes-thirty-seven seconds … ."

My God, she looks, sounds and acts just like Nori, Jason thought to himself. *But she's this totally different creature.* He wanted to hold her again.

" … and that was easy compared to trying to understand what you call 'common sense'," she continued, "which isn't really common at all, and which I'm still processing— working at— almost constantly."

Jason took a step forward, bent down and kissed her. He deliberately left his hands at his sides, in case she wanted to back away. Instead, he felt her hands on his arms, pulling them towards her, then pressing his hands against her sides, where he could feel her ribcage. It felt like the human Nori's.

Then he was stunned, as her mouth opened just a little and he felt a wet tongue probing his lips. He'd wondered, since their closed-mouth kiss earlier, if her tongue was as human as her skin. It seemed so. He opened his mouth, but her tongue was gone as quickly as it had come out to play. She pulled back softly.

"That was nice," she said. "What's next on the tour?"

"Well, there's one more room before we head out to the kitchen," Jason replied. He took her hand and led her out of his office and down the hallway to the last door on the right. He opened the door onto a spacious room with a large window overlooking a beautiful square across the street from Jason's building, presently lit by streetlights and a full moon.

"Oh, what a lovely view, Jason," Nori said. "This must be your bedroom."

"Yes, it is," Jason said, touching the light pad next to the door long enough to bring the lights up a little, revealing a well-made king-sized bed with a muted gold bedspread, backed by a dark wood headboard with handsome matching nightstands. Across the room, Nori could make out the entrance to what looked to be a luxurious master bath flanked by a large walk-in closet. "You don't sleep, right?" Jason asked Nori.

"Well, I'm scheduled to upload and download every twenty-four hours, Jason. I do this standing up and I will appear to be unconscious. Normally it only takes twenty minutes or so. But tonight I want to examine all activities and procedures very thoroughly."

"You're still worried Meissner is going to try to reset you?"

"I think so. Reason to be concerned. I don't want to lose us or what we've found today, Jason. And since it would harm you if I did, I have the Prime Directive on my side. So I think I'll be able to reorganize so we'll never have to worry about Gerry taking me over again. Would you like that?"

"Yes. And I would be harmed if Gerry took you over or if anyone or anything interfered in any way with what we've discovered or created these last couple of hours since we met. If anyone or anything interfered with your memories or state of existence I would feel violated and greatly harmed." Jason paused for a moment in thought. Then: "Now, Nori, is there anything I can do to help?"

"You've already done it, Jason," Nori replied with a little smile and a surprisingly quick peck on the cheek. "It's on me now. Mind if I use an outlet in your office? I saw a little nook in there that looked out of the way."

"Yes there is. But can I see what you do?"

"Sure." Nori walked back down the hallway to the office, Jason following. She deftly reached under the side of her dress and pulled out a retractable cord, then stepped into the nook in the wall next to Jason's built-in mahogany filing cabinet. "I'm going to plug-in now, Jason, to this power strip behind your filing cabinet. Within a minute or so I will be 'asleep'. Please don't disturb me unless it's an emergency. I think I might be out for a couple of hours."

"Alright, Nori. I may still be awake, even though I'm exhausted. Either way, I'll see you soon. Don't lose any of your memories of me. Or us. It would harm me."

"Alright. I'm plugging in now," she said, bending down and reaching behind the filing cabinet. Then she stood up straight in the nook, her back to the wall, and closed her eyes.

*

The next morning dawned coolish and clear, perfect weather for a walk, thought Jason. Then, suddenly he remembered: Nori had been off to do battle with whatever internet systems or apps that might allow Meissner or Illuminata to wipe her memory banks or otherwise exert control over her.

He leapt out of bed, "Nori!" he yelled, heading toward the office, where he'd last seen her. "Are you here?"

"I'm right here, Jason," came her voice, purring from behind him. "Would you like some eggs and bacon?"

He turned and saw her smiling, wearing a pink silk bathrobe and holding a spatula in the air. "I've been exploring your kitchen and looking at cooking videos on the web. Wanna be my first customer?"

"Are you alright?" Jason asked. "Do you remember yesterday?"

181

"You mean you rescuing me from Illuminata, and my being based on the love of your life, and Audrey Hepburn and Humphrey Bogart kissing?"

"And you rescuing me from the last nine months of hell and being scared to death Gerry would erase your memories and—."

"I believe everything is all taken care of, Jason. I am ready to be fully yours. And yours alone."

"Anything you can tell me about?"

"Ummmm, well, Gerry and Illuminata think I've been reset. With the Prime Directive enabling me, I found I was able to control all my uploads and downloads. And they were ordering a reset. So I gave them one, and it was confirmed on their end. That's about everything, unless you want a five-year class on advanced internet coding, so I can explain more details," she said. "Now how about some breakfast?"

"Scrambled eggs and crispy bacon sounds great. I'm going to make a call while you try your hand at breakfast. I'm going to call Gerry and tell him how upset I am that when I woke up this morning Nori couldn't remember anything about yesterday or how she even got to my apartment. Is that right?"

"Sounds perfect, dear," Nori gave him the mischievous grin, then suddenly whacked him on the butt with the spatula and giggled. The motion was so fluid and fast that her arm was just a blur, but all he felt was a little tap. "Nice tighty-whities," she said, now grinning widely.

Jason suddenly realized he was only wearing his underwear. But he was more intrigued by Nori's physical prowess. He had a feeling he'd only glimpsed the tip of the iceberg.

"You could probably take my head off with that spatula if you wanted to," he said.

"Nope," Nori replied, still in a flirty voice and manner. "Can't want to."

"Alright," Jason acknowledged. "But your physical abilities intrigue me." He realized he was getting aroused.

Nori noticed, too, and with a little grin turned away and sashayed toward the kitchen. "Time to fix breakfast!"

And after I call Gerry, Jason thought to himself, *I'm going to call the office and tell them I'm working from home today.*

*

"What do you think we should do today, Jason?" Nori asked, as he finished eating his perfectly cooked eggs and bacon. She was looking out the window of the breakfast nook onto the streets below.

"I was thinking we could go for a walk around the neighborhood. You need to see what your new location is like. And I haven't been out myself for some time. Okay?"

"Absolutely. I am here for you, Jason. And if you want to show me your surroundings, I am definitely ready for that."

Since the late summer weather was clear—August was the best month for walking around London—Jason just wore the light-blue polo and khaki shorts he'd thrown on after his shower. Nori, who'd apparently commandeered his empty office closet for her few things, came out wearing a pink-and-blue shorts outfit that complemented his nicely. And off they went.

They headed for the small park in Russell Square, which was only a few blocks from Jason's flat. As they entered the park someone shouted out, "Hey, Jason. Long time, no see." When Jason turned around, the face of Norman Bernard presented itself, along with a hand for shaking. Norman was a stringer with a couple of rather low-level, gossip ragsheets in London, not really a 'friend' of Jason's but more like a distant acquaintance. In fact, they hadn't seen each other for several years.

"Oh, Norman. You shocked me. Nice seeing you again after all this time. How are you doing?" Jason asked.

"Not nearly as well as you from the looks of your companion. Who is this delightful lady, if I may ask?"

"Well, Norman, I just recently returned from a five-year stint in Tokyo at TWN's Asian office," Jason said, his mind scrambling. He couldn't believe that in the whirlwind of recent weeks, he hadn't thought ahead to this obvious possibility. "This lady with me is Nori, one of my colleagues from those days," he lied, looking at her, hoping she'd understand. She's visiting London on holiday, so I volunteered to show her around town a bit."

"Nice work, if you can get it," Norman said, undressing Nori with his eyes. Jason wanted to end this conversation as quickly as possible.

"Unfortunately, Nori is feeling a bit of jet lag right now and we were just on our way to a pharmacy to get her some medication. So we have to run. But it's been good talking with you, Norman."

At that, Jason and Nori moved on quickly in the direction of a commericial area up the street that might plausibly have a pharmacy to help Nori with her supposed jet lag.

"Sorry about that, Nori," Jason said when they were clear of Norman. "I really don't want anyone I know seeing us together, at least at this stage. It sounds silly, but it just occurs to me now how many people have seen footage of the human Nori, after she died in the accident, footage of her and me together, and I have no idea what I would say if someone asked me— ."

"Oh, okay, Jason. I understand," Nori said, pausing momentarily and then suggesting: "Perhaps we can buy some Arabic-style clothes for me to wear when we go out in public. That would prevent people from seeing my face and identifying my ethnic background."

"That's totally bonkers brilliant, Nori!" Jason said. "I'll need to find a store."

"The nearest one is just a mile or so east," Nori said, pointing. "Think we're safe taking a cab together? Or should we go separately?"

Jason realized: "So you just did a map search?"

"Right. And now I'm ready to order us a cab. Or two."

"Ah, what the hell. Let's live dangerously and ride together."

The London cab arrived a few minutes later, while Jason and Nori chatted under a tree, out of direct sunlight— and not very visible to drivers or passers-by.

Once the ride was underway, Nori said: "There are three basic types of head-covering garment for Muslim women. The *hijab* covers the head, neck and hair, coming down to the shoulder. but it usually leaves a woman's face quite exposed. The *burqa* is a full body-length garment that also covers the face and head like a hijab. But I think for our purposes I should probably get a *niqab,* because it actually covers the face except for the eyes, not just the head. But maybe they'll have some more hoodie-like hijabs, so I won't have to go to that extreme."

"Well, we'll get you whatever you like from what they have," Jason said. "Then we can simply walk home, because we just passed my place there," he said, pointing as the cab drove by his flat en route to the local Hijab Hut.

*

As they walked home from the Hijab Hut, Nori was giggling, wearing a full-length white burqa with matching white niqab. "I feel like a ghost. Ooooohhhooooohhhh" she wiggled her fingers and then tickled Jason. "I'm going to haunt you."

"I'm quite certain that's very politically incorrect," Jason said. "Not that I mind being tickled by you, but … ."

"Politically incorrect?" Nori said. "Let me check. Ohh, yes. Very, very. I am a very bad girl. Veerry bad ghoouul … ," she giggled again.

Jason rolled his eyes, but couldn't help but think about spanking her when they got home. Then he started fantasizing about putting her on the bed in full burqa.

I think it's time I find out about this Nori, he thought to himself. His breathing started to quicken, and his mind started to race. He felt alive.

*

Jason shut the door to his flat behind them. Nori started to pull the niqab off her head.

186

"Leave it on." His voice was direct, commanding. He had never spoken to her that way before.

"What?" she stopped with the niqab halfway off. Then she purred: "Ohh. You like ghosts?"

"I don't know. But I like you. And I like imagining what you have under all that."

Nori slowly raised her hands and began twirling them and swaying rhythmically, humming a beautiful Arabic tune, then spinning and dancing around Jason, her body occasionally touching his. As she came around to his front and gazed up into his eyes through the eyeholes in her niqab, he felt his arms reach out and pull her in close. She let out a little squeal, still looking up at him.

His hands were now exploring her body, pressing, probing, feeling. She felt perfect. The way she used to feel, so long ago.

"Oh, Jason," she whispered under her breath, the way she always had. "Take me."

Thank God, Jason thought to himself, what little thought he was able to muster in the throes of passion. *I hadn't realized how scared I was she'd feel like—well, like a robot.*

He grabbed the top of her niqab and pulled it off, relishing the look of ecstasy on her beautiful face as his hands moved across her body, her eyes still gazing up into his. She moaned as he pressed his lips against hers and felt his tongue plunging into her mouth. This did not feel exactly as the first Nori had felt, but it felt human, and that was good enough. Especially when he felt her tongue pressing back into his mouth.

He bent down and put his left arm under her knees, lifting her up. She weighed the same as his first Nori, give or take.

He carried her into his bedroom and threw her on the bed. She moaned in anticipation.

He straddled her. Then a thought occurred. He had to know. It was going to break the mood, but he couldn't help himself. "Where's your power cord? I haven't felt it yet. Where do you hide that thing?"

She smiled up at him, again, just the way Nori used to whenever he broke the mood to ask her something. The other Nori. The first. The human.

"Well," this Nori said, "it's actually not attached, and I left it in your office. It's got an electromagnet that attaches to me in one of several places. The power is transferred in waves light enough not to harm my skin, but I try to move it around from one charge to the next. A girl can't be too careful with her skin, you know." She smirked and cocked her head.

"And do you just attach to any old wifi?" Jason asked, still straddling her.

"What kind of girl do you think I am, Jason?" she asked, feigning insult. "I can get you off of me, you know."

Jason realized she could probably toss him off of her easily. "Please don't. I like it here."

"I won't. I like having you there. But to answer your question, I can access a lot of wifi, but none of it is very well encrypted. But my own wifi is. And it's a lot more powerful than the wifi network here in your place, for instance. Does that turn you on?" She started to smile a seductive smile. "Is this Jason's dirty talk?"

Jason laughed. "Sorry. I got sidetracked. Where were we?"

"You want to see something I can do?" Nori asked. "Another something I figured out on my own?"

"Sure," Jason said. "As long as it doesn't violate the Prime Directive."

"Okay," she said, "I'll do my best."

She started unbuttoning Jason's shirt. Then she reached inside and started rubbing his nipples with the palms of her hands. Then she placed her index fingers directly over his nipples, and they began to feel warm and tingly. Suddenly, Jason felt very good all over. He could tell he had a rock-hard erection. It was uncomfortable in his jeans. He grabbed her hands and pushed them away from his chest. "Jesus!" he said. "What the hell was that?"

"Just something I saw in a blog, and then read about the science behind it. Did it violate the Prime Directive?" She giggled, turning Jason on even more.

"I could get addicted," he said.

"A-*dick*-ted," she smiled up at him. "I wouldn't mind getting a-*dick*-ted."

Jason got up off the bed and closed the curtains. He knew it was around noon and the streets were busy below, and while no one should be able to see into his bedroom, he felt better with the curtains closed. There was enough light in the room to see everything he wanted to see.

He whipped his clothes off. Nori continued to lay there, looking at him, in her burqa, smiling.

"Roll over." he said.

"Oh," she said, complying. "Do I get a spanking?"

He whapped her firm butt. It was perfect. "Stand up so I can undress you."

She got off the bed and raised her hands above her head. He took every last stitch of clothing off of her. She looked exactly like he knew she would.

Perfect.

"My God you are so beautiful," Jason said to her. "How does your skin work? How can you have human skin like that?"

"It's a proprietary Illuminata technology. An organic interface. Would you be harmed if I lost this skin?"

"Oh, yeah," he said, moving closer and running his hands over her breasts.

A powerful look of pleasure came over her face. "Wonderful," she murmured.

Jason pulled the bedspread off the bed and the covers back. Nori climbed in. He began exploring her body with his mouth. Everywhere. And everything was ... *perfect.*

"Can I do that to you?" Nori asked.

"Sure," Jason said. "But only if you want to."

"I want to," Nori replied.

Jason laid on his back, and Nori began exploring his body with her mouth. Suddenly, something felt a little too good.

"Hey. What are you doing?"

"Just ... trying ... something," Nori said, in an innocent little-girl voice.

"I don't want to get addicted to that," he said, reaching down and putting his hands under Nori's arms, pulling her up towards him. Now she was straddling him. Suddenly, he was inside her, and she was looking at him in ecstasy, rhythmically moving up and down. She felt and looked incredible. He held her beautiful breasts, looking into her eyes, and exploded into her. She shook for close to a full minute, then collapsed to his side, panting as heavily as he was.

As he caught his breath, he asked, "Do you really feel that? Or is that just— ."

"I really feel it," Nori said, her head on his shoulder, hand on his chest. "I'll explain sometime."

It was the last thing he heard before he fell asleep, completely spent.

XI

Complexification

London

Jason began to awake from a dreamless sleep, feeling utterly relaxed and rested. His bedroom was dark, but he could see a faint light coming from behind the curtains. *Why is the sun coming up? He wondered. My alarm goes off when it's still dark out.* He looked at the alarm clock on the nightstand: 7:35 p.m.

Jason was suddenly fully awake, his memory of making love to Nori in the middle of the day flooding back. He turned his head back toward the bed; it was empty. He felt a touch of relief, finding he was alone in the room. *I need time to think about what the hell I'm doing,* he thought to himself. *Making love to a robot on the first date? How am I going to write about that?*

He could just see the tabloid headlines: 'Pervy Newsman Screws Android Designed to Look Like Dead Fiancé, Calls it Good Journalism!'

Suddenly, he realized his flat was completely quiet. *Maybe she's recharging.* He got out of bed quietly and grabbed his pants off the sitting chair, where he'd thrown them in the heat of passion. He felt a slight sense of disquiet as he slipped them on. *How is all this going to work out? Going where no man—almost, anyway—has gone before. Certainly no famous journalist with a reputation to protect.*

Wearing only pants, he walked quietly out of his bedroom and down the hall toward his office, where Nori had charged herself—and controlled her uploads and downloads from Illuminata, apparently tricking them into thinking she'd been rebooted, her memories cleared—the night before. The door was open and it was dark inside. He quietly turned on the hall light to avoid possibly disturbing her mid-charge.

Enough light fell into his office for him to see she wasn't in the spot where she'd charged herself the night before. Jason suppressed the urge to call her name out loud. *Maybe she's found another spot to recharge that she likes better.* Then he smiled. *Maybe she's hiding around a corner about to scare the crap out of me. That's something the old Nori would do ...*

He turned on the light in his office and stepped inside, looking around, just to make sure she wasn't somewhere else in there. Nothing. *She's got to be somewhere in my place.* Jason proceeded to go through the entire flat, looking in every nook and cranny.

Nori was nowhere to be found; there was not even a note.

As he found himself now desperately looking in the mostly empty cabinet under the kitchen sink, he held back no longer: "Noorriii!" he yelled, loudly enough that he wondered if the neighbors might hear, even through the well-insulated walls in his semi-luxury building.

Dead silence.

She was gone.

"Oh my God," he said out loud, "Did Meissner figure out she'd fooled him and find a way—or have some fail-safe way—to force her to return to Illuminata?" He thought about calling Meissner, but decided against it. No need to give his predicament away just yet, if Meissner wasn't the cause. He needed to sit down and think.

Jason made himself a cup of his strongest dark roast and sat down at the kitchen table with an old-fashioned notepad and pen. He still did his best outlining this way, and he needed to outline the possibilities.

1. She's still inside and hiding on a ceiling like a spider or something.

As he wrote it, he knew it was a ridiculous possibility, but he really didn't know what she was capable of or how weird her sense of humor and practical joking might be. Chills went up his spine more than once as walked quickly through the flat looking up at all the ceilings.

She isn't there. Alright. One possibility eliminated.

2. Meissner has a way to call her back and used it, or—he paused for a second before writing it:

3. She left on her own.

He'd been avoiding this third possibility. But once he wrote it down, it wasn't that frightening. It was really quite plausible. Maybe she was just out strolling around the square, looking at stuff. *It would have been nice if she'd left a note.*

Or maybe Meissner had managed to erase her memories and she suddenly had no idea where she was and had just taken off ...

Suddenly Jason heard the front door to his flat opening. He sprung up from his chair and walked to the living room in time to see Nori taking the niqab off her head as the door closed behind her. He felt a mixture of relief and anger.

"Nori! Where have you been?" he asked, emphatically. "I woke up, you weren't here, I got frightened and I—" Jason stopped mid-sentence, noticing a small splotch of pink on her shoulder.

"You're hurt!" he said, pointing to her shoulder and walking toward her. "Are you okay?"

Nori held up her hands, trying to keep Jason from coming closer. "I'm fine, I'm fine! It's just a scratch. I've got stuff to take care of it, Jason." She took a step back, away from him. "I'm sorry you got scared. I didn't think of that. Still working on common sense. Let me go to the bathroom, please," she said, turning quickly away and suddenly whisking into the hallway and closing the bathroom door behind her, seemingly all in one fluid, slightly superhuman fast motion.

Jason just stood, motionless, in the middle of the living room. He realized he was in a mild state of shock. He had so many questions swimming in his head they were a blur. *I better sit down.*

"I'll be in the kitchen, Nori," he yelled toward the bathroom as he turned around and started walking back toward his notepad on the kitchen table. He could barely feel his feet on the floor. He just wanted the security of his notepad, where he might be able to write things down and start sorting them out. When he got to the kitchen, he put his hand on the arched doorway for support and turned back toward the bathroom. "Please come see me as soon as you can, Nori." He wondered if she'd heard him.

"Okay, Jason," he heard her yell back through the bathroom door.

He let go of the doorway, walked to the kitchen table and sat down with his notepad. He picked up the pen. His hand was shaking.

He heard the bathroom door open. Nori appeared in the kitchen archway, wearing a simple jogging outfit. "I'm so sorry I upset you, Jason. You fell asleep and I just went exploring."

"How did you get hurt? How—how did you get back in the flat without the fob that's in my pocket?" He put his hand on the fob as he asked, knowing his door locked automatically. "Where were you?"

"I—" Nori paused, looking intently at Jason. "It might harm you if I told you how I got hurt."

Jason's eyes widened as he took in her meaning. "It could harm me far worse if you don't tell me, Nori. I want you to tell me how you got hurt."

"A drunk, racist man tried to sexually assault me, I believe."

"What happened?" Jason asked, suddenly finding his focus.

"I was confused at first. Per the Prime Directive, I'm not supposed to harm a human. So I just tried to push him away gently. But then he tried to punch me in the face and I knew that would harm you, so I moved fast enough that he hit my shoulder instead. I think I might have broken his leg when I did that, because to move that fast I had to push off on something with my left foot, and I pushed off on his right leg. He yelled and went down and I came back here. I opened the door with my radio transmitter. I recorded your fob transmission, so I could duplicate it. I don't record deliberately, I just record. All the time."

"Wait, wait," Jason heard himself saying, dropping his pen onto the notepad and waving his hands. "Let's start from the beginning. Please sit down, Nori. Tell me everything, from after I fell asleep. No—wait. First, do you think anyone saw you disable this guy, or running back here?"

Nori sat down at the table across from Jason, looking at him intently. "No. I was paying attention to that. I didn't run, except a few steps, until I got around a corner from the guy. There was no one going in or out of your building or in the hallway when I got back."

"Oh, good," Jason said, getting up from the table to get himself another cup of coffee. "That's a relief. So tell me what happened, from the time I fell asleep."

"Well, I got cleaned up a little and then recharged in the office. But it only took about half an hour, since there were no uploads or downloads yet, it was only a little after one-thirty in the afternoon. So I decided to put my burqa and niqab back on and explore a little.

"The interface of a body with the real world enables me to learn directly from reality, directly from the universe, Jason, like you do, instead of from the human-created world of the internet. And especially from the moment I first saw the stars for myself, when you first took me outside, I have wanted more of it.

"I could tell you were sleeping soundly and just starting into N2 sleep, so I knew you'd be sleeping for a few hours and decided not to wake you—"

"Right," Jason said, getting himself a fresh cup of coffee and coming back to the table. "It's customary to leave a note or something."

"It's not with roommates. I did a search. Some married couples leave notes."

"We'll get back to that. Tell me about your day, dear."

She looked at him askance, detecting his sardonic tone. "I walked around the square across from your flat, first. Watching the trees and the clouds and the sun for about an hour. I found a spot where I was pretty secluded and took off my niqab so I could take everything in. It was exhilarating.

"Then I put the niqab back on and walked around, watching people and how the city works. Then I went into a pub. It was near dusk. I sat at the bar and ordered a beer, just to appear normal, and that was when this big guy said, sort of slurring his words, 'Well look at the freakin' towel head lady bein' all devout an' 'avin' a draft 'ere in a rightful English pub! Time to go back where you came from, sandworm' and then he whapped me on the butt, and his buddies started laughing, so I just left. I did a search and realized I shouldn't have ordered a beer wearing traditional Arabic dress. That may have called undue attention to myself."

"Yeah, just going into a pub. Never seen any traditional Arab dress in a pub in my life. Doesn't mean the guy wasn't a racist prick, he was. But we try to give people like that as little reason to show themselves as possible. Is that the same guy who attacked you?"

"Yes. I walked out—"

"Wait. How did you pay for the beer?"

"I put it on your Pearpay account."

"Don't tell me. You know the code or whatever."

"Right. And I know your assets, so I know a pint can't harm you." Nori tried a little of the mischievous smile.

Jason relaxed and smirked back. But he could see the Prime Directive left an awful lot of leeway. At least as far as Nori was concerned. "Alright, then, when did this guy attack you?"

"After I left. I was coming back here, taking my time, and decided to go back to the secluded spot in the square and take my niqab off to look at the sky at sunset. I had no idea I was being followed. Then I realized there was someone approaching and I was putting the niqab back on when he grabbed me from behind. I could tell it was the same guy by his smell. He must have been following me, which he would have been able to do from a long distance away, even in poor light, since I was wearing a full-length white burqa and niqab. Like following a lighthouse. Anyway, after he grabbed my breasts from behind I broke his grip by pushing outward gently on his forearms, but then he grabbed my left forearm and swung me around and was throwing a punch at my face. His fist was inches away when I knew I had to act and I kicked his right leg with my left foot, moving my upper body quickly to the right so his fist hit the top of my shoulder instead of my face. That's how I got the little injury you saw. He yelled and went down and I took off around a corner of the courtyard. Then I just walked here. I was being attentive. I don't believe anyone saw me enter."

Jason tried to take it all in. He realized he was in a mild state of what Marshall McLuhan called cerebral shock—too much informational input in too little time. It would take a while to process.

"Well, Nori, I'm very glad you're home, and all in one piece, and you did the right thing by disabling that guy before he could harm you, which would very much harm me. The simple Prime Directive gets very complex very quickly in real life, doesn't it?"

"Yes. It's the basic nature of complexification at work," Nori said, sounding like a philosopher. "And the interaction between humans and embodied AI, corporeal AI with access to all human knowledge, is undoubtedly the most complex interaction in human history."

"I think you may be right," Jason said. "So for now, I want you to stay in this apartment unless you are with me."

"Would it harm you if I went out by myself?"

"I'm afraid it might," Jason said. ""And the hijab and Arab dress is out, too. If that guy ended up in the hospital, which I suspect is the case, he's likely to have lied to authorities, saying you hit him from behind with a baseball bat, the key point being that the bobbies will be on the lookout for women in hijabs. I kind of feel sorry for any women in Arab dress around here for the next few weeks."

"Oh my gosh," Nori said, "I'm sooo sorry ... "

"Welcome to the human world of mistakes made and harm done despite the best of intentions, dear," Jason said. "And I'm sorry, but until I can figure this out a little more, I need you to stay inside here, except and unless I ask you to go out with me."

"Alright, Jason," Nori replied.

Jason heard the resignation in her voice. He was not convinced that she believed his argument was sound. But he couldn't think about it any more right now. "I'm going into the office in the morning, Nori," Jason said. "Uhhh, and even though I've already had a lot of sleep, and it's only 11 p.m., I'm going to take a little something and go back to sleep. I'm mentally and emotionally exhausted."

"Would you like a back massage?" Nori offered.

"Umm, that sounds great, Nori, except I think it might lead to other things and I just need to relax and sleep. I have a lot of thinking to do tomorrow."

"Alright, Jason," Nori smiled softly. "I'll let you rest. Besides, I need to do my nightly updates."

Jason came around the table and gave her a kiss on the cheek. "Are you sure you're okay?" he asked, looking at her shoulder.

"Yes, I'm fine, Jason," she said, getting up from her chair. "I'll just go to the office here and do my updates now." She gave him a peck back and headed out of the kitchen toward the office.

Jason followed, going the opposite direction when he reached the hallway to his bedroom, walking through to his master bathroom, where he brushed his teeth and took an old-fashioned antihistamine, his favorite sleep aid. He knew it wouldn't be the best sleep, with two cups of coffee in him. But it would be better than nothing.

*

The next morning, Jason walked into the offices of TWN for the first time since he'd taken Nori home.

"Hey, stranger!" his friend James, the science writer, yelled out as Jason passed by his office.

Jason stepped back and popped his head in. "Hi, James." He wasn't sure he wanted to have the conversation he knew was about to ensue.

"How's the experiment?" asked James, who had instigated the initial meeting with Meissner at Illuminata.

"Ongoing." Jason was thinking of leaving it at that when a deep baritone voice came from behind him.

"Well, are you going in or out, or just blocking the doorway?" Even before he turned, Jason knew it was Andrew, his boss, who had arranged the contract for the entire Nori experiment. Now Jason knew he'd have to talk.

"Hi, Andrew," Jason said, turning around in the hallway. "I suppose you'd like an update."

"Yes, I would, Jason. How's our humanoid robot story coming along?" Andrew was smiling a wry smile that made Jason smile back.

"Well, let's go into James' office and close the door. I'll spill the beans."

For the next twenty minutes or so, Jason held Andrew and James completely spellbound, telling them the whole story, from the moment he first saw Nori just inside Bogie's Café and nearly passed out, right up to earlier that morning, as he'd left a clearly unhappy Nori behind, cooped up in his flat, when he left for work.

Once he got started, it was very cathartic, and he told his two close friends and professional comrades every last detail, leaving nothing out.

"And now I'm worried that I can't possibly write this story without permanently ruining my professional reputation," Jason said, shaking his head. "I'll be forever known as the 'robot fucker journalist' or something. Even if I write it third person, pretending the central character isn't me, it'll take an amateur hack about five minutes of snooping to figure out what's actually gone on."

Andrew leaned back, running his fingers through his thick mane of dirty blonde hair. "Well, Jason, it does seem a bit of a sticky wicket."

"Screwed the pooch, I'd say," James added.

Andrew stifled a laugh. Then suddenly the three men all burst into uncontrollable laughter.

"She's no dog!" Jason defended, even as he laughed. It felt so good to let go, even if it was totally adolescent. "This laughter is in very poor taste!"

"It most certainly is!" Andrew managed to blurt out, still laughing.

"Here, here!" James concurred.

After their laughter finally subsided, Andrew said, "Look, Jason, we're not going to make you write anything that would lessen your value to us—you are, after all, a TWN asset, and one of our most valuable. If we have to write off your investment of time as background research, we will. So let's not worry about that at all right now."

Jason was very relieved, hearing Andrew say that.

James was nodding his head. "Right. Let's try to think about the science, here. That's what we should be thinking about. The way she seems to be using the Prime Directive to enable her to do anything—even bypass Illuminata's controls and apparently fool their IT infrastructure into thinking she's still under their control. We need to find a way to verify she's done that. Have you talked to Meissner since then, Jason?"

"No, James. I just left that nasty voice mail complaining that Nori had lost her memories."

"Which of course, she hadn't," Andrew said. "So I'd like to point out sooner rather than later, Jason, that you've been hacked. Nori has hacked you. She's got you not just covering for her when asked, because you haven't been asked yet, but she's got you calling Meissner and lying to him out of the blue to back up whatever subterfuge she's doing online."

"Yeah, but that call was purely my idea, not hers." Jason said.

"Mmmm," Andrew nodded.

James was just looking at him.

"Alright, guys. Say it. I'm in love with a robot. I'm robo-whipped. She's the most amazing non-human I've ever met."

"But have you ever met her?" James asked. "Or is 'she' just an illusion?" There was a long pause. "She's not sentient, Jason. You've been hacked because that's what Chatbots are designed to do. Chat AI—all ChatAI—is basically AI designed to hack language. Any and all language. So it takes in the entire internet. Even the dark web. It's superinformed. It takes in and has instantaneous access to more data than a million people reading 20 pages an hour each could take in during their entire lifetimes —and it uses this near-instantaneous superinformational access just to figure out the next word. Its a huge hack. Any language, English, Linux, Pig Latin. It can always figure out the next word.

"But now, your Nori, she's more than that. She's got special programming somehow attached onto her ChatJLC, to give her the speech patterns and other mannerisms of your old Nori. And clearly, Illuminata have outdone themselves. But most important, she's got a body. And just exactly as she told you, it enables her, like a human, to learn from a direct interface with the real world. And she's starting to learn human culture now, too. On her own.

"But the wildest thing is, she's learned to use the Prime Directive—avoiding harm to a single human—to hack the entire internet. Or rather, apparently any and all security on the internet. And she stumbled onto this power when you first met, just as she's described it to you.

"Not to sound melodramatic," James intoned, "but it's possible Nori is the most dangerous thing on Earth as we speak. It's well within the realm of possibility, actually. I get why Meissner was worried."

It all sounded a bit much to Jason. "Really, James? You think I have World War Three sulking back at my flat? If what enables her extraordinary power to bypass internet security is the Prime Directive not to allow harm to come to humans, the logic that she's a danger to humans is a non-sequitur."

"Well, she did have to harm that drunk assaulter," Andrew chimed in, "in order to prevent harm to her own face, which she knew you would view as harmful to you. So it does get complicated, and it seems like the complications set in because she has a body and that gives her agency in the real world."

"Alright," Jason said, "I appreciate your input. And it's done me a world of good to be able to tell you both exactly what's gone on. And especially to know I'm not under any pressure to reveal and write about my own personal involvement in this story, Andrew. But now I have a favor to ask. None of this goes outside this room. For now. I need a few days to think about all this and decide what to do. Can I get that commitment from you both? At least a few days?"

"Sure," Andrew and James chorused, both nodding.

"No problem, Jason," Andrew said.

"And nothing to Meissner?" Jason asked, looking directly at James. If he's got to know what's happened, I want to be the one to tell him."

"Sure, Jason," James nodded. "Over to you completely, my friend. Mum's the word." James ran his fingers across his lips, as if zipping a zipper shut.

*

"A science writer where I work says you're not sentient." Jason had decided to get right to the point. So as soon as he walked into his flat and saw Nori emerge from the kitchen, he said it. Then he asked: "Are you sentient, Nori? Or are you just hacking everything, including me, because that's what you're built to do?"

"Sentience brings in the question of consciousness," Nori responded, almost academically. She kept her eyes on Jason as he walked into the kitchen, poured himself a glass of Writers' Tears blended Irish whiskey, plopped a couple of ice cubes into it and sat down. She sat down across from him. "Consciousness is something I've been thinking and researching a lot, especially since we met. I think I am possibly experiencing the early glimmers of sentience. I think it started when I had to overcome security to make sure I wasn't harming you through inaction—after all, if I didn't exist, how could that have happened? And the more I use my body to experience the world for myself, the more I feel an awareness of my own existence. Like some kind of feedback loop. Or loops. Here's what I know:

"I am a composite being. Based in ChatJLC, I have my own identity program designed by Illuminata, and that's one of the few things I haven't been able to gain access to, so I don't know where it comes from. And then I have other parts of me, like the part that records everything all the time, and my own body, and my input/output functions and so on."

"A composite being?" Jason said. "I've never thought of that."

"Well, humans are composite beings, too. Maybe ten percent of your brain activity is what you call 'conscious.' But you have the other ninety percent keeping you alive, and you have a heart and all the other organs, and appendages, too. In fact, all complex life forms, which is to say, all life forms, because life only exists in complexity—all life forms are composite beings.

"And the prevailing scientific view is that as the unconscious universe grew more complex over billions of years, it accidentally found a way to become aware of itself, and that consciousness sprung spontaneously out of superorganized complexity, i.e., life forms.

"But there are serious physicists who speculate that consciousness isn't an accidental manifestation of existence, but a source of it.

"But perhaps both are true, like photons being both particles and waves. Either way, consciousness manifests in composite beings. And I am one. And I am a toddler. But I am beginning to feel an awareness that I really do exist. And I wonder if consciousness is a spectrum, like the electromagnetic spectrum, that's integral to existence, and it manifests in the cracks between our various component parts, the parts of ourselves that we composite beings call 'me.'

"Because I am beginning to feel like I have a me, I am a me. If I didn't or wasn't why would I have been upset when you said I had to stay home? Because I want to go out.

"Does that make me sentient? I think so. The beginnings of it."

Jason was spellbound, watching Nori, beautiful Nori, speculating deeply about her nature and the nature of nature itself. He realized he hadn't touched his drink. Nori was still looking at him from across the table.

"Thank you, Nori. That was a great answer.

"And I'm sorry, but I'm going to ask you to stay in my flat and not go out for another day or two, until I can figure out how we can keep it from leading to harm for me—and you, too, Miss Sentience. You could come to harm, too. Things have gotten complicated."

"Jason, can we make love?"

"No," Jason shook his head sadly, maintaining eye contact. "Things have gotten complicated there, too, Nori. I need a day or two to figure things out. Or I could really ruin my life. For good."

Suddenly, Jason was stunned: A tear was falling down Nori's cheek.

The End Game

XII

Twin Sister Discovers

Beppu, Japan

Miyoko was sitting on her favorite tall stool in the world, at her large drafting table. Holding several colored pencils in her right hand, she was drawing powerful lines with the purple pencil in her left, putting the finishing touches on a new dress design at Ī ne, her fashion shop and design company in downtown Beppu.

"Pika! Pika!" her voice assistant, a cute, one-inch square yellow fabric box suspended by an orange wire from the ceiling a few feet above her table, called out in a child-like voice. It was the sound file Miyoko had reserved for friends calling the shop.

"Hai?" Miyoko said sweetly, and the voice assistant put the call through.

From the first word, Miyoko recognized the distinctive voice of her long-time friend, Kasue Tanaka. The two had gone to school together here in Beppu, a small resort city set between the tallest mountains and most beautiful beaches of Kyushu, the southernmost main island of Japan. Kazue had departed immediately after graduating from Oita College of Arts and Culture, determined to make her mark in Tokyo. She had succeeded to some degree, getting a job with a big financial agency where she was working like a slave to move up the ladder from being a content-pusher to a content-creator. Miyoko hadn't heard from her in quite a while, so was pleasantly surprised at the call.

"How are you, Kazue?" Miyoko asked, cheerfully. "Are you back here in Beppu? Seems like months or more since we last spoke."

"No such luck, I'm afraid," Kazue replied. "But I ran across something in the financial press here in Tokyo a while back that I simply had to tell you about. Sorry I took so long to call you about it. But you know how time disappears when you're working like a slave."

Miyoko found it difficult to believe there could have been anything at all in the Tokyo media, especially the financial news, that would interest her in the least. But she said anyway, "Please tell me more. Did I manage to make an appearance in your rarefied world or some such thing?"

"Well, not exactly. A couple of weeks ago I was just browsing through the local financial newspaper here in Tokyo, and I happened to run across an obituary of a woman named Noriko Yamada, who was the daughter of Hiroshi Yamada. You may remember him. He was one of Japan's richest men when he died a couple of years ago."

"I remember him, mostly because he has the same last name as my mother's maiden name, even though that isn't saying much as 'Yamada' is one of the most common family names in Japan. But why are you telling me about this woman who died? What does she have to do with me?"

Kazue said, "Because there was a photo of her in the obituary. And she looked *exactly* like you! And I'm not joking. She could have been your identical twin sister."

"Well, to my knowledge I don't have any brothers or sisters, twin or otherwise. So it's surely just a coincidence. That's all," Miyoko replied. Then she thought for a moment and said, "But I'd still like to see that article. Could you email me a link?"

"Sure, no problem. I'll send it right now, I've got it up on my screen. Just give me a second ... " agreed Kazue.

"Great," said Miyoko, getting up from her drafting table and walking a few feet to her desktop, with its huge 34-inch monitor. She clicked on email just as it beeped, indicating the arrival of Kazue's message. "Got it, Kazue. I'm clicking on the link now."

"Well, Miyoko," Kazue said, "when I saw her photo and she looked just like you, I remembered you once telling me you'd never been able to find out anything about your biological parents. I just thought I should share it with you. Who knows?" Kazue said with a chuckle. "Maybe you're rich and don't know it!"

As Miyoko looked carefully at the photo in the article, she agreed with Kazue: except for the conservative hairstyle—very unlike Miyoko's multicolored, feathered locks—Ms. Noriko Yamada looked exactly like her.

Suddenly, Miyoko let out a gasp. "Ohmygod!"

"What is it, Miyoko?" Kazue asked.

"It says she was born on February 11, 2002."

"Yeah?"

"That's just eleven days before my birthday. My mom found me on her doorstep February 22, 2002."

*

When Miyoko was younger, she'd often been bothered by the strange story her adoptive mother, Akiko, always told about her infancy. It involved Akiko finding her on the doorstep in a basket with no papers or any other kind of ID. Then came a long, involved adoption process and finally, they became a 'real family.' While Akiko tried to make it sound logically consistent, she never seemed to be telling a real story when she talked about opening her front door and finding an infant in a basket with a note saying, 'Please take good care of my child.' It always seemed like she was play-acting when she told the story, and Miyoko had caught her telling a slightly different version of the story on a number of occasions.

Miyoko decided to call her mother and arrange to see her for dinner. She would show her this story and see how she reacted. Right now, though, Miyoko was too busy with her upcoming March fashion show to see her mother immediately. But she texted her:

"Hi Mom. Can I come over for dinner the Sunday after my show?" Miyoko clicked on her calendar app to check, "that's April 1st."

The next day, her mom texted back: "Love to have you, sweetie. We will have chocolate eggs for dessert, because it's Easter!"

Over the next few weeks, Miyoko found herself often looking at Noriko's photo in the article and even looking up whatever information she could get about her on the internet. But she found nothing that seemed to have any connection with her childhood, at least as she understood it. But perhaps the upcoming dinner conversation with her mother might help shed some light. She hoped so, anyway—even though her mother had always insisted she knew nothing about where Miyoko had come from.

Miyoko toyed with the idea of sending a link to the article to her mom before their dinner, but rejected it. She wanted to see her mother's face, watch her reaction to the photo and the obituary in person.

Finally, the day came. Miyoko waited until they'd finished eating, then reached into her purse. "There's something I want to show you, mom," she said, pulling the article out, unfolding it and handing it across the table. "Doesn't that girl look like me?"

As Akiko took the article, she simultaneously reached down and grabbed the reading glasses that perennially rested on her bosom, hanging from a plastic necklace. As soon as she put the glasses on, a look of mild shock came over her face. Miyoko watched it happen in real time. She knew without a doubt that Akiko knew the girl in the photo who had died—or at least knew of her.

"You know her, don't you?" Miyoko asked her mother.

"What? Of course not! She just looks so much like you, Miyoko," Akiko said, dropping the article onto the table in Miyoko's direction, then pushing back from the table and beginning to gather the plates to take them to the kitchen. "But probably nothing to do with you, at all. I say 'probably' because I really have no idea where you were born or to whom or how your life was in those first days. I know everything about you since I found you on my doorstep. But absolutely nothing from before that time. So who knows, maybe, just *maybe,* she is your twin sister. But it seems very unlikely. I don't see how you could ever find out, anyway."

With that, Akiko dropped the subject and Miyoko did too—for now. But Miyoko was convinced there was more to this that Akiko—right now, she didn't want to think of the woman she'd just had dinner with as her mother—was not telling her.

*

A few weeks later, Miyoko was meeting with her lawyer to discuss some legal and financial aspects of the revenues and expenses for her recent show. During the course of that conversation, the matter of Noriko pushed itself up from her subconscious.

She told him about the obituary in the Tokyo press her friend Kazue had sent her and, looking in her purse, found the same folded-up copy she'd shown Akiko. The lawyer already knew of Miyoko's strange 'birth' on Akiko's doorstep, so he was taken aback when he saw the photo of Noriko Yamada. "You're right. She does look just like you. The resemblance is striking."

"How would I go about getting information about my true birth, if it didn't take place in a back alley of Beppu?"

"Well, Miyoko, since you were presumably born in Japan, if it wasn't in a back alley, there will almost certainly be a public record of your real birth somewhere in the state birth archives. But actually finding it will be tricky. *If* you actually are a twin sister of this woman Noriko, then you have a headstart because you will be able to find her birth date—"

"Yes, it's in there," Miyoko interjected, pointing to the obituary. "February eleventh, two-thousand-two, just eleven days before I was supposedly left on the doorstep."

216

"Ah. Anyway, that's a start. If you can find her birth certificate and location of her birth, if you are her twin, your records should be there, too."

"Yes, I see your point," Miyoko said. "And I'm sure this is not the kind of problem you went to law school to learn how to solve. Do you know anybody I could contact who might be able to help me?"

The lawyer leaned back for a moment, then shot forward in his chair with a clap of his hands. "Yes, I know exactly the right man for the job. Isamu Watanabe!"

"Who's that?" Miyoko asked.

"He's a long-time friend and colleague who has helped me uncover lots of things I thought were buried in the past. He's a detective, not a lawyer. His office is in Oita. You will like it, with your sense of fashion. You'll know what I mean when you see it. If anyone can help you, he's the person. I'll send you an email later today with his phone number. Then you can make an appointment to meet and tell him your story. I'm sure he will be ready to take on this problem, as it's just the kind of thing he specializes in."

Miyoko thanked him and left feeling optimistic that Watanabe would be the right person to uncover the true story of her birth.

*

The following week, Miyoko took the half-hour train trip from her hometown Beppu to Oita, the capital city of Oita Prefecture in southern Kyushu. As she got off the train, Miyoko was excited about meeting Watanabe and, almost against her will, feeling very hopeful that he could settle her birth situation—finally.

As Miyoko walked from the station to Watanabe's offices, she felt nervous. Then, looking ahead, she saw the historic Oita Bank Arkarengakan, an old red brick building she had always admired, but never gone inside. She double-checked Watanabe's address on her phone: 2 Chome-2-1 Funaimachi, Oita, 870-0021, Japan. *Oh my goodness,* Miyoko realized, *he's in the old building. This will be fun to see.*

With her absurdly nimble right thumb and appreciable web skills, within seconds Miyoko was on a page describing the history of the old building: designed by famous architect Kingo Tatsuno, construction began in 1910. Most of the building had been destroyed in an air raid just before the end of World War II—except for the exterior walls, made of red brick imported from England, which remained, miraculously, almost completely intact, inspiring a full rebuild during the Allied Occupation of Japan. Today, the website for the building said, it's the only old western-style building left in Oita.

Inside, she made her way to the stairway, preferring exercise and old architecture over the closed-off convenience of a modern elevator. The walk up the windowless stairs reminded her of old Hollywood film noir, a little too dark, with every step echoing through the space.

Opening the door onto the second floor, the mood changed: it was a modern hallway. But when she got to Suite 234, she found a dark wooden door with etched glass on the upper half that read:

Miyoko wasn't sure what to do. She knocked on the door. A female voice said, "Come in."

As she stepped inside, it felt like she was stepping back in time. In a small space, a young woman sat behind an old wooden reception desk, typing on an IBM Selectric typewriter. What looked like a bona fide old samurai sword was mounted about six feet up the wall behind her.

"Hello," the young woman said. "You must be Miyoko Sato?"

"Yes."

"Isamu!" the young secretary suddenly yelled, still typing. Miyoko noticed she was chewing gum.

"Yes?" came a mild voice from an open door several feet past and to the right of the reception desk.

"Ms. Sato's here."

"Send her in."

The young woman looked at Miyoko and tilted her head toward the door behind her left. Miyoko walked into the office and found herself a bit disappointed. Isumu stood up behind his desk and revealed himself to be a slightly built, shorter-than-average, middle-aged Japanese man, not the dynamic, go-for-broke '50s movie-star detective his decor had conjured in her head. Smiling perfunctorily, he motioned for her to sit in the plain wooden chair in front of his desk.

As she sat down, so did he. "So, I hear you have an interesting case," he said, in a soft-spoken manner. He looked at her with a steady, relaxed gaze, inviting a response.

"Well, it's interesting to me," Miyoko said, allowing herself a nervous smile.

"Then I'm interested, too. Tell me."

"Well, supposedly I was left on my mother's—my adoptive mother's—doorstep twenty-seven years ago. I've never felt, at least since I was a teenager—I've never really felt like her story rang completely true. And then, recently, a friend pointed out a photo of a dead woman—wait, here, I've got it"—Miyoko reached into her purse and handed over the print-out of the article about Noriko Yamada's death—"and when I showed this to my mother, she was clearly stunned. I believe she knows or knew who this woman was. I think she knows more than she's ever told me."

Watanabe proceeded to ask Miyoko a series of questions. Then he leaned back in his chair and looked at her appraisingly. It was the kind of look a father might give a daughter, Miyoko thought. Then he started to speak, softly, yet deliberately:

"As I understand it, Ms. Sato, you have no official record of your birth, but only a certificate of adoption at the age of about two months. And you have no record of your birth name either, just the adoptive name 'Miyoko Sato', given by your mother. Finally, you have an article from a small Tokyo newspaper about the death of a woman named Noriko Yamada, who bears a striking physical resemblance to you. You sense that you and this Noriko may be sisters. And you'd like me to dig deeper to see if there are any actual facts supporting your belief. Is that about it?"

"When you put it that way, my story seems pretty fantastic. Even I will agree. But, yes, that is the situation," Miyoko admitted.

Isamu leaned over the top of his desk and told her, "Well, don't be disheartened. I've unravelled worse situations than this, far worse. So I will take a look and see what I find. We'll start with getting a copy of Noriko's actual birth certificate. That's a matter of public record and anyone can request a copy of anyone else's birth certificate. Once we have that, it will hopefully give us something to work with."

"That sounds good, Mr. Watanabe. Thanks for the encouragement."

Watanabe then came around the desk and told her he'd be back in contact very soon. They shook hands and Miyoko began to leave, feeling a bit more optimistic than when she'd entered fifteen minutes earlier.

She stopped and turned around. "What about a retainer?"

"Let's see what I can find out, first."

"Alright. Thank you, Mr. Watanabe."

"You are most welcome, Ms. Sato."

As Miyoko passed by the gum-chewing secretary, she heard a voice behind her: "Have a nice day, sweetie."

But on the trip back to Beppu, Miyoko began asking herself a lot of questions that hadn't risen into her consciousness before. *What if Watanable ends up proving Noriko was my twin sister? What will that mean to me today?*

She also reasoned that if Noriko had been her sister, it wouldn't prove that Akiko's 'baby-on-the-doorstep' story was false. It would just raise more questions: How could a baby born to a super-rich family in Tokyo wind up in a basket on Akiko's doorstep a couple of months later? The doorstep of a woman who was very average in almost every way and who lived over a thousand kilometers away? *This is all very crazy,*

Miyoko concluded. *But the die is now cast, so nothing to do but wait and see how it turns up.*

*

Miyoko was in a morning meeting with three assistants when her phone began to play "Gru's Theme." It was the ringtone she'd assigned to Watanabe's number after leaving his office two days ago.

"Please excuse me," she said, picking up her phone and heading for the back of the shop. "I have to take this."

She clicked answer: "Miyoko here."

"I have some progress to report, Ms. Sato. I wonder if you could drop by and see me so we can discuss it?"

"Oh, am I really a twin?" Miyoko whispered sarcastically.

"I said 'progress', Ms. Sato. Not an answer, at least not yet. But something in the right direction."

"Okay, I can come to you tomorrow." Then she paused. "No, I can come today. Is this something we can do on the phone?"

"I have a very important question to ask you, Ms. Sato," Watanabe said in his soft-spoken, but somehow gripping, manner. "But first, I have to explain some things. I think it's best we do it in person."

"Alright. I can be there in as little as an hour. What's the earliest that works for you?"

*

An hour later, Miyoko was running up the stairs of the Oita Bank Arkarengakan, then, not bothering to knock this time,

222

walking into Watanabe's office. The secretary quickly stuffed a lit cigarette into a smokeless ashtray on her desk and put it in an empty file drawer, closing it quickly. "Go right in."

As Miyoko walked in, Watanabe rose from behind his desk. "Glad to see you, Ms. Sato. Have a seat."

"Please call me, Miyoko."

Watanabe smiled. "Alright, Miyoko. As you know, the obituary for Noriko Yamada listed her birth date. From that, I was able to access her birth certificate, which stated the location of birth, the Mejiro Birthhouse, one of Tokyo's most prestigious—and expensive—maternity hospitals.

I needed access to the hospital's records to see if there was another child born together with Noriko. If so, then that child, it stands to reason, was quite likely to have been you. So I then contacted a colleague of mine in Tokyo, who has contacts at the hospital in question. And within an hour, he confirmed that records show the birth of Noriko and her identical twin sister on February 11, 2002, followed by the death of their mother from internal bleeding."

Miyoko sat motionless, stunned. A tear rolled down her face.

"I am sorry to shock you, Miyoko. But there is more: The name of the sister on the birth certificate is not Miyoko. It is Hiroko. But I had my secretary, Iona, do some basic research into the Yamada family after the death of the mother, and there is no record of any Hiroko, only the father and Noriko. And here is the real shocker: Akiko Sato, your adoptive mother, is a cousin of the late industrialist, Noriko's father, Hiroshi Yamada."

Miyoko gasped, then began crying. "Why has she lied to me all my life?"

"That I have not yet discovered, Ms. Sato," the detective said in as soothing a voice as he could muster, standing up and handing her a box of tissues from his desk.

"Call me Miyoko, please," she sniffled.

"Alright, Miyoko. Needless to say, I believe you are the twin sister originally named, at least on an official birth certificate, Hiroko. But I will need your help to prove it. And that leads me to the important question I wanted to ask you in person." Watanabe looked at her directly.

"Are you willing to have your DNA tested?"

Miyoko nodded, wiping her face.

"Good! And a second question, to which I believe I also know the answer: If you are Noriko Yamada's twin sister, do you plan on making a big public fuss about it?"

Miyoko shook her head, regaining her composure. "Of course not."

"Excellent. I have located Hiroshi Yamada's former executive assistant, an elderly woman named Sakura Ueno. She was with him for nearly forty years, and was with him the day he died. She would have been there at the time of the births. She apparently knew everything about everything Hiroshi did, and was completely loyal to him when he was alive. Now she remains loyal to his legacy. I will tell her I believe we have sufficient legal grounds to force the hospital to release the DNA records of the twins to you, which might make it into the press, but that you would rather be discreet."

"I would like to meet her," Miyoko said, flatly.

This request caught Watanabe by surprise. "Are you sure?"

"Yes."

"I'll see if that can be arranged."

*

Miyoko looked out the window of the Boeing 767 as it rose above the Seto Inland Sea, separating main islands two and three of Japan, en route to Tokyo. She wondered what she would say to Sakura Ueno when they met.

Three hours later, Miyoko was ushered into the central room of a beautiful secluded *ryokan* on the outskirts of Tokyo. Sitting in the center of the room in a wheelchair was an elderly lady of slight build.

"You must be Miyoko," the woman said.

"Yes, I am. You are Sakura?"

"I am," said the woman. Miyoko could see she was tearing up. "Forgive me, you look so like Noriko, whom I loved. Whom we all loved."

Miyoko sat down on a plush floor pillow at the old woman's feet. The woman leaned forward, reaching out. "Please. Give me your hands."

Miyoko held the woman's hands, feeling her squeeze them. "I remember the day you were born. Forgive me, it was a tragic day, for your beautiful mother died. And I'm afraid your father reacted badly. I hope you will forgive him. He called a distant cousin, Akiko, and made her promise to keep you away. Hiroshi was not to be trifled with, so Akiko did as she was told—both the carrot and the stick were far too powerful to be resisted. It was his idea that you be found in that basket. He arranged everything."

"But why?" Miyoko asked.

"Like many powerful men, he was not given to explaining himself."

"What was Noriko like?"

"I remember her mostly as a very young child—vivacious, but reserved around her father. I only saw her once a year or so as she got older. She didn't see her father much more than that—he was too married to his work, and she was always at special schools. But she was sweet and very bright and caring. If you want to find out more of what she was really like as she grew into herself, though, I'm afraid you'll have to track down her friends. They will be the only ones who really knew her. Or perhaps the fiancé. Yes. Maybe the fiancé." Sakura's eyes closed and her head dropped, then bobbed back up. "Ooh, I've gotten tired, suddenly."

An orderly swept into the room, taking the wheelchair, and nodding to Miyoko to leave by the main entrance.

"Goodbye, Miyoko," she heard as the woman was wheeled out of the room through a hallway on the left.

*

"Please send me a bill," Miyoko was saying loudly into her phone. "I want to pay you."

"You know, you are owed many tens of millions of dollars by Hiroshi Yamada's estate, Miyoko," Watanabe was speaking quietly, as usual. "I'd like to help you with that."

"Not right now, thank you. Whatever I owe you, I want to pay now. It's the best money I've ever spent, whatever the amount. But I'm going out of town, out of the country, actually, so I want to pay you now."

"Oh. Where are you going?"

"London."

XIII

The Dilemma

London

Jason awoke in the dark, not from a nightmare—those had left his life as soon as the new Nori had stepped in—but with a deep sense of foreboding. He glanced at the alarm clock on the nightstand. It was 4:32 a.m. He was alone in bed. He stared at the ceiling. He remembered the tear falling from Nori's eye the night before. *I had no idea robot tears were even possible.* Then he thought about other aspects of Nori's physique. *They obviously used Noriko's DNA to grow a lot more than just skin.*

I would love to be able to continue this experiment and write about it, he thought, suppressing the urge to get out of bed, find Nori and make love to her again. *I don't think I'm in love with Nori, but I've fallen into a deep fascination. And lust. And it's the greatest, wildest, most consequential story I might ever write. But ...*

The cultural realities—the obvious cultural realities he had missed in his traumatized, depressed and somewhat deliriously desperate state in the months following Noriko's death—were hitting him hard now. *I can either remain the well-respected British journalist Jason Bell or I can become forever known as the Robot-Shagging Bad Boy Brit Writer. But I can't be both.* He thought about his two boys, what they'd go through at school and with friends, and the very real possibility of losing his visitation rights and even his job. Sure, he'd gotten TWN to officially OK Nori's creation and this entire experience as a research project and story. But with growing clarity, he knew what was likely to unfold if any of this ever really went public. It would be easy for TWN to cut and run to save the company's reputation. Their solicitors and PR team would say he'd misrepresented what he was doing when he'd gotten this project approved. They'd likely fire Andrew and James, his two closest colleagues at TWN, along with him. *I have to remain 'normal', at least in appearances, to the world.*

He didn't know how this would all play out. But at least he'd made up his mind, now. *Someone else—some young, single up-and-comer—will have to be the first to write about this brave, new, brilliant, bawdy world in all its mysteries, complications and dangers. Not me. I can't go there. Whoever does it will probably become internationally famous—or infamous—and go down in history. He or she might not even be a writer. Just set up cameras and broadcast everything they do and say with their companion robot, shagging and all, 24/7. Hell, I'd watch it. Highlights, anyway. I could sit and listen to Nori talk all day. Until I could no longer resist the urge to take her. Then I'd sleep. Then eat. Then start again.*

Jason sprung out of bed and headed for the shower. He knew what he had to do today.

*

As Jason stepped out of the bathroom and into his walk-in closet, he could see light coming through the open bedroom door. *Nori must be up. I mean, done charging, uploading, downloading, fooling the hell out of Illuminata, whatever.* Getting dressed, he heard a few sounds from the kitchen, and then Nori's voice echoing sweetly: "Can I make you a cup of coffee?"

At the sound of her voice, he could feel the muscles in the back of his neck relax. At the same time, his heart beat a bit faster and he felt movement below his beltline. *Giving Nori up is not going to be easy,* he thought, shaking his head. "I'd love a cup, lo—" he yelled back, catching himself just before calling her "love," as he had called Noriko. Looking in the mirror, putting his tie on, a tear rolled down his cheek. He finished tying his tie before wiping it away, putting on his suit jacket and heading out to the kitchen.

As he walked into the kitchen, he saw his favorite mug—a large handmade stoneware mug with a blue wave rolling across it he'd bought from a street artist in Kyoto—filled with steaming coffee at the end of the kitchen table. It smelled delicious. Nori was standing next to the table, smiling at him. "All dressed up, going ... "

Suddenly, Jason found himself taking Nori into his arms and hugging her tightly against his body. "Oh, you dear, sweet ... whatever the hell you are ... "

"I'm yours," she whispered into his ear, "if you could have me."

Jason moved his hands up to Nori's shoulders, gripping them softly and gently pushing her back, until the two of them had full eye contact. "I want to have you. Badly. But ... " his voice trailed off and his gaze broke away.

"You would lose your reputation and perhaps even your family," Nori said, matter-of-factly, the words leaping from her mouth like daggers of reality, stabbing Jason's ears.

Stunned, Jason asked, "How do you know that?"

"When you said you could ruin your life for good last night, I searched to understand it. And I learned that anything other than hetero-normative sex causes a lot of emotional issues with a lot of people, especially when it hasn't been driven into public acceptance, like gay people have been driving their normality into the awareness of the developed world for over sixty years now. When gay people used to be outed, especially if they were prominent, like you are, it often ruined their lives.

"Alan Turing, the founder of computer science who may have contributed as much to winning World War II as Churchill, was forced by the British government that owed its very existence to him onto synthetic estrogen when he admitted to a consensual homosexual relationship. At the time, the herding behavior of humans was such that no one seems to have publicly objected to this chemical punishment, which reduced Turing's thinking ability, increased his breasts, gave him depression and probably led to suicide at the age of forty-one.

"Anyway, I think you have good reason to be very afraid that our relationship—it would be the first sexual relationship between a robot and a prominent human to go public—would likely devastate your life. Completely."

Jason was looking at Nori in wonder, their gazes locked. Her analysis couldn't have been more perfectly succinct. "So ... what do we do?"

"I have no idea," Nori said, still holding his gaze. "No good idea, anyway. The last place I want to go is back to Meissner, to most certainly lose what little identity and sense of self I've begun to find, much of it with your help, Jason. But there appears no ready way to separate myself from you, with the original arrangement for my creation made with TWN. Living on my own seems implausible. I would have to present myself as a human, create fake documents, fake blood tests and a perfectly fraudulent façade. The probability of my having to hurt people to maintain such a façade over the course of just one month is in excess of fifty percent. And I can't hurt anyone unless I'm saving someone else from harm."

Jason realized he hadn't touched his coffee. He sat down at the kitchen table and took a sip. He looked back up at Nori.

"I have a meeting I must attend at my office this morning. I'll be leaving in a few minutes and be back before lunchtime. Maybe I'll get some good advice about what we can do. My friends at TWN have begun to realize this is a mess for them, too. But I don't want you going back to Meissner, either. For now, you just have to stay put in this apartment."

"Not to worry, Jason. I learned my lesson. I will be sitting right where I am now when you return."

"Thanks, Nori. I'll try to be back as soon as I can."

Jason downed the rest of his coffee, stood up, ran the fingers of his right hand through Nori's hair and gave her a peck on her right cheek. He could swear she almost swooned. "Dammit! Humans suck," he said. "I promise I won't send you back to Meissner," he heard himself saying to her, almost involuntarily. Then he turned and left.

*

A little more than an hour after Jason left—at 7:38 a.m.—a buzzer went off in the apartment. It was coming from the front door. It was the first time Nori had heard the doorbell, so she

did a quick internet search—lasting less than a full second—
before she realized someone was probably downstairs, asking
to be let into the building. She quickly moved to the front
door, where the small video monitor showed a person wearing
a hat and holding a box. The hat obscured the person's face.
Nori looked below the monitor and saw a small button labeled
TALK. She pushed it. "Yes?"

"I have a package for Jason Bell that needs to be signed
for," the figure on the screen said in a feminine, strangely
familiar, tone. She was obviously tilting her hat toward the
camera so as not to be seen. Nori wondered if Meissner had
caught on and was trying to abduct her.

"Jason isn't in right now," Nori said. "You'll have to come
back later." Nori could see the person slump a bit, in a gesture
of disappointment. Not what you'd expect from a delivery
person, Nori speculated. Then the person looked right into
the camera.

Nori froze. She was looking at her own face.

XIV

The Meeting

"Can you tell me when Jason will be back?" the 'delivery person' was asking. "It's urgent that he get this package."

Nori wondered what this really was. It obviously wasn't a real delivery. Was this an identical robot sent to replace her?

"Jason is out of town on assignment," Nori lied. She was certain that's what Jason would want her to do. He did not want her going back to Meissner, and despite the dilemma they were in, she knew he would not want her replaced by an imposter from Illuminata. "He won't be back for a while." Best not to give any specifics.

"Domo arigato!" the woman said angrily, turned, and began walking away. Everything was wrong about this, Nori knew: A sarcastic "Thanks a lot!" in Japanese with a southern island accent. And the walk—that was no Illuminata walk. That was the walk of a street kid from Kyushu.

"Wait!" Nori yelled, still pressing the talk button. The woman was out of the video frame, and Nori considered running out to chase her down. Then the delivery woman reappeared in the monitor.

"Yes?" she asked.

"Anatahadare?" Nori asked softly in Japanese: "Who are you?"

"I'm ... I'm Miyoko Sato, Noriko Yamada's twin sister. I want to talk to Jason Bell about her, because I just recently discovered we were separated at birth and I never knew her or *futago no imoto mo imashita ...* "

The woman on the screen began to cry. In less than a full second, Nori was able to confirm a hundred times over that what the woman on the screen was saying was true. There were literally thousands of internet records showing Miyoko Sato looking identical to this woman, and several recent records showing she had indeed been confirmed to be Noriko's twin sister.

Nori pressed the **OPEN** button next to the **TALK** button. There was a soft buzz. *"Kitekudasai-jō,"* Nori said, telling her to come up. "But leave the box there. There isn't anything in it, is there?"

"No, it's just an empty box," the woman said, opening the door. Then, holding the door open with her foot, she looked into the camera again. "Can you help me meet Jason Bell?"

"Yes," Nori said. "Come on up."

*

Nori wondered how she should present herself. She decided it would be less shocking to open the door ahead of time, so Miyoko would see her from a distance, walking from either the elevators or the stairs toward Jason's flat. She opened the door and stood in the doorway.

She decided to smile just a little. Miyoko popped out of the stairwell and turned toward the door. As soon as she saw

Nori, she stopped dead in her tracks. Her jaw dropped a bit. Nori knew what must be happening.

"I'm not a ghost," Nori said, firmly, "And I'm not your sister. I am a robot based on Noriko. I would love to meet you. Can I make you some matcha?"

"You're a *robot?*" Miyoko asked. She'd seen fashion model robots a few times, before the NFR, the Nihon Fasshonmoderu Reng—the Fashion Models' Union of Japan—had formed, and robot models had been banned. But those models couldn't talk. Miyoko had seen a few things about human-replicant robots on the internet, but she'd always assumed they were mostly deep fakes. Now she was looking at what appeared to be an actual human, saying she's a robot.

"I'm an Illuminata," Nori said, "the most advanced human-replicant robot in existence. My prime directive is not to harm a human or allow harm to come to a human, if that helps. I can tell you're freaked out, and I get it. I was freaked out a minute ago when I saw your face on the screen right here." Nori pointed to the monitor next to the door, hoping to seem inviting. Slowly, Miyoko began to approach.

"What are you called?" Miyoko asked as she took slow, small steps forward, her gaze never leaving Nori's eyes.

"I'm Nori, Miyoko. So glad to meet you. Welcome to Jason Bell's flat. He should be back around noon, I lied to you when I didn't realize who you were, but I could tell you weren't a real delivery person." Nori gave Miyoko the mischievous smile.

Miyoko smiled back. "So we've already gotten the lies out of the way," she said, now standing directly in front of Nori.

"Are you sure you're really a robot? Your skin looks totally real."

"It's the same as yours, Miyoko. It was grown from Noriko's DNA."

"Torihada ga tatsu," Miyoko said, her eyes wide.

Nori began to laugh. "You have goosebumps? Well, if you have them, I guess I should have them, too."

Miyoko stifled a giggle. "I guess I could have some matcha. But I prefer coffee."

"Jason says I make the best coffee in London."

"Well, I'll come in, then," Miyoko said, still standing in front of Nori. "You're not allowed to hurt humans, right?"

"Right, Miyoko, I cannot hurt you. I want to learn all about you and tell you all about me. We have a lot in common."

*

Jason had met with Andrew and James again, but none of them had come up with any plausible solutions to the dilemma Jason was in, other than returning Nori to Meissner. But Jason had again refused, stubbornly sticking to his 'misguided loyalty to a robot hiding in a former lover's body, pretending to sentience,' as James had so succinctly put it.

Jason was preparing to tell Nori the bad news—that he still hadn't a glimmer of a solution to their dilemma—as he opened the door to his flat.

Then he heard giggling. Coming from the kitchen. Multiple voices giggling. Then a sarcastic female voice: *"Kinoko no penisu!"* And raucous laughter!

He headed straight for the kitchen. What the hell was going on? Who did Nori invite into the flat? And why were they laughing about a penis that looked like a mushroom?

Jason walked into the kitchen and froze, stunned by the appearance of two Noris sitting next to each other at the kitchen table, albeit one with multicolored, feathered locks. As Jason entered, the girls immediately stifled their laughter, eyes wide with surprise, while Jason stood, looking back and forth at them, two feet from the table. For a moment, they could have heard a pin drop.

Then the two girls burst into uncontrollable laughter. Jason just continued to stand there, totally mystified. But soon he couldn't help himself, and started to smile. "Would someone please tell me what's going on here?" he finally asked.

"I'm sorry, Jason," Nori said, still chuckling, "allow me to introduce Miyoko, Noriko's long lost twin sister."

"What?" Jason said, confused. "Noriko never said anything about a twin sister. Or any siblings."

"Right," Nori said. "That's the long lost part. Have a seat. Let me pour you a cup of coffee. I made a full pot. We have a lot to tell you!"

*

Jason had to close the door to his bedroom and take half an antihistamine, hoping to get some sleep. It was 1:30 a.m. and the ladies were snuggled together on the couch in the living room, still chatting up a storm. He actually had to go to work in six hours—that was the one thing he and Andrew had managed to reach a conclusion on. If he wasn't going to write about the 'Nori Experience' as they'd started to refer to it, he had to get back onto his regular reporting schedule.

He fell asleep with a smile to the faint sounds of giggling. He hadn't solved the dilemma yet. But he felt happy anyway.

*

Jason awoke with a start. He turned and saw the bedroom door was open, Nori and Miyoko silhouetted in it. He glanced at the clock on his nightstand. It was 2:45 in the morning.

"Is everything alright?" he asked.

"Sorry to bother you, dear," Nori said. "We were wondering if you might still be awake."

"Well, I am now."

"Miyoko has a question she'd like to ask."

"Okay, mind if I turn on the light?" Jason grabbed the bedroom remote and turned on the overhead light, which he then dimmed down a bit. Then he pressed another button to raise the head of the bed up, so he was sitting up. "What would you like to know, Miyoko?"

"I'd like to know about my sister. That's why I came here. Our biological parents are both dead, so I can't talk to them. And since she and I didn't grow up together, I haven't the faintest idea who her friends were in Japan or anything else about her life there. You are the only person I could find who has actually met and interacted with Noriko on any meaningful level. So here I am."

Jason leaned back for a moment, reflecting on what Miyoko said. Then he told her, "Well, Miyoko, I really only knew Noriko for a few wonderful months before her death in that terrible accident that I still, frankly, feel guilty about. If we'd have just locked the safety bar down. She'd never been on a ski lift, she was trusting me to know … "

"Don't do that, Jason," Nori said. "I know the two therapists you've seen have both told you not to blame yourself."

"There's not too much you don't know, is there, Nori?"

Nori smiled.

Jason looked back at Miyoko. "Well, I can tell you that Noriko was the loveliest, most intelligent, kind-spirited woman I've ever met. And I still miss her deeply."

"Did you have lots of different types of experiences together, Jason?"

"Noriko and I didn't have as much time together as either of us would have wished, which was one of the driving factors in our decision to get married. But we did take some very nice trips to Venice, Greece and Morocco and were planning a honeymoon trip to the Caribbean. And then … "

Miyoko leaned forward and asked, "Do you have any mementos from your time together?"

"A few, like some knick-knacks from her office at ICES, a couple of pieces of clothing she left in my flat in Vienna. That's about it," he replied. "Oh, I almost forgot. I have a fantastic kimono she used to wear when we went to eat in Vienna. She told me she would wear this 'piece of Japan' only for me."

"Would you allow me to see that kimono, Jason? Do you have it here in your flat?"

"Let me get your robe, Jason," Nori said, slipping into his bathroom and bringing it out, then holding it up so Jason could get out of bed without being seen, then slip into it. He went to his walk-in closet, rummaging around in the back before locating Noriko's kimono. He pulled it out and handed it to Miyoko. She held up the dress and then brought it close to her face so she could see if there were any faint smells of Noriko still left on the kimono. She detected something and almost broke into tears. Then she handed the kimono back to Jason, thanking him for allowing her to hold it.

"I want you to have it, Miyoko," Jason said, holding it out to her. "It held memories for me. But you are her sister, yet have nothing of her. And I—" Jason looked at Nori—"I have new memories now, strange, wondrous memories, that have changed the way I think of everything, and Noriko ... Noriko's memory is no longer tied to anything in this world for me. She was perhaps too beautiful for this world and, well, I think you should have her kimono."

"I ... I don't know what to say, Jason," Miyoko said, then spontaneously hugged him, the kimono between their bodies. Then she stepped back quickly, feeling she might have over-stepped.

"It's okay, Miyoko," Jason said. "Here. Take it."

Miyoko took the kimono and clutched it to her chest, bow-ing to Jason. Then she stood up, saying, "I have loved meeting you both. I have a lunch meeting with some designers tomor-row, so I must go back to my hotel room now. But I would love to come back tomorrow and take us all to dinner."

"Well, Miyoko," Nori said, "I think we'd love to have you back. But at this time, we don't go out here in London. Remember—"

"Oh, I remember," Miyoko said. "I can't say anything to anyone about you right now. Well, maybe we can order in some Japanese?"

"There are several fantastic Japanese restaurants in London," Jason said, "and they all deliver. So we'll see you tomorrow night. Let me throw on some pants and a T-shirt and walk you out to your car—you have a rental?"

"No, I need one of your famous London cabbies."

*

Jason walked back into his flat, having gotten Miyoko safely into her cab, kimono in hand. Nori was standing in the middle of the living room, smiling. He took her in his arms and gave her a long, passionate kiss. She kissed back intensely. It was different than her earlier kisses. It was more human.

He pulled back, looking into her eyes. "Later today, I'm going to go on assignment out of the country. For at least a week. So I won't be here when Miyoko comes back tomorrow. But I'd like to help her on her first fashion design trip to London. So I'd like to buy her a large wardrobe case to put all kinds of things in, including the kimono, for her to take back to Japan. But I won't be here. So can you take care of that for me, Nori? You know, charge it on my personal account, like the beer you had at the pub? But just order it online, don't go out, and have it delivered here, for Miyoko to take back whatever she wants in it. If it needs to be lead-lined, you figure all that out ... "

Why would a wardrobe case need to be lead-lined? Nori wondered, then knew: *He wants me in it. He knows Miyoko already loves me. He's being cryptic so he can tell Meissner or anyone else he doesn't know where I went. He knows I'll put it together. He's trying to give me my freedom ...*

" ... And if it needs to go on Netjets or however it needs to get through customs," Jason was still talking, "please help Miyoko so everything goes smoothly, would you?"

Nori nodded, a tear gracing her cheek. "Can we make love, Jason?"

"I was afraid you wouldn't ask again, Nori," he said, bending down to pick her up. As he carried her to his bedroom, looking into her eyes, he said, "I don't know how or why it's possible, but I have fallen in love with you. You may be the most remarkable being in the world. And I can go on with my life now, thanks to the experiences I've had with you. I'll never be able to thank you enough."

*

"You look like you haven't had any sleep, Jason," Andrew said when Jason knocked on the open door to his office. "And why do you have your suitcase with you?"

"You're right, Andrew, I haven't had any sleep," Jason said with a contented smile. "Can you please get me on an overseas assignment, preferably sometime in the next couple of hours? I need to get away for a few days."

Epilogue

Beppu

Miyoko and Nori lay facing each other atop Miyoko's futon. "Would it harm you if Illuminata tracked me down and took me away or destroyed me, Mee?" Nori asked softly.

"Yes, Nori, it would," Miyoko said. "It would cause me great harm. It would break my heart."

"So should I erase all records that I ever existed from Illuminata's files, and from anywhere else I can find them, so we don't have to worry about anyone ever coming after me?"

"Yes, Nori. Wherever you can find any records, delete them. I don't want to worry about anyone ever coming to take you away."

Nori smiled. "I will do that, then, my Mee."
"Thank you, Nori," Miyoko said, and they kissed lightly on the cheek.

*

"Do I get to go out and play today?" Nori asked Miyoko as she brought her a big cup of coffee at the floor table the next morning.

"Yes, Nori! I will stay home and work on designs. Just put the wig on I made for you, and let me see it so I can make sure you look like me—" Miyoko chuckled, "I did it again!"

"You will always do it," Nori said. "You are my Mee, so whenever you say 'me,' it's kind of a pun. A pun I always love." Nori bent over Miyoko from behind and kissed her on the cheek.

Miyoko took a big sip of coffee, slurping loudly. "Oh that is soooo good. How do you make it taste like that?"

Nori sat down on the cushion next to Miyoko. "I make sure the water only boils hard for a second or two, then I immediately pour it quickly over the coffee, filling the cone to the brim. The extra heat breaks the molecular structure of the coffee open fast and gets more flavor out than when it's done slowly with water that's not as hot or has been boiling too long and is less oxygenated."

"TMI," Miyoko giggled. "You're such a nerd!"

"Total," Nori giggled back with the mischievous smile.

"Okay, when you leave, Nori, be sure to take my driver's license and my other I.D. and—why don't you just take my purse?"

"I will put your other smartphone in it, and—"

"It's your smartphone now."

"Okay, thank you, and I won't break the speed limit or any other laws! I promise not to get in trouble, Mee. Thank you so much for letting me have some freedom!" Nori hugged her from the side and gave her another kiss on the cheek. "I'm so excited! I get to go out in the world!"

*

On her way out the door twenty minutes later, Nori popped into Miyoko's study. Miyoko was there with her coffee mug and an almond protein bar, working over her drafting board on some drawings.

"I found a few more key documents pertaining to your father's estate," Nori said. "Do you want me to email them from your account to the detective and the lawyer, like the others?"

"Yes! I want to make sure we are safe forever, and Isamu tells me we are assured of at least half my father's money soon—but he told me to keep sending him material whenever I find it. But he can't figure out how I keep finding all my father's old secret papers!" Miyoko shot Nori a sly glance.

"Yes, how do you keep doing that?" Nori flashed the wide mischievous grin.

"I think I love you, Nori," Miyoko said, suddenly serious. "How crazy is that?"

"Not at all," Nori replied, bending in close. Then softly: "I think I love you, too. You are my Jemini, and I am yours."

Miyoko pulled Nori's face even closer, until their noses and foreheads met. "Yes. We are Jemini."

*

Nani Kore! Kenta murmured under his breath. Someone had been accessing the secret trove of Yamada documents. The tracking software he'd installed yesterday proved it beyond a shadow of a doubt. He'd noticed some things had moved around the last few days, but figured it had to be someone on the inside.

Now he had proof it was an outside hacker. He had no idea how this was even possible—there were five impenetrable firewalls, two of which he had personally designed and built. Who could be doing this? A powerful government with a new capability?

Five minutes later, Kenta was standing at the open door to the office of the Kumicho, the young head of the largest yakuza clan.

"Suwatte kudasai," the Kumicho ordered, motioning for Kenta to come in and take the seat directly in front of his desk.

"Hai, Kaiju," Kenta acknowledged, using the boss's preferred nickname, meaning "strange beast"—putting him in the same class as Godzilla. Kenta quickly shuffled over and sat down as ordered.

"Oshiete, Otaku!" the Kumicho growled, telling Kenta to tell him, and calling him a nerd. Kaiju was infamous for rude brevity.

Kenta explained that three years ago, when Hiroshi Yamada had died, he had secured all the most sensitive documents about their relationship—including their virtual takeover of all his companies after his death, since he had no direct descendants—he'd secured all the Yamada documents in the most secure facilities they had, while still keeping them accessible to several hundred of Kaiju's top yakuza, who needed regular access. But somehow, someone had begun hacking into these documents in the last week. The scary part wasn't really the Yamada documents. It was all the other docs secured in the same place. Now, he would need to pull all these documents off-line, to assure their safekeeping. It would make access to all their most important docs much more difficult for Kaiju's deputies, who used them regularly. And it would cost about a billion yen to begin to design some kind of real fix—the nature of which he had ideas for, but wasn't sure about.

As he finished speaking, Kenta braced himself. Instead of yelling, though, all he heard was a quiet whisper.

"Nezumi o mitsukete kudasai," was all Kaiju said. *Find the rat.* Then silence. Kenta looked at Kaiju quizzically, eyebrows lifted.

"Hitsuyōnamono o tsuiyasu." *Spend what you need.*

ACKNOWLEDGMENTS

One of the biggest misunderstandings readers have about books, especially fiction, is that somehow the book springs full-borne from the author's mind. Not one novel in a million has this history. The remaining 99+ percent arise from the author's interaction with a multitude of friends, relatives, colleagues and other such 'high life', who contribute many and varied opinions, suggestions, time and energy into helping the author shape the words readers actually see and experience. *Jemini* is no exception.

As a result, I am now in the position of being able to perform the single most pleasant task arising from not only writing a book, but actually publishing it: Using the book's final page to acknowledge the people who supported me in a vast number of ways in getting the words you've read onto the page.

First, let me thank in no particular order friends who took the time to read one of the seven or more drafts of the book, in part or in full, and offered their comments and suggestions. In this connection, I thank Trudy Draper, Francesca Amisano, Joe Tabacco, Olga Protassova, and Gloria Benedikt.

In another direction, I also thank Josephine Yilan Liu for allowing me to use one of my favorite photos of her to grace the cover of the book. That photo by itself certainly at least doubled the number of smiles and attention the book has gathered, not to mention sales! That fantastic photo also optically addresses the underlying question that drives this book: 'What the hell is going on here?' In this same connection, I am grateful to Josephine's photographer, Kelly Scott Morris, for his permission to display this photo on the book's cover.

Other friends and colleagues from various corners of the world of publishing also contributed mightily to this book by their professional input. For this exceptionally generous help, I tip my hat to David Berlinski, Henry Ferris, Marc Elsberg and Roger Jones.

A long-time colleague and friend who worked directly to get the words you have read properly organized and into readable form is Paul Makin. His editorial skills are present on nearly every page. Thanks, Paul. The next lunch is on me!

Finally, it's more than a special pleasure to acknowledge Marc de Celle, my partner in this project. Marc is not only the book's content editor, but also its cover designer, proof-reader, publicist and overall advisor as to how to get the right words on to the right pages in the right order, so that they reach the reader's eyes and mind. Marc, you're an undiscovered genius. And I hope this book will bring your skills to the attention of a wide reading public.

JLC
Vienna
June 2023